WHAT
WE
HARVEST

WHAT WE HARVEST

ANN FRAISTAT

DELACORTE PRESS

Text copyright © 2022 by Ann Fraistat
Jacket art copyright © 2022 by Marcela Bolivar

Visit us on the Web! GetUnderlined.com

Educators and librarians, for a variety of teaching tools, visit us at RHTeachersLibrarians.com

Library of Congress Cataloging-in-Publication Data
Names: Fraistat, Ann, author.
Title: What we harvest / Ann Fraistat.
Description: First edition. | New York : Delacorte Press, [2022] | Audience: Ages 12+. | Audience: Grades 10–12. | Summary: The farms of Hollow's End were blessed with miracle crops, especially the shimmering, iridescent wheat of Wren's family farm, but then the quicksilver blight came, and the blight destroys everything: crops turned to silver sludge, animals sickened and blinded, even people; Wren believes she is responsible, and desperate to save Hollow's End she turns to her ex-boyfriend—but they find that there is a lot they do not know about their town and its miracle crops, and that their ancestors have a lot to answer for.
Identifiers: LCCN 2021012256 | ISBN 978-0-593-38216-5 (hardcover) | ISBN 978-0-593-38219-6 (trade paperback) | ISBN 978-0-593-38217-2 (ebook)
Subjects: LCSH: Family farms—Juvenile fiction. | Plant diseases—Juvenile fiction. | Secrecy—Juvenile fiction. | Responsibility—Juvenile fiction. | Fathers and daughters—Juvenile fiction. | Interpersonal relations—Juvenile fiction. | CYAC: Farms—Fiction. | Diseases—Fiction. | Secrets—Fiction. | Responsibility—Fiction. | Fathers and daughters—Fiction.
Classification: LCC PZ7.1.F72 Wh 2022 | DDC 813.6 [Fic]—dc23

The text of this book is set in 11.5-point Sabon LT
Interior design by Ken Crossland

Printed in the United States of America
10 9 8 7 6 5 4 3 2 1
First Edition

For Grant, Shawn, Mom, and Dad & Pam,

And for Kylie Schachte,

to whom I specifically dedicate Teddy

CHAPTER 1

So, it had finally come to kill us, too.

The sickest part was, I'd started to believe we were invincible—that somehow the miracle of our farm might protect us. I'd seen Rainbow Fields survive crackling lightning, hail, devouring armyworms, eyespot fungus. No matter what came from sky or earth, the field behind our house still swayed with towering, iridescent wheat. Crimson, orange, yellow, all the way to my favorite, twilight-blazed violet: each section winked with its own sheen.

My whole life, the wheat had soothed me to sleep through my bedroom window with its rustling whispers, sweeter than any lullaby, or at least any my mom knew.

My whole life, until now. When I realized even rainbows could rot.

I stood at the very back of our field. A gust of wind caught my hair, and the cascading waves of wheat flickered into a rainbow, then stilled back into a field of shivering white gold. At my feet, a sickly ooze crept from their roots. It wound up their shafts and dripped from their tips.

The quicksilver blight, we called it, because it gleamed like molten metal. But the stench gave it away for what it really was—a greedy, hungry rot.

So far, I'd only spotted six plants that had fallen victim. No surprise they were at the back of the field, closest to the forest.

The blight in those woods had crept toward us for months, devouring our neighbors' crops and pets and livestock. Our neighbors themselves. Every night, the grim white eyes rose like restless stars, watching us from behind the silver-slicked trees.

The air hung around me, damp—cold for late June in Hollow's End. Spring never came this year, let alone summer. Even now, the forest loomed twisted and bare. From where I stood with our wheat, I could see streaks of blight glinting behind decaying patches of bark.

My breaths came in tiny sips. If I closed my eyes, if I stopped breathing, could I pretend even for a second that none of this was real?

The field was hauntingly quiet. Wheat brushing against wheat. The farmhands had packed up and fled weeks ago—like most of the shop owners, like most everyone in Hollow's End except the core founding families—before the quarantine sealed us off from the rest of the world. In the distance, our farmhouse stood dark. Even Mom and Dad were out, off helping the Harrises fight the blight on their farm. They had no idea our own wheat was bleeding into the dirt.

Dad had tried to keep me plenty busy while they were

away, tasking me with clearing out brambles near the shed. He and Mom didn't want me anywhere near the back of our field, so close to the infected forest. But today, they weren't here to check for crop contamination themselves— and they also weren't here to stop me.

I was our last line of defense. The least I could do was act like it.

Hands gloved for protection, I grabbed the nearest stalk and heaved it up from the festering soil. I could barely stand to hoist it in the air, its suffocating roots gasping for earth. But this plant was already good as dead. Worse. It would kill everything around it, too.

Even me, if I wasn't wearing gloves.

As I ripped up plant after plant, the stench, syrupy like rotting fruit, crawled down my throat. I hurled the stems into the forest and spat after them.

The wind answered, carrying a distant tickling laugh that squirmed into my ear.

I froze, peering into the mouth of the forest—for anything that might lurch out, to grab me or bite me or worse.

Only silent trees stared back. I must've imagined it.

The blighted didn't wake until nightfall, anyway, and the sun was still high in the sky. Maybe two o'clock. I had time to deal with our infected wheat, before my parents raced back from the Harrises' in time to meet the town curfew at sundown. Before the blighted came out.

Not a lot of time. But some.

Mildew stirred in my sinuses, like it was actually under the skin of my face. A part of me.

A sour taste curdled behind my teeth.

I spat again and turned to kick the dislodged earth away from our healthy wheat. My foot slipped—on a patch of glistening blight. The puddle splashed into tiny beads, like mercury spilled from a broken old-fashioned thermometer. Shifting, oily silver dots.

My stomach dropped. No. Oh no, oh no.

It wasn't just in the plants. It was in the soil. How deep did it already run?

I needed a shovel.

I threw off my contaminated gloves, kicked off my contaminated shoes, and ran. Dirt dampened my socks with every pounding step down the path to our shed. Seven generations of blood, sweat, and toil had dripped from my family into this soil. That was the price we paid to tame this patch of land—our farm. Our home.

That wheat was everything we had.

As long as I could remember, my parents had sniped at each other over our thin savings. With my senior year looming ahead this fall, their fighting had kicked into overdrive—and that was before the blight came, before the farmer's market had shut down in April.

For the past several months, the blight had been eating its way through the other three founding farms. So now that it was our turn, I knew what it would do. It would take more than this year's harvest. More than our savings. It would take the soil itself—our entire future.

Mom had never loved Rainbow Fields like Dad and I did. Since the blight appeared and shut everything down, she'd been asking what we were clinging on for. If she knew it had reached our wheat . . .

The blight would fracture my family and tear us apart.

Some heir I was. I kept seeing that look on Dad's face—the horror in his eyes—when he realized how badly my efforts to help us had backfired, that I was the one who'd unleashed this blight on all of Hollow's End.

A fresh wave of shame bloomed in my chest. I shoved against the shed's splintered doors. It felt good to push back. I grabbed spare gloves, the rattiest pair hanging by the door, caked stiff with crumbling mud—the ones I wore when I was a kid. They barely fit anymore.

Armed with a shovel, I raced back to the infected soil at the edge of our farm.

With every gasp, every thrust into the earth, numbing air bit into my lungs. And I realized I hadn't put my shoes back on. Dammit. Now my socks were touching contaminated soil, and I'd have to leave them behind, too.

The sharp edge of the shovel dug against the arch of my foot as I pressed down with all my weight. I pulled up the dirt and scoured it, praying for smooth, unbroken brown.

But there were only more silver globs—beads of them crawling everywhere.

I could dig for days, and I'd never get it all out. My hands ached, and I dropped the shovel with a dull thud.

It took everything in me not to collapse beside it.

The blight had burrowed too deep. There was only one way I could think of to slow it down. I had to dig up the fence from our backyard and sink it in here, hard into the soil. I had to block off the corrupted back row of our farm, and the forest looming beyond it.

Yes. That was a plan. Something Dad himself might've thought of. I could do that. I could—

My sinuses burned. I sneezed into my glove, and the mucus came out like the soil, flecked with silver.

I stared at it, smeared across my fingers. The whole world lurched.

No way.

I swatted it off against my pants so hard I was sure I'd left a bruise on my thigh, and scanned the fields—could anyone have seen what just came out of me?

But there was only me and the swaying wheat. The empty sky.

I couldn't be infected. I hadn't touched it.

I had to keep telling myself that. I knew way too well that if any of the blight rooted inside me, there was no coming back. It was worse than a death sentence. It was . . .

I needed to shower.

Now. And then move the fence.

I stripped away my socks and gloves. In cold bare feet, I pounded back to the house, jumping over rocks where they studded the path.

The nearest farm wasn't for two miles, so I did the teeth-chattering thing and stripped on the porch. I paused at the clasp of my bra, the elastic of my underwear. No one was watching, but these days the forest had eyes. And it was hard to forget that laugh I thought I'd heard from the trees. My bra and underwear were fine, so I left them on. As for my beloved purple plaid shirt and my soft, work-worn jeans . . . After my shower, I'd have to wrap them in plastic and dump them in the trash.

Last time Mom took me shopping, I saw how her eyebrows pinched together when she reached for her credit card. There wouldn't be replacements—that's for sure.

Pimpled with goose bumps, I charged inside, straight to my bathroom, and cranked the hot water. With any luck, it'd slough off the top layer of my skin. I scrubbed at my arms and legs. I scalded my tongue rinsing out my mouth. When I spat down the drain, the water came out gray. A little dirty.

Or was I imagining it?

Everything was far away, like I was twenty feet back from my own eyes. A gunky heaviness clung under the skin of my cheeks and forehead.

I don't know how long I stood there, surrounded by cream-white tile, steaming water beating my body. By the time I blinked myself back into reality, under my head-to-toe dusting of freckles, my pale skin had turned lobster-pink.

I threw on overalls and combed my fingers through my shoulder-length hair, before the chestnut-brown waves tangled into a hopeless mess.

As if it mattered how I looked. My brain bounced all over the place, trying to forget that it was much too late for normal.

I went down to the kitchen and called my parents from the old wall-mounted phone.

The calls dropped to voicemail immediately. I took a deep breath. That wasn't surprising. Reception was so bad out here that cell phones were practically useless, and Wi-Fi was pathetic—Hollow's End was stuck in the dark ages, with landlines and answering machines. Back when we still had tourists, the town's community center played it off as charming: "Just like the good ol' days! A simpler time!" In reality, though, it wasn't as simple.

Pacing the kitchen, I tried the Harrises next. As the phone rang in my ear, I stopped in front of our fridge. Pinned under a magnet shaped like a loaf of bread was the hazard-yellow flyer stamped with the official US seal on the front: PROTECT YOUR FAMILY FROM "QUICKSILVER BLIGHT." It was one of the early flyers they'd passed out at the end of February, when the government responders arrived in town. When they still came door to door, and we really thought they might help. Now, they stayed holed up in their tents blocking the bridge out of Hollow's End. Every couple weeks they flew a helicopter over, dropping the latest flyers—littering our farms and fields, so we had to trudge through with trash pickers, shoving them into bulging recycling bags.

The flyers never said anything new. At the bottom, in big bold letters, this one shouted:

**IF YOU SUSPECT YOU OR SOMEONE ELSE MAY
HAVE BEEN EXPOSED TO "QUICKSILVER BLIGHT,"
IMMEDIATELY CONTACT YOUR EMERGENCY
TRIAGE CLINIC.**

They said the triage clinic could treat us for mercury exposure. Although we all knew the blight was more than mercury. That was, however, the official story being fed to the outside world—Hollow's End was suffering from an extra-nasty mercury spill—and somehow, any photos or videos we posted online disappeared minutes after they went up, like they'd never been there at all.

As for the dozen folks who had gotten infected and turned themselves in to the clinic this spring, their families hadn't been able to get any word about them since. Not one had returned.

The truth was: there wasn't any treatment, let alone a cure.

The phone stopped ringing. "Hey there, you've got the Harrises . . ."

"Mrs. Harris," I blurted, "it's Wren! Are my parents—"

"Or you don't yet, because we're busy. If you're calling for a quote on our stud fees, or to join our puppy wait list, don't forget to leave a callback number!"

Shit. That awful message *always* got me.

I dropped my forehead against the fridge door. At the beep, I mumbled a plea for my parents to call me back and slammed the phone into its cradle.

My empty hands wouldn't stop shaking.

I couldn't move that fence alone, not if I wanted to make any real progress before sundown.

Who else could I call, though? My "friends" from school had barely spoken to me since I was quarantined. They all lived across the bridge in Meadowbrook anyway, inaccessible now, thanks to the government responders' barricade. All except for Derek. And things with Derek were over—*extremely* over. Now he was nothing but deleted texts and unanswered calls.

But . . . he was the only option, wasn't he?

I allowed myself a good long sigh at the phone, then picked up the receiver and stabbed out his phone number.

It was too late for normal. Too late for feelings, too.

CHAPTER 2

I hadn't spoken to Derek Pewter-Flores in two months. Ten minutes after I hung up, his dented Dodge Ram roared into the driveway—and, spread out as Hollow's End was, that meant he'd driven *fast*. His truck jerked to a stop next to my sunshine-yellow pickup, an ancient Chevy with old-school round headlights. The two vehicles side by side in my driveway was like a picture yanked straight out of my memory. It splashed me back to all our lemonade-soaked summers together—the electric tang of the melon Popsicles we used to lick on my porch, juice trickling down our wrists faster than we could catch it.

He stepped out of the truck slowly. These days, an emergency call from a neighboring farm only meant one thing. Derek had dressed accordingly. He wore stiff boots, long sleeves, gloves, and his rattiest jeans. A blue bandana was slung around his neck.

He'd cropped his straight black hair short for the summer, same as always, even though it wasn't hot this year.

Trying to pretend, just like me, that everything hadn't changed. Like most of us in Hollow's End, he wore his outdoor work in the broadness of his shoulders and the chapped blush of his windburned cheeks. The sun had bronzed his brown skin, highlighting the scar of his repaired cleft lip. I knew he hated it, the old pale line that jagged over his upper lip, but I'd seen it smudged blue with Popsicle juice, felt its ridge when we'd kissed. No matter how much his body changed—his chest widening, voice deepening—that scar never did. I loved how it proved he was, without question, still the same boy I'd grown up with, hand in hand.

At least, I used to love it. It was some kind of torture now.

He stood in my driveway, gazing up at me on the porch.

"Wren." He swallowed hard and tried to hide it with a flimsy smile. "We're talking again?"

I didn't taste those Popsicles anymore. Just cold, stale air. "Derek—"

My voice choked off, and I took a step back. I don't know what it was with me, but my dad did it all the time, too—this nervous step backward like we could outrun a tough conversation. Teeth grinding, flinty eyes darting. "The ol' Warren lockjaw," Mom called it, shaking her head. "A family legacy." Whenever I did it, her lips pinched in that disapproving way. I don't remember when her resentment of Dad got bad enough that she started hating every little thing that reminded her of him—even when it was also a piece of me.

Derek was familiar with the Warren lockjaw. Way too familiar.

11

He sighed. "So, we're not talking. You just want me to shut up and help."

It sounded awful when he put it like that.

"For old times' sake?" I tried. "Please?"

Derek's shoulders stiffened, his mouth sealing into a grim line.

But he nodded.

My chest unclenched with a tiny flood of tenderness. "Thank you. Seriously."

The stickiness in my throat caught up with me, and I hacked like a fifty-year smoker into the crook of my elbow.

Well, tender moment broken.

"Wren, you didn't . . . ?" Derek's face got sharp and urgent. "You were careful, right? When you found it?"

"Obviously!" I ran a hand through my tangled hair. "I didn't touch it. I tossed my clothes."

"Where's your bandana?"

"Bandana?"

"To cover your face." Derek lifted his own, holding it over his nose and mouth. "Or face mask. Anything to stop you from breathing it."

Of course. Dad had been wearing a bandana this morning, hadn't he? A dignified gray, a shade darker than the silver of his hair. I'd noticed the knot at the back of his neck as he prepped for the Harrises' cleanup, filling a sky-high travel mug with black coffee and itemizing my chores for the day. Dead serious, as always. His normally pin-straight hair was sticking up at the back of his head, where he couldn't see it. I'd had to bite my lip.

"You can't get infected like that, though, can you?" I asked. "Just from breathing? I know not to touch it, but the flyers didn't say—"

"The flyers." Derek rolled his eyes in bitter reflex. "People and animals wouldn't infect you that way. I mean, maybe if they breathed straight into your mouth—though, let's face it, they'd be biting you by that point. But blight collects in plant roots. When you dig them up, it stirs into the air." He tossed this off like it was common knowledge.

Maybe for anyone allowed to assist with blight cleanup, it was. Derek had been battling it on his own farm for weeks. Unlike my overprotective parents, his mom actually trusted him enough to let him help. She'd been sending him out to assist our neighbors, too.

My parents' rule was clear: Stay the hell away from blighted anything. Plain and simple. It was one of the few things they could agree on.

"It's okay," Derek assured me, "as long you didn't pull up any plants."

Whatever look paralyzed my face, it was enough to freeze Derek, too.

"Wren?" His voice had dropped.

People told me I wasn't easy to read. Animals always knew what I meant, but Derek was just about the only person who did.

"I feel okay," I said softly, more to my porch boards than to him.

"Then you probably are," Derek returned, way too

quickly. "I'm sure you're fine. Just use a bandana this time. No need for unnecessary risks, right?"

I glanced up—to see if there was any chance he actually believed that.

He'd pulled his shoulders back, nodding. He even smiled. So, yeah, maybe he did.

And maybe he was even right. It was only six plants I'd dug up. I'd showered right away. I definitely didn't have any wild urges to run off into the woods to join the others. At least, not yet.

I managed a smile back. "Right," I said, and went inside to get a bandana.

There was nothing Derek and I could do but move the fence. Luckily, Dad had built that thing tough, with solid planks and no gaps. He'd made it for Teddy back when she'd still been our dog, to keep her in the yard and out of the forest. For all the good that had done us.

Derek and I ripped it up, section by section, and hauled it all the way to the back of the crop field. We wedged it deep into the earth—between the violet-tinged stalks still standing tall and the inky mud pit I'd dug earlier. If Derek and I could buy a little time and keep the blight back overnight, at least that'd be a tiny scrap of hope I could offer my parents once they got home.

But my foot wouldn't quit slipping from the shovel. I was shivering and sweat-drenched, even though we couldn't have been working for more than an hour. I'd always been on the puny side, shorter and smaller-framed than was ideal for farm labor, but I was used to working double time to keep my noodley arms in pace with Derek. It'd never stopped me before.

"Take a breather." Derek paused in his digging. "I can keep going." He was working to maintain that lukewarm mask of his, but just like he could read me, I could read him. Spot the fear in the back of his dark-brown eyes, in the slight crumple of his forehead.

Now that I'd confessed to breathing in blight, everything was loaded. Stopping would only validate his worst fears—and mine. Besides, if this was hard on me, it was what I deserved.

I shook my head and kept working. The scraping of shovels was once again the only sound.

As hours slipped away and the sun leaked out over the horizon, our digging grew desperate. Faster. Deeper. My shoulders screamed. My sweat-sopped shirt clung to my back. I kept squinting at the house and driveway, looking for Mom's missing Jeep. All the while, my ears strained toward the forest, nearly sure I heard the hoots and shrieks of nasty night birds, waking with the twilight.

Another sound, too, like slithering over leaves. Drawing closer.

We had the last panel halfway in when Derek looked over his shoulder to the trees.

"Okay, let's go," he said. "I saw eyes."

"That's impossible." I jerked around so sharply my neck twinged. "It's too early." Curfew didn't start until the sun went all the way down, at eight-thirty. This was closer than my parents had cut it before, but no way they'd miss curfew.

I dug for my phone and tapped it awake. A little past seven-forty. I held up the screen, so Derek could see for himself.

He sighed and leaned against his shovel, wiping his forehead with his sleeve. "I have to head back soon anyway, you know."

Right. Yes. Of course. I'd been so fiercely focused I'd only seen one target: save the wheat. But Derek needed time to change and drive home.

Still, it wasn't like him to make excuses. If he wanted to go, he would've just said that.

"You really saw something?" I asked him.

"No, I just thought joking about it would be real funny." Derek stared at me flatly.

I mean, I kind of deserved that. "Fine," I muttered. "Let's go."

We dropped the shovels and tore off our shoes and gloves. We left them in the dirt, this growing collection of useless accessories and rags.

Neither of us wanted to be the first to start running, heading back to the house. It wasn't exactly cool to admit the fading light scared you. He broke first, into a light jog, one he could almost pretend was carefree. But it took all of two seconds for me to break, too, and then neither of us felt that bad about picking up the pace.

As we reached the porch, I glanced over my shoulder

to the woods. The shadows between trees were deepening with the coming dark.

Derek paused beside me. "Where should I . . . ?" He ran an awkward hand over his neck. "I brought a change of clothes."

I pointed around the side of the house. "You can go over there, and I'll, um, change here, I guess."

My cheeks burned. God, I was turning funny colors, wasn't I?

His mouth turned up at the corner with a touch of old fondness, like he suddenly remembered I could be cute.

Unfortunately, that reminded me right back, how warm I knew his full grin could be. How much I missed sharing it.

Curse him. "Shoo." I waved him to the side yard.

Off he went, with a mostly swallowed chuckle.

I did my half-naked dance in record time, jamming arms and legs into the change of clothes I'd left for myself on the porch. When Derek tracked back around the front, I held out a trash bag so he could dump his sack of blight-soiled clothes in with mine.

"You don't have to pitch those," Derek said. "Mom figured out how to wash out the blight with bleach and a metal tub in the yard. I can take care of them for you, if you want."

I hesitated to cash in yet another favor, but it was such a waste to keep chucking clothes. And, to be painfully honest, an excuse to see Derek again was starting to feel a little tempting.

Slowly, I nodded, and handed my bag over.

"Well," he said. "Guess I'm gonna . . ." He nudged his thumb toward his truck.

I could've just said thanks and bolted into the house. But in the driveway, Mom's Jeep was *still* missing. I'd heard them roar away this morning while I was brushing my teeth, and I hadn't even bothered to wave out the window. It was dawning on me now exactly how naive that had been—taking little things for granted.

"Stay for dinner." It slipped from my mouth. "Or at least a glass of water. Hot chocolate?"

Derek frowned up at the sky, rawer red than the front rows of our wheat.

"I know you don't have much time. But just for a little while?" I shrugged, hands curling in my overalls' deep pockets. After all the work he'd done on my family's behalf, it'd be awful to send him away without offering any real thanks. "My folks still aren't back, and . . ."

"Yeah." He smiled, just a little. "Hot chocolate sounds nice."

Hot chocolate, my butt. He ate half the kitchen.

To be fair, though, I guess I offered. The humiliating truth was that I would've given him every crumb we had to get him to stay with me in this empty, creaking house.

We sat across from each other at the old oak table. My heart pinched at how automatically Derek had taken his usual seat. I refused to glance at my parents' empty chairs to my left and right. The owl clock by the back door swung its pendulum steadily away. A little past eight. Through the window over the counter, the horizon had dimmed from bloody to bruise-dark. Derek would have to leave soon. I couldn't believe how close my parents were cutting it.

This was all backward. I was sixteen. Shouldn't my parents have been the ones eyeing the clock, heaving disappointed sighs over my lateness?

I cupped my peacock-blue glazed mug and breathed in the sugary embrace of marshmallow. The steam was a welcome balm on my clammy skin.

Derek dug into a hearty serving of casserole leftovers. Mom's latest questionable creation. She called it Harvest Surprise. Emphasis on "surprise." She'd throw together anything in our yard that was overripe, then toss it with macaroni and the cheese closest to expiring. She'd been good enough to remind me about it as I crunched sleepily on cereal this morning, while touching up her sunscreen in the hall mirror. "Remember to eat a good lunch today, baby—there are leftovers in the fridge." She'd poked her head around the kitchen corner, lipstick bright as her red plaid shirt, with a somewhat evil grin. "Your favorite."

And I tried not to gag.

Derek would eat anything, so he didn't bat an eye at the cabbage and old goat cheese. He polished off that plate in a way that would've made Mom proud. "You're not hungry?" he said, pausing in his fork-cleaning ritual, midlick.

I shook my head and raised my hot chocolate. "This is fine."

Honestly, it was a struggle to eat at all. A nasty new taste hunkered at the back of my throat. One that dragged me back to that fall when the acorn-squash seeds we'd got-ten from Derek's family did way too well. Mom roasted three squashes every night for dinner, but we still wound up with an overflowing crate in the cellar. Come March, we had a knee-high pile of rotting mess. Like autumn got sick all over our basement. Decaying leaves, sour mold.

That's what I tasted now, at the root of my tongue.

Derek went into autopilot, washing his plate clean—even wiping it dry with a hand towel and clinking it back into the cabinet. Since his dad disappeared five months ago, he'd been doing half the cooking at his place. Clean-ing, too.

He frowned at the window over the sink, the lemon-yellow curtains dotted with tiny blue tulips. "These new?"

Hard not to notice the color pop. Dad had always insisted our house uphold the Warren tradition of frugal, no-frills decor—same as when his parents had run the place, and his grandparents before. Any hint of rainbow belonged in the field. Inside, it was cream walls and dark wood.

Mom had practiced her forced smile as she replaced the aged lace that Grandma Peg had hung decades ago. "Maybe this kitchen needs a touch more color," she'd said. "Some-thing cheerier." She'd dumped the old curtains in the trash, where they were swallowed up by tea leaves and banana peels, before Dad could demand she put them back.

That was a little over two months ago, right after I lost Teddy and stopped talking to Derek. When it was finally becoming clear the blight might take everything we had. It was Mom's sunny little act of defiance.

I nodded. "Since April."

Derek turned his back on them, scowling.

We'd missed so much in each other's lives. Lord knows kitchen curtains were the tip of a towering iceberg.

For the first time since he'd arrived, I looked at him— *really* looked at him. Shadows had collected under his eyes, slashed into the broad planes of his cheeks. Red blisters glared from the pads of his fingers and palms. It took an awful lot of extra work to blister hands as callused as his or mine.

He was worn-out, exhausted in a way that came from weeks, months—not hours.

"Derek . . ." I licked my suddenly drying lips. "Listen, thank you for coming today. My whole life's falling apart, and I—"

"All our lives are falling apart, Wren." Derek stiffened. "My dad's still missing—thanks for asking. The blight has been on my farm for months. Reached us maybe a week after you broke up with me. Did you even know?"

"Of course I knew," I said. I was haunted by the thought of his missing dad. And when my parents told me about his farm, I lay awake that whole night, curled into the tightest ball. Even the wheat's murmur couldn't drown out my thoughts of Derek and his mom finding those festering melons and the exhausting hours they'd spend fighting to save the rest. No way it'd be enough, especially not with his sister, Claudette, away for freshman year at college. They'd lose a ton of crops. The money they needed for Derek's college fund.

"You didn't help us." Derek folded his arms, leaning back against the sink. "You didn't say a thing to me."

I couldn't, though.

I could still barely handle being in the same room after what he'd done to me. And if he had any idea what *I* had done to all of us, to Hollow's End, he'd hate me forever. I could keep it hidden from everyone else, like Dad had made me promise, but Derek knew how to see all the way through me. If he asked the right questions, made the right accusations . . .

"I'm sorry." I stared at my mug, running my thumb over the chipped handle.

"You don't mean that. You can barely even look at me."

My whole face steamed up.

"You know what, Wren?" Derek loosed a breath somewhere between a laugh and a scoff, shaking his head. "I should probably get going."

He'd have to leave soon or not at all. Curfew was already too close.

My gut seized up as he moved toward the door. "No, Derek—"

He paused.

"Please," I said.

Please don't leave is what I wanted to say. *I have no idea how I feel about us or anything right now, but you spent two months begging me not to walk away. All I know now is, I need you here, too.*

But I could only make that one word come out.

Derek's gaze flicked all over my face, and I hoped he

22

understood the part I couldn't speak, like he so often had before.

The pendulum clock ticked out our silence. One swing, two swings, three . . .

"Fine," Derek muttered.

He crossed to the kitchen phone and called his mom to tell her he wasn't coming home and not to worry—a hell of a lot more than my parents had done for me.

And then, rigidly, he came back to the table. Reclaimed his chair across from me.

I wanted to thank him, but I was afraid saying anything would undo this. Jinx it. I picked at the stray dirt under my nails, burning under his stare.

He sighed. "How much wheat did it get?"

He was just veering us back toward a safer topic, but it worked.

"Six of the violet," I said. "So far."

He nodded. He still hadn't touched the hot chocolate. "I don't know why I thought if anything would be safe, it'd be the wheat."

The whole town did. Rainbow Fields was one of our four local farming miracles, but even among Derek's family and their silver-veined ghost melons, the Murphys' golden yams, and the Harrises' prized horses and dogs, our wheat was the most spectacular. Tourists overbooked our guided tours and posed with selfie sticks for the better part of thirty minutes, clicking shot after shot until the wind caught the rainbow in our wheat just right. Then they'd crowd by the ribbon-wrapped pole we'd planted to mark the only spot with reliable Wi-Fi—unfortunately, like three feet from our front porch—to post.

We told everyone that Dad's ancestors lucked into our wheat, that the only credit they could take was for knowing a miracle when they saw one.

They knew we were lying, but no one had ever figured out the truth.

A couple times people had snuck in after dark, sliced off stalks to run away with and replant. Mom and Dad just laughed, watching from the window. They knew what those stolen wheat berries would grow: plain straw-colored two-foot-tall wheat.

Our five-foot-tall shimmering rainbow remained ours alone. Our supply was small, so our prices were high. But for any bakery that could afford us, the local specialty was a pale seven-plaited loaf, one glittery-flecked strand per wheat color. Unicorn braid. It had a cult following—people who swore by its supposed healing properties. Every flu season, our orders skyrocketed.

I wasn't sure about its virus-fighting abilities, but I'd spent enough sick days with Dad serving me a fresh hunk dripping in wild clover honey to find it comforting.

Actually, if there was anything I could eat now . . .

I pushed up from the table and dug into the breadbox behind me to find a loaf from my favorite bakery partner, Harvest Homes. The bread melted as I chewed, each plait a different kiss of our wheat's natural flavors: peppery red, malty-rye orange, grapefruit yellow, celery-seed green, salty blue, eely indigo, and that last note, blackberry-sweet violet.

The unicorn braid tingled against my tongue, over-whelming that sickly sour rot in my throat. At least for a moment.

"How are you feeling?" Derek asked, his tone suddenly soft. He turned in his chair to watch me leaning against the counter, eyeing me in a way that turned my face hotter.

The bread stuck in my throat as I swallowed. "I still feel okay."

A cough tickled up—one I only half-choked back.

"Well," I admitted, "*mostly* okay."

"You do have allergies, though," Derek offered up. "Or it could be a cold."

I couldn't answer. All I could think of was Benji Thomas. After he'd gotten infected, his parents locked him in their barn, leashed like an animal, anything to keep him from running wild into the forest. He'd strained against his ropes until he snapped his own neck.

I stared out the window to the tangle of trees past our wheat. Soon, those flashes of white eyes would be weaving through the dark, hunting for a fresh place to dig their teeth. "What if it's not allergies?" The words dragged from me, slow and heavy. "What if it's not a cold?"

"Even if . . . if you are . . ." Apparently, Derek couldn't even say it. "There has to be some way to fight it."

I shook my head at his clenched fists. "What are you gonna do, beat up the blight? It's not like—"

Scritch, scritch, scritch . . . I turned toward the sound. It was coming from outside.

Near the porch.

I jolted back from the counter.

Derek leapt up from his seat.

Scritch, scritch, scritch . . .

Again. Louder.

Coming up the back steps.

Derek grabbed my arm, nestling me in toward the heat of his body as if it was safer there.

"Wait," I tried to tell him, "it might be—"

"Shh!" Derek jabbed at the dimmer switch beside us. Above the kitchen table, the glass pendulum went dark.

Scritch, scritch . . . On the porch, getting closer.

"Don't move," Derek whispered. In the darkness, I could see his shadowy form pointing something at the back-door window. A pistol.

Whoa, since when did he start carrying?

"Hey!" I jerked away. "What do you think you're—"

Scratch! At the back door.

Now I knew for sure what it was, but a hard click came from beside me—Derek cocking his gun.

"Derek! *No!*" I darted between him and the door, throwing my arms wide.

"Jesus, Wren!" The pistol fumbled from Derek's hands and clattered to the ground. He forgot all about staying quiet. "Why would you *ever* jump in front of a gun? That can't be your parents! It sounds like some animal!" He dropped to his hands and knees to retrieve his weapon.

I stared at his outline in the dark, my chest still pounding with panic. "Just don't point that thing at a target you can't see." I punched the knob of the kitchen light back on. "Not in my house."

I moved toward the door.

Derek gaped up at me, still on the floor. "What are you doing?" He grabbed my ankle. "Wren, don't—"

"It's fine!" I shook my ankle to throw off his hand. "It's Teddy!"

Just in case, I peered out the window. We'd gotten into the habit of keeping the porch light off, the lights inside dim. Nothing brought them out of the forest like light.

"Teddy?" Derek gasped. "But Teddy is . . ."

On the murky porch, something waited. Wolf-shaped. Shaggy and ragged. Dragging its nails down the back door.

My dog.

Gun in hand, Derek scrambled back to his feet.

"Would you chill?" I said. "I'm not letting her in!" I rummaged through the breadbox for the stale hunk of unicorn braid I'd set aside. It was a smidge moldy, but she wouldn't mind.

"Psst, Teddy! Up here, baby girl." I cranked the handle to inch open the window above the counter.

The shadowy shape paused, shifted. Teddy lumbered across the worn wooden boards, stopping under the window. Those hollow eyes, white like moth wings, stared up at me.

"You're *feeding* her?" Derek's voice came from behind me, half-choked. "You should be putting her out of her misery."

"Derek," I said, "you put a bullet in my dog, you are dead to me. Now and forever."

He stepped back with an injured scowl, but he lowered his gun.

His family didn't have pets. They had livestock. Goats in a shed. He didn't understand what Teddy was to me. He hadn't been there that day when I was nine, when my parents finally caved and brought me to see the Harrises' newest puppy litter. The yipping fuzzballs had rolled over each other, tiny tongues flopping. Their coats gleamed with the trademark Harris-bred auburn.

Of course, I wanted the runt. The tiniest one, her coat a bit closer to mahogany than the Harrises preferred. In her rush to greet me, she got trampled by the rest.

The Harrises worried about her health. Wondered if she'd even make it. "Choose another," they'd encouraged me. "What about this one? Such a cute white patch on his chest."

Nothin' doing. I held out my arms for Teddy, and I waited like a concrete statue until they gave her to me. She wriggled happily in my hands, ribs ridging from her sides. The first thing she did was reach up and kiss me under the chin with a soft pink tongue.

My puppy. I'd never let her go.

Not then, not now.

Outside the window came a stabbing whine, one that started high and ended low, edged like a growl. A rancid stench wafted up to me.

"Teddy," I said, "sit."

The old porch groaned as the shadow shifted back on her haunches.

"Good girl." I tossed the bread, and she snapped it into her jaws, silvery threads of spit glistening by the light of her eyes.

I cranked the window shut and turned back to Derek, my arms preemptively crossed. "What?" I said. "All she'll do is drag herself around the porch. She'll be gone before morning."

Derek had his arms crossed, too, unconvinced. "Uh-huh."

"She still listens to me," I said, not sure why I was bothering. I didn't have to explain myself to him. But I pressed on anyway. "As long as she listens, she's in there, okay? So, I can't . . . I'm not gonna just . . ."

I squeezed my eyes shut, barricading the heat building behind them.

"Anyway, is that what you're gonna do to *me*?" I waved a hand at his gun. "Put me out of my misery?"

Derek's face fell. "What? No, I—"

"Then why do you even have that thing? You don't use it on them, do you?" I pointed toward the forest.

"Not on people!" He shoved the pistol into the back of his waistband, out of sight. "On animals! We've had problems at our place. Possums, a moose . . ."

"You shot a moose?"

"I *tried* to shoot a moose. Claudette shot a moose."

"Right. That makes more sense."

He'd practiced for years with his sister, shooting cans off their fence, but he still put more bullets in the fence than actual targets.

"Besides," Derek said, "we don't know you're infected, right?"

"Right," I mumbled, rubbing at the sting in my forehead. It had spread from the center into my temples, and was now itching deep under my skin, a place I couldn't scratch.

God, I was tired. I never would've said it aloud, but more than anything, I just wanted my mom.

What the hell were she and Dad still doing out?

Teddy was here. She was awake. The rest of the blighted had to be waking up, too.

I shot a glance at the clock: 8:30. Outside, it was dark.

My parents had officially missed curfew. No more pretending they'd just gotten caught up and cut it too close.

Derek followed my gaze. "You already tried calling them?"

"Earlier." I nodded. "But I'll try again."

I called Mom's cell. She didn't pick up. And neither did Dad. The Harrises' phone rang eight times and jumped to: *"Hey there, you've got the Harrises . . . Or you don't yet, because we're busy. If you're calling for a quote on our stud fees—"*

I hung up. Slowly. Stiffly.

"No one answered?" Derek paced between the fridge and table. "Your parents, the Harrises . . . they can't still be out there."

If they were, something had gone horribly wrong.

Derek and I froze, eyes locking. I might be bone-tired, it might be after curfew, but . . .

"I have to drive over there," I said.

"What?" Derek glanced out to the forest, to the dim white dots in the dark. "Can't we just call the police?"

But we both knew they'd stopped answering those calls. Sure, tomorrow morning, they'd go survey and write up a report, but it'd be too late to help anyone who was outside now.

I couldn't really blame them, the few who'd stayed behind with us when the responders closed the bridge. They'd lost officers to the blight, and they had families of their own to think about.

So did Derek.

"Listen," I said, "you can wait here or head home. Don't feel like you need to come. It's not safe."

"Yeah. It's *really* not." He stood in front of the back door, crossing his arms like a bodyguard, ready to block the exit. "Look, I get wanting to help them—of course I do—but how is putting yourself in danger going to make anything better?"

He was being rational. But my heart beat against my ribs like it might burst. The soles of my feet twitched, like every second I wasted here was another mini-betrayal of my parents.

"Derek. *I have to go.*" It burst out of me, that same desperate fire that had fueled me when I jumped in front of his gun.

He searched me with scrutinizing eyes. His lips parted, like he wanted to ask again what this was really about, this painful desperation he'd seen in me more and more since March. Since I'd realized the blight was my fault.

Everything it did—every death, every farm lost, every life ruined—all my fault.

I looked away, fixating on the relentless tick of the owl clock so I didn't have to see his disappointment. He'd spent weeks asking me questions. He knew damn well I wasn't going to answer now.

Derek sighed, scrubbing his palms over his face. "If you're going, I'm going."

Warm relief melted the tension in my chest. Of course I

didn't want to do this alone. But if Derek came out of guilt and something happened to him . . .

"Don't," I said. "Please don't. The risk isn't worth it for you."

Derek pinned me in a burning stare, eyes dilating dark. "Shouldn't I be the one who decides which risks are worth it to me?"

I didn't know how to argue with that.

Worst of all, I didn't want to.

I nodded, and turned away so he wouldn't see me blot my eyes on my sleeve. "Then let's go," I said.

CHAPTER 3

There was an immediate problem with our plan. It was hunkered down and waiting on the porch.

I snuck a glance out the window.

Yep, what had been Teddy still lay out there. Her head was rested on her folded paws, but her shock-white eyes stayed peeled. Her patchy tail thumped slowly side to side.

She usually stayed all night. At first, my parents would chase her away. But then sometimes we heard other sounds. Shuffling, or the creak of porch steps. Teddy would cough out her hoarse bark, her nails skittering over the wooden planks as she chased it—whatever it was—away.

So my parents let her stay, but they were stern as steel: I was not to interact with her in any way. She'd lunged at Dad once when he took out the trash.

She was sick and confused.

She was a creature of the wild now.

Derek and I pressed up against the front door, listening, but all we heard was the shrill, scissoring calls of crickets.

Teddy was still around the side. We only had to make it to the driveway without her catching us. I touched my truck keys in my pocket, just to reassure myself. Of course they were there. I'd already checked five times.

Derek's hand twitched toward the back of his jeans.

"No guns," I whispered.

He dropped his hand. "This is a bad plan. A *really* bad plan."

"Then don't come."

I took a deep bracing breath and put my hand on the doorknob. There was no real point in stealth. Teddy could hear a rabbit rustle in the wheat from fifty feet away. No matter how quiet I tried to be, she'd hear me.

I burst into the restless June night.

Before Derek could slam the front door shut behind us, a ragged bark broke out from the side of the porch.

That wolf shape charged around the corner, barreling toward me.

"Teddy!" I shouted. "Fetch!"

I hurled the steak I'd pilfered from the fridge as far as I could—off the porch, toward the garden. If she knew how to sit, she still had to know how to fetch. *Please, please, please—*

She snuffed at the air, wheezing as the meaty projectile arced over her head.

With a hearty woof, she pulled an about-face and raced after it.

Good dog.

"I can't believe that worked," Derek said as we dashed across the porch.

"I know my dog."

Still, Teddy was on that steak before our shoes left the last porch step. She snapped it up in fierce jaws, an unholy squelch sounding out as she sucked it down her throat.

The moon shone wet on her bloodstained snout as she turned back to us.

"Any other plans to deal with *your* dog?" Derek asked.

I didn't have time for a smart-ass answer. "Shut up and run!" I shoved Derek ahead of me.

With one last longing lick at the grass, Teddy vaulted across the garden toward us, slobber streaming in her wake.

Pebbles flew under our feet as we raced across the yard to my truck, Teddy's loping strides pounding the ground behind us.

Good thing I'd left the truck unlocked. Derek yanked open the passenger door with a shriek of unoiled metal. He was almost safe.

But Teddy wasn't after him. She was after me.

We used to play like this when she was a puppy—chase. We'd run and run, and then she'd tackle me from the back. When I was eight, she pounced me down so hard in the driveway that gravel sliced every bit of my exposed skin, my knees and shins and forearms carved into bloody pink patchwork. That's when Mom said I had to stop playing chase with Teddy, and I did.

Until now.

Gravel crunched and shifted under me as I sprinted for the safety of the driver's seat, Teddy a stride from my heels. The muscles in my legs felt too loose, like I couldn't push hard enough against the ground. I was faster than this. I knew I was. But my head start meant nothing. Teddy kept gaining and gaining.

Something happened to creatures the longer they lived with the blight: It sped them up, gave them extra strength. But it also made them clumsier.

Behind me, rocks skittered, and Teddy crashed with a yelp. It killed me not to check if she was okay.

To be fair, she was trying to eat me.

I tore at the flimsy chrome handle of my truck door and pulled it open. As I stepped up, I chanced a glance at her.

Oh shit. Teddy was back on her feet, an arm's length from my dangling ankle.

In a wild blur, I dove inside and slammed the door.

The metal crunched hard—a distinctly dog-sized crunch—as she hit the other side of the door.

"Teddy!" My heart stopped. Oh my God, did I just bludgeon my dog to death with a truck door?

I couldn't help cranking down the window, terrified I'd find some crumpled mass with a caved-in skull lying on the ground.

"Baby girl?" I called timidly out into the vast night.

"Wren!" Derek sat up sharply from his panting slump. "What are you doing?"

With a low whine, Teddy hauled herself to her feet and gave her head a hard shake, flinging gooey spit all over my tire. Her pale tongue lolled out to one side as she looked up at me.

I should've known she was tougher than a truck.

"Good girl," I whispered down to her.

Teddy's tail pounded the gravel. By the dull starlight, I caught a white glimmer near the rotting tip. Jesus, was that bone?

"'Good girl'?" Derek said, butting into our quiet moment. "She tried to kill us! What are you praising her for?"

For staying alive. But I doubted Derek would appreciate that.

I shrugged. "For *not* killing us?"

"Not sure she's gonna pick up on that nuance." Derek rubbed at his forehead, catching the sweat dripping into his eyebrows.

"Stay," I told Teddy.

I rolled up the window and turned my key in the ignition. The growl of my truck's sputtering engine startled both me and Derek, feeling twenty times louder after curfew, in the dark.

I cleared my throat. "Well, we handled that," I said. "We can handle whatever's at the Harrises'."

Derek, white-knuckling the passenger door, gave me the smallest grunt of acknowledgment.

We both wanted to pretend that whatever was at the Harrises' wasn't going to be a million times worse.

We set off down the winding driveway, rocks grumbling under the tires.

In the side mirror, I watched the shadow of my dog until the glowing pinpoints of her eyes faded into the night.

Derek and I lapsed into twitchy silence, scouring the tree line on either side of the narrow dirt road.

Every time a moth fluttered in front of the windshield, my heart spasmed.

Mom had been ferrying me to the Harrises' for weekly riding lessons since I was old enough to sit in a saddle. I knew the drive by heart, even in the dark, from Rainbow Fields, in the northeast part of the peninsula, to the Harris Red Horse Ranch, in the southwest. Thirty minutes. And that was if I went the short way, cutting through town—the heart of Hollow's End, nestled dead center between our four farms.

Even before the blight and the quarantine and curfew, our quaint three-hundred-person population had been far outmatched by farmland and forest, so it wasn't uncommon to drive for a stretch without meeting another pair of headlights. The closer to town, the more folks would pop up—passing locals waving through windshields, lost tourists flagging down directions.

Tonight, the road was empty.

By the time Derek and I reached Main Street, the ancient dashboard clock read 8:51. But I was gambling the cops wouldn't be out to catch us breaking curfew, not even here.

The whole town sat dark, even the streetlamps.

The dim sweep of my headlights passed over one locked door after another. CLOSED signs were plastered over shop windows. The red, white, and blue barbershop pole outside the Thomases' had been unlit since Benji got infected.

Even the places that still opened by day—the General Store, Ted's Hardware—had taped Sharpied updates in their windows, outlining their dwindling hours.

It'd been awful enough to lose the spring festival this year, when the Harrises would usually set up their petting zoo and haul their newest pup litter into town. They'd prance and play-fight in makeshift pens hemmed with hay bales—and whimper irresistibly at passersby. All for sale, of course, for thousands apiece. We'd host our spring rainbow cakewalk and weave our wheat into wreaths with baby's breath, for people to wear proudly in their hair.

The summer festival, when the Pewter-Flores ghost melons were the star, should've been kicking off now. It was supposed to be when the carnival came. We couldn't fit much—but a small Ferris wheel and a Tilt-a-Whirl went a long way—flashing hot pink and purple against the black sky like fireworks. Main Street transformed into one big whiff of sugary kettle corn and fresh-fried corn dogs and ghost melonade, with its sweet, cooling tang, a pale, unearthly blue that glowed in the dark. Kids ran through, shrieking and bopping each other with balloons.

Now, the only life on Main Street was an empty plastic bag, wafting like a wraith from one sidewalk to the other.

It was so quiet I could hear the unsteady echo of my own breath, the seat springs cringing as Derek fidgeted. My old truck didn't have bucket seats—just a cushioned bench. Derek's shoulder was only a foot from mine, his musky body spray wrapping around us. The kind of closeness we definitely hadn't minded when we were dating. But now . . .

He found an awful lot of other places to look, none of them at me.

No doubt he was breathing me in, too. I hadn't remembered deodorant after my shower, had I?

No. Definitely not.

Not that it mattered, because we were probably going to die anyway.

I rolled to a grudging halt at the stop sign beside the white-bricked Cormac Murphy Community Center. Every public building in Hollow's End was named after one founding farmer or another. It probably didn't hurt that the mayor and town council were usually distant relations. But I'd always had a soft spot for this building, even more than the Thomas G. Warren Library, because of the enormous mural on the community center's side—the four founding families standing in a circle, holding hands around an enormous cornucopia. It was whimsical and rainbow-bright, with both a sun and a moon in the sky. Whenever I walked by growing up, I'd run a hand along the Crayola purple wheat spilling from the cornucopia, then boop the nose of the frolicking Clifford-red pup that looked like Teddy.

But tonight, the truck's headlights cast strange, slanting shadows across the mural. The colors were too glaring, even as the old paint curled and crumbled. The grins of the founders were too toothy and wide.

On the billboard beside us, missing-persons posters fluttered in the night breeze. There were so many, layered, the newer ones blocking the first—from January, when the blight showed up at the Murphys' farm and folks helping with their crops started disappearing. We'd figured the blight had made them delirious, that they'd wandered away and died in the cold, feverish and freezing.

Then, in February, one lunged out of the forest at night, eyes glowing white, and nearly tore off the arm of a cop. That's when we realized that whatever the blight was doing to the people infected, it was a lot stranger than death. It was just like those "rabid" animals that had started staggering out of the forest after sundown.

The posters still said MISSING. It was too dangerous to search at night. By day, the cops scoured the forest, but they couldn't find a single blighted person—not even a blighted animal.

So, the flyers just accumulated and accumulated.

Would my parents be up there next?

Amber Murphy's picture glared at me from the dark. Her bright-red hair. The freckles like mine. A fellow founding-farm heir, and a junior at Meadowbrook High, bused over early in the morning with the rest of the Hollow's End crew, at least until we all started learning to drive.

She'd escaped the early round of infections at the Murphy farm. But in late April, she'd driven after curfew to visit a friend. They found her truck by the side of the road— a big dent in the front, glass from her smashed headlights scattered across the road. The driver's door lay several feet away, yanked from its hinges, raked through with claw marks.

Blood smeared the ground, trailing off into the woods.

Amber's disappearance was enough to end any grumbling about the curfew. No one I knew had broken it since.

And yet, here we were. Staring at her face after dark.

I swallowed hard and tried to steady my grip on the wheel as I drove us to the other side of town. Soon, the mostly empty houses thinned back into trees.

"Maybe you should turn on the high beams," Derek said. He kept craning forward to squint at the road and into the trees.

I shook my head, hard. "The brighter the lights, the faster they'll find us." It was bad enough to have any headlights on at all, but we didn't have much choice on these pitch-dark roads.

"Right." Derek winced. "Well, let's at least turn on the radio." He reached for the knob.

"We need to be able to hear! Would you stop trying to get us murdered?" I grabbed his hand without thinking.

We both jolted at my intimate impulse, a relic of our long-since-canceled relationship. I snatched my hand back.

I was immediately sorry I'd let go so fast. Derek used to make me feel safer than anyone else did.

I clutched at the cold grooves of the steering wheel instead.

"Sorry," Derek mumbled. His gaze darted back to his window. "It's just, I can see them out there. The . . . fireflies."

Mom liked to call them that, too, the white flashes in the dark. It was better than saying "eyes."

"Where?" I asked. "How far from the road?"

"A ways back. It doesn't look like they're rushing at us. Just watching, I guess."

"Watching . . ." I bit the inside of my cheek and pushed harder on the gas.

It was still a long fifteen minutes until we saw the faded sign for the Harris Red Horse Ranch, then, up ahead, their roadside farm stand, closed for the night. A placard propped on the counter said WE'LL BE BACK WITH THE GOODS. SEE YA BRIGHT N' EARLY!

We turned past the booth and started up the long driveway—a series of hills and dips hedged by wild clover, overshadowed by trees that had staked their claim on this land far longer than any of our families.

My ribs constricted tighter and tighter as we crept closer to the house and barn. God, I needed some harmless explanation for why my parents hadn't called, why no one was answering the phone.

Pickup trucks clogged the driveway in front of the house, so we parked beside Mom's Jeep in the grass. They'd called in a lot of folks to help. I recognized the Murphys' truck, too.

An awful lot of vehicles for no lights to be on in that house. It stood dark, no sign of movement inside.

"Maybe something happened and they didn't want to risk turning on a light, not even a dim one?" Derek wasn't half-bad at bullshitting.

Even as cold, slimy dread splashed in my stomach.

"Maybe," I said.

With a thick, sour swallow, I unlocked my door.

"You're getting out?" Derek's eyes went wide.

"I have to check the house, at least. You can stay in the

car." I opened the door and turned back. "Seriously, I'd understand," I said, and slid out, tapping the door shut behind me as quietly as I could.

The night outside was nearly silent. Rattled by a breeze. Overhead, an owl hooted.

I jerked my head up. Perched high in the ancient oak leaning over the driveway, the barn owl peered with wintry, foggy eyes, its speckled feathers mottled against the branches.

I pointed it out to Derek as he slipped out of the truck. "Blighted owl. Watch your head."

Derek muttered a curse as he circled around to stand at my back.

I would've done the same for him, even after our falling-out, but he was the one being forced to prove his steadfastness. I hoped he had any idea how much it meant to me. I gave him a little nod over my shoulder. It was the most I could manage in that awful moment, standing on the Harrises' empty farm.

He nodded back, like he knew what I meant.

For now, that would have to be enough.

We tiptoed up to the house. No porch, which thankfully meant no creaky old boards leading to the door. Derek peered in the front window and turned to shake his head.

I pressed the doorbell and held my breath. The distant melody of "Amazing Grace" chimed inside the house.

But no footsteps followed.

A far-off clang came from somewhere past the house.

The barn?

Derek and I met eyes. The barn was farther from the

truck than it was wise to wander, but the alley around the side of the house was too narrow for us to drive up.

Well, at least Derek and I were pretty fast runners, if it came to that. We'd made it past Teddy.

Together, we trudged through the dry grass, wincing at its every rustle against our jeans.

The open barn doors creaked with a slight sway in the breeze.

While the Harrises were known for their exceptional horses and dogs, they kept a modest number of other animals, too. A dozen pigs, several sheep, a small herd of fat-sided goats. They usually filled the air with muddy-nosed snorts and stamping hooves.

Now, all I could hear was the trilling of peeper frogs, hiding in the grass.

In the barn's doorway, dozens of hoofprints were trampled in the dirt and scattered hay. My stomach closed into a fist. Someone must've let the animals out in one mad rush. A desperate move—one you only pulled if there was no time to lead them to safety.

Deep in the barn—a thud.

So, if someone had let out all the animals, what was in here now?

I didn't want to know, but if there was even a chance it was a person . . .

I took one step in, instantly enveloped by the familiar odors of hay and tangy manure. "H-hello?" I called down the aisle. My voice had always been higher and thinner than I would've liked, but it sounded extra-small now. The empty barn ate it right up.

Derek kept watch behind us, making sure nothing lurched out of the swaying cornfield.

The barn sat silent.

I tried again, a little louder: "Hello? Anyone in here?"

Scuffling—near one of the back stalls. Whatever it was, it wasn't gonna make this easy.

I led us in deeper, one shaky step at a time. Without the moonlight from the open doors, everything grew murkier. I pulled out my phone and tapped on the flashlight. At this point, the darkness was more dangerous than a little light.

My beam found empty pens and smashed gates. Hay particles swirled through the light. To my left, something gleamed. A half-rusted pitchfork leaned against the wall. It made me sick to contemplate using it, but I grabbed it before I could stop myself.

"If you get a pitchfork, I get a gun," Derek muttered, sliding the pistol from his waistband.

Another quiet clang, now just thirty feet away, stopped me from arguing.

I took one more step forward. The quiet clang became a loud clang.

Something bigger than me or Derek burst out from the back stall.

It reared up with a high whinny, and clattered its hooves down against the concrete floor. The beam of my light caught a cinnamon-red coat. Deep-brown eyes, orbed with over-dilated black.

The horse wasn't blighted. It was just terrified out of its mind.

A champagne-pale shock of mane spurted out between

its ears. I'd know those frizzy bangs, the uneven white blaze down the nose, anywhere.

"Buckwheat!" The Harrises' youngest filly, a two-year-old with fighting spirit. "Buckwheat, shh!" I dropped the beam from her eyes and set down the pitchfork, approaching with an outstretched hand.

She clomped backward, tossing her head. I'd never ridden her, but hopefully she remembered my weekly visits. All those crisp green apples I'd fed her.

She paused when her flaring nostrils got a whiff of my scent.

My eyes caught on a bucket mounted on the wall next to me. I dug in and pulled out a flaky fistful of oats. "It's okay, Buckwheat. It's me." Inching closer, I held it out to her, flat-handed.

With an uncertain whicker, she shuffled closer and shoved her velvet nose against my palm, licking with her strong tongue.

I smiled and fed her another fistful. She let me pat her side.

"Um, Wren?" Derek glanced behind us. "Touching as this is, not sure we have time to play My Little Pony."

"We can't leave her here to die."

Derek groaned, gesturing toward the fields beyond the barn. "Look, we have no idea what's out there. We haven't seen any sign of anyone—"

"I know," I said. "That means we should search the fields, and we can't get the truck over there. Don't you think it might help to have a horse? A *Harris* horse?"

It was the Harris family motto: "Nothing beats a Harris

horse, except maybe a Harris dog." As the proud owner of a Harris dog, I'd always loved that. Now it hit me with a different kind of pang, salt in the gaping wound of losing Teddy.

Rumor had it, the first of the Harris horses and dogs came from the forest itself. Frankly, I didn't buy it. If my family was lying about our miracle wheat to throw people off our scent, why wouldn't the Harrises do the same? But wherever the animals came from, there was no doubt: they were lit from within. The Harris dogs and horses were all that same disarming auburn. They grew bigger than normal dogs or horses. Stronger. Faster. The Harrises made a fortune studding their stallions.

Derek sighed. "Okay, just . . . hurry, yeah?"

"I'll be fast. Let me calm her down and get her saddled up."

Buckwheat was on her third fistful of oats. She let me scratch the bristly hair under her forelock. Maybe a fistful or two more and I'd reach for the bridle hanging by her stall. She'd bolt if I tried too soon.

Derek looked over his shoulder. "I'll go check out there, make sure nothing's planning our imminent deaths."

I jerked my head up. "Don't go out there alone! It'll just be a minute—"

"Someone needs to watch the door!"

"Don't go far." I pointed a warning finger, like Mom did to me when she got dead serious.

"Like I'd go playing around on an abandoned blight-wrecked farm." Derek's tone had eye roll all over it as he retraced our steps, muttering, "But that's cool. Don't come with me or anything. God forbid we risk the *horse's* life."

Pretty sure he knew I could hear him.

Maybe he didn't get why Buckwheat mattered so much to me. But something bad had gone down on this farm. Really bad. All the trucks were still here. The bridles and saddles hung by the empty stalls. If anyone had escaped, they were on foot—out there, somewhere in the night. Maybe that's exactly what my parents had done. With every fiber of my muscle, pulse of blood, ounce of soul, I *needed* that to be what my parents had done. If they hadn't . . .

I didn't know if I could help them at all anymore. What I knew was simple: I could save this horse, and maybe, if things went south, this horse could save us.

I mumbled soothing nothings and slipped the bridle over Buckwheat's head.

She startled at the straps against her cheeks, but I palmed the metal bit past her teeth before she had time to spit it out. She snorted in indignation as I saddled her up, and stomped her back foot when I tightened the girth. A drama queen.

It'd be better if I could find cloth for her hooves. Her horseshoes would be quiet enough on the grass or dirt, but not on the barn's concrete. Not on asphalt.

I glanced toward the barn doorway, expecting the re-assuring silhouette of Derek's broad shoulders.

But the doorway was empty. No Derek. No silhouette. Nothing reassuring.

"Derek . . . ?" I half whispered.

Buckwheat whickered, flinching under my uncertain touch.

Probably he'd just roamed away from the barn's entrance. Probably he was checking around the sides, or wandering out to scan the perimeter of the cornfield.

Probably, probably, probably.

Probably wasn't a fun game to play.

Okay, screw the hoof padding. With a grunt, I hauled myself into the saddle, throwing my other leg across the horse's back. We clicked one horseshoe after another out of the barn, both pairs of our nervous eyes darting. God, I hoped nothing would rush at us from the shadows. I *really* hoped Buckwheat didn't throw me and smash my skull into the ground. A helmet would've been a good idea.

Too late now.

"Wren!"

The call was distant, out from the fields.

Dammit, Derek. That was way farther than he should've wandered. And what the hell did he think he was doing, shouting like that?

He must've found something.

"I'm coming!" I dug my heels into Buckwheat, and we lunged out of the abandoned barn, the night air whipping my cheeks.

"I said, 'Wren'!" Derek was closer now. He was running hard, the corn crashing in the field.

"I said I'm coming!" I yelled, turning Buckwheat toward the sound.

"No! Not 'Wren'! 'Run'! I'm telling you to *run*!"

Oh. Oh no.

From my perch on Buckwheat, I saw the cornstalks swaying and snapping. A line that must have been Derek cut pell-mell across the field. Uncountable lines converged behind him, all leading from the forest.

He'd found something, all right. Or rather, it had found him.

My jaw dropped in a voiceless scream. The stench of fungus rolled in from the field, chokingly thick.

The ground under Buckwheat's hooves vibrated with the approaching stampede.

She whinnied and waffled, ready to bolt.

I pulled her to our left, running parallel to the field. "Derek! This way!"

The fierce crack of Derek's gun rang out, close, followed by a groan and a crash and Derek's muffled cry. Something was almost on him.

His crackling path through the corn veered to meet us.

Behind him, the other lines shifted to follow.

"Come on, come on . . ." I bit my lips raw, charting his path, racing to align my own.

Derek would never have come here if it weren't for me. Whatever else happened, I had to get him out. I gripped Buckwheat's reins so tight the leather cut into my palms.

In front of us, the stalks parted.

Out burst Derek, wild-eyed. His face and hands were nicked bloody by the sharp edges of the corn plants.

He looked back at the stalks snapping behind him.

I needed to get him out of there. Now.

We charged straight at him in a thunder of hooves. At

this speed, Buckwheat might just mow him down. I hauled at her reins, and she tossed her head with a furious whinny—like, didn't I have any idea what was coming our way?

I wound her in a circle, forcing her to slow to a trot. "Come on," I yelled to Derek. "You have to climb up!"

Grunts came from the swaying field beside us. A rising growl.

Derek stared at me. His family was better with machines than animals. But he grimaced and charged for us.

As Buckwheat circled past, he seized hold of the saddle and lifted his foot to the stirrup.

Behind him, only a few feet away, the crops smashed apart. A savage roar raised every hair at the back of my neck.

A black bear stared us down with cloudy, glowing eyes. Its torn mouth gaped, jaw hanging by gory gob-ridden tendons, lips rotting back from its shark-sized teeth.

I froze. So did Derek, one hand on the saddle, one foot in the stirrup.

Buckwheat unfroze first. Her front legs reared from the ground. Under me, the saddle slid.

"Hey!" Derek cried, slipping. "Hey—"

I yanked the reins. "Buckwheat! No!" But one of my feet was out of its stirrup. I pressed down on the other heel, trying to find purchase.

My calf quivered, weak—weaker than it should have been. My fingers couldn't hold their grip.

Derek and I crashed down with a breath-whooshing thump. My teeth tore into my tongue as my bones slammed against the packed earth—and Derek's torso.

Buckwheat galloped off without us, while we spat in the dirt.

"Dios freaking mio," Derek wheezed as we scrambled to untangle.

The bear rose to its back legs before us, looming seven feet tall, a vicious tree with fangs and claws.

Derek staggered upright. In a steely flash, he raised his gun and fired. Dead-on, at the bear's face.

Glops thicker than saliva flew out, slapping wetly against cornstalks. The bear reared back, dropping to all fours.

Derek drew his shoulders tall, looking awful proud of himself.

Until the bear turned and locked us again in its milky, hot stare. Its jaw was gone entirely, blown back into the field. Its tongue, thick and pale as a trout's belly, flopped from that gaping pit in the bottom half of its face. It roared again—a gurgling choke that sprayed out more molten bear bits.

I grabbed Derek's hand and bolted toward the barn. Again, something writhed in the muscle of my calf, this strange twitching tug, threatening to trip me to the ground.

I fought against it—landing every step with all the pounding precision I could muster.

I peered past the shadowy tractor and fences for a horse-sized flash of red. "Buckwheat!" I wasn't worried about making noise anymore. Everything in that field knew exactly where we were. They were already coming.

The bear thundered behind us, clumsy but determined. Behind it came the sound of hooves and growling from

God-knows-what. I sure as hell wasn't turning around to check.

I tugged Derek, scanning more and more frantically for Buckwheat. We'd never make it back to the truck.

In the distance, over by the backyard, dogs began to bark.

Oh shit. The dogs. Teddy's mom and dad and brothers and sisters. The Harrises had kept a veritable pack, until one by one, they'd lost them to the woods.

Like they said, "Nothing beats a Harris horse, except maybe a Harris dog."

Buckwheat streaked out from behind the barn, the dogs hot on her heels. Big as wolves, jaws slathering, eyes like moonstones. They drove her, snorting and wild, back toward us.

As she charged past, I caught her reins. "Derek! Get up, get up!" He'd have to pull me after him. Mounting any horse without a stepstool was a feat for me, at five foot two.

He was right behind me. This time, he managed to grab hold of the saddle and get himself up.

I caught his hand, and I landed with a whump in the front of the saddle. Hard enough for Buckwheat to grunt and toss her frizzy mane.

Bless that horse. She refused to let our clumsy mounting slow her down—not with hell's wolf pack on her heels, a bear barreling toward her, and a horde of more half-rotting creatures pushing out from the corn to lunge after us.

I clutched the reins like they were a lifeline. Derek's arms wrapped around my waist, the skin under my shirt jumping at his touch. Because my brain stem refused to

54

realize this was a terrible time to care about things like that.

We only had time to run.

So Buckwheat ran. She ran and ran and ran. Her breaths came in huffs and heaves, her coat lathered with icy sweat. There was no time to stop for the truck, not with the dogs nipping at her flying hooves.

I glanced back once, before we turned the corner down the winding driveway. In the fields, all I'd seen were frenzied beasts. But I had to know . . .

Well, the humans were the slowest. They brought up the rear.

Behind the howling dogs and roaring bears and yipping foxes and more shapes than I could make sense of—there came the runners on two legs.

Tripping past possums, running in tattered clothes, teeth bared . . . Short and tall and every shape in between.

Running like one united frothing herd.

It was too dark to find faces beyond the flashes of eyes and teeth.

My parents wouldn't be among them, anyway. Not yet. Once the newly blighted went into the forest, they didn't come out for a good long while. No one knew what they did in there, and no one could ever find them. All we knew was, it took time for them to get to this point.

How much time, though?

My tongue probed at my back teeth, filmed over like moss.

CHAPTER 4

Once we hit those rolling hills, Buckwheat's hooves beating against the dirt driveway and kicking up dust thick enough to choke, the dogs began to fall back. She pumped her legs in a vicious gallop until her horseshoes clanged against the empty road, until we'd left the Harrises' farm behind. She would've kept going, but finally I stroked her neck, murmuring to slow her down.

She couldn't run like this forever, and we might need her to do it again before the night was through.

As adrenaline loosened its grip on my aching muscles, I was again very aware of Derek, our gulps and gasps puffing tiny clouds into the air. The twitching in my calf had slackened, replaced by an extra heaviness that settled into my ankles and feet, bowed my neck.

We clopped down the middle of the road, the trees whispering to each other on either side. No headlights now. Even with the moon close to full, everything was an indigo murk. All I could do was nudge Buckwheat toward the faint yellow dashes on the hard pavement. That was as close as we were getting to a yellow brick road.

"I'm sorry I wandered out so far."

At the low sound of Derek's voice, his warm breath against my sweat-slicked neck, I spasmed and nearly threw us both from Buckwheat's back.

"I heard something," he continued, "and I hoped . . ."

I already knew that if he'd found anyone in that field, he would've told me. Still, I couldn't stop myself. "You didn't see anyone when you were out there?"

"No, but maybe your parents ran away," he said. "You know, before . . ."

I swallowed hard, with one swift nod. "I'll go back to-morrow morning, as soon as the sun's up. Get a better look when it's safe."

"I'll come with you." Derek's voice vibrated down my back.

I let my eyes shut. Just for a second, I wanted to hold that feeling close. I leaned back against his chest the tini-est hair.

He leaned forward the tiniest hair, too, to catch me. "We're going to my place, right?" he asked.

We . . . were. Huh. I hadn't made that decision con-sciously. I was on autopilot. Well, that was embarrassing.

"It's closer," I mumbled.

"It is." Derek's hands tightened around my waist, by a possibly unintentional centimeter. "You should definitely stay. At least for tonight."

Dammit. If he was inviting me to his house—into his home, with his family—I had to tell him. "Derek, I'm not sure yet, but I think . . . My throat tastes moldy."

"So? We've been around the blight all day. I can practically taste it myself." Derek replied too quickly again, refusing to leave the slightest gap for my words to sink in. "We shouldn't assume the worst. You're not acting weird. We'd have a lot more warning if you were dangerous."

Pretty funny coming from Derek, after the way he reacted two months ago, when we'd found Teddy with that blighted bird in her mouth. Teddy had still looked like herself. Acted perfectly normal.

My jaw tightened.

But I needed him to be right. It was impossible to wrap my brain around the alternative. That I was a time bomb. Soon it could be me running with that horde, white-eyed and brain-dead, gnashing my teeth at my neighbors.

If I was blighted, we'd have more warning before I truly lost it. Right?

Flickers followed us behind the trees—a whirl of shadows, a wink of white. Just the right height to be a human looking out at us. Or what used to be a human.

Any second, something could lunge into the road and block our path. Sneak up behind us. Barrel out from the tree line to T-bone Buckwheat's side and crush our legs.

For now, they watched.

Thank God Derek's house was close. At the speed my heart kept pounding, I would've passed out before we got to mine.

Soon, we saw the sign: PEWTER-FLORES FARM-FRESH MELONS.

The only founding farm with a sign made of clean wood and still-bright paint, on account of its name change.

In Hollow's End, if you were born a Harris, Pewter, Murphy, or Warren, that was your name for life. Founding family names took precedence over a spouse's. Derek's mom had made a huge gesture when she changed their farm's name to Pewter-Flores. I'd asked her why once, and she said it was out of respect for Derek's dad. "He does half the work," she'd said. "He should get half the credit."

Mom had nudged Dad in the ribs when I'd told them. "You hear that?"

Dad's face didn't change. He just said, "You already took the Warren name. Your name is on that sign, same as mine or Wren's."

I'd so often wished my parents could be more like Derek's. But now that Mr. Flores was gone, the sign was another painful reminder.

I clutched too tight at the worn leather of the reins, back teeth grinding.

No one had seen Mr. Flores since he left that night in January, after a blowup with Mrs. P. It wasn't like them to fight. Mrs. P wouldn't say what it was about. But he never came back from his walk, not for his stuff or to say goodbye. He never answered his phone. And he left his truck—the truck we now called Derek's.

The family reported him missing to the police. By that point, a few folks had disappeared after contact with the

Murphys' blighted farm, but Mr. Flores hadn't gone any-where near it. Mrs. P had insisted this was different, that he had left her, like her first husband. Even though that seemed like something Mr. Flores would never do. Derek had tripped over the words as he told me, like the shapes were all wrong in his mouth.

As weeks passed and we learned more about the blight—that infected creatures were attacking people and dragging them into the woods—what went unspoken was the obvious conclusion: Mr. Flores had most likely never left Hollow's End at all. He was probably, even now, lum-bering around the forest. Had maybe even been part of the horde we just outran.

But no one had ever spotted him, so we didn't know for sure.

Poor Derek. How must it be for him, driving past this sign all the time? I felt a pause in his breath where our bodies leaned together. He shifted to look away, watch the other side of the road.

A weight dragged my heart down.

I clucked my tongue to get Buckwheat to pick up the pace as we rode up the drive, toward the fields. Icy glim-mers, low to the ground, jolted me with instinctive panic. But, as I had to remind my shot nervous system, these lights weren't the watchful white eyes we'd been running from.

This phosphorescent glow curled across the fields, winding through the melon vines.

By day, ghost melons weren't much to look at. To be honest, they were slightly creepy. Unlike the netlike peel that crisscrossed cantaloupes, ghost melon rind looked and felt like the clammy, pale skin of someone's arm, bulging with veins, thick with silver instead of blood. The cool flesh inside was bluer than honeydew, the thinnest cerulean wash, studded with silver-fuzzed seeds.

But by night, the ghost melon blossoms bloomed like moonflowers.

They reminded me of that summer three years back, when a rare red tide had swept into Harvest Moon Bay and carried with it bioluminescent plankton. Living lights. On the rocky beach after dark, Derek and I had watched as the blackened waves sparkled electric blue, like tiny stars washing into shore. All those glimmers had reflected in his brown eyes.

Ever since, it was all I could think of when I saw the ghost melon fields and their twinkling blue blossoms: a sea of fallen stars.

There were fewer than I remembered.

But if rainbows could rot, stars could, too.

At long last, we found the squat line of Derek's house. A candle flickered in the windows of the kitchen and the living room, promising safety, sanctuary.

There was no stable for Buckwheat, so we took her to the goat house. She nearly smacked her head on the doorway as I led her in. The goats, hunkered cozy in their straw, only flashed a horizontal pupil or two and sighed. I got Buckwheat settled in, untacked and brushed down, as Derek brought her water and a bucket of feed. That went a long way toward settling the last of her uneven breaths, and her long-lashed eyes started fluttering shut. With a final pat and a murmur of praise, we left her to doze.

Once Derek padlocked the animals in safe, we trudged to the porch, shoulder to shoulder.

God, I knew how Buckwheat felt—my bones were liquid with exhaustion.

We were only a few feet from the bottom step when a red dot of light flared on the porch. A shadow shifted against the window.

Derek and I reeled back.

Then a wry hard-knock voice I knew too well said, "What are you jackasses doing out here?"

"Claudette's back?" I whispered to Derek. When he'd mentioned her shooting a moose, I figured it was just how she'd spent her spring break. Pretty on-brand for Claudette.

"For a while now." Derek sighed. "When it really started hitting us in April, she dropped her semester. Don't mention it in front of Mom, because she is still hella pissed. And whatever you do, don't tell anyone there's even a chance you're . . . you know."

"Are you serious?" I stopped walking. "I can't do that. They should get to decide for themselves if they're okay with it."

They deserved at least that much. Derek's family didn't owe me shelter—not at the cost of their own safety.

"It's fine." Derek waved me forward with an impatient hand. "You're not going to do anything tonight, and where else are you supposed to go?"

I waffled on the front path. The night sky loomed

behind me, gaping, except where trees clawed up to snatch at the stars. The unblinking eye of the moon stared down, shivering into my skin.

My truck was gone, left behind at the Harrises'. Buckwheat was exhausted. And Teddy was probably still waiting on my front porch. Open jaws and all.

"Wren." Derek's fingers curled into my sleeve.

Under the heat of his hand, there was the strangest sensation—like the purple of my shirt might blossom into a richer plum. But that's how Derek always used to make me feel. Like all the colors billowed brighter, even in the dark.

"Please," he whispered.

Like I'd begged him in the kitchen. He'd stayed for me then, understood everything I couldn't say. I knew well enough what he meant now.

Slowly, I nodded.

"What are you lovebirds whispering about?" The rocking chair creaked to a halt as Claudette's lanky shadow rose to meet us at the long, low porch steps. She leaned against a wooden post. "Been a while since I've seen you, Wren. You two patch things up?"

"No," Derek said, dropping my sleeve to fumble with his hands. "It's not like that."

"Too bad. Because now I've got nothing to be happy about, and I'm just plain pissed."

Claudette slapped Derek upside the head. Hard. "The hell you think you're doing, running around this time of night? Mom said you were staying at Wren's."

"What about you, dipshit?" Derek shot back, rubbing

his head. "Out on the porch? *Smoking?* Something could sneak up on you at any time—"

The porch beside us creaked. A new shape moved against the dark.

Derek yanked out his gun. "Holy—"

"Hey, guys," the shadow said.

"Angie!" Derek cried. "Don't sneak up like that!"

"Sneak up?" Angie said. As she joined us at the front of the porch, the moonlight popped against the sherbet-pink of her sweatshirt. "Sorry I'm not glow-in-the-dark pale like Claud, but I've been standing here the whole time. And this sweatshirt is as close as it gets to reflective gear without going, you know, full nighttime-jogger-chic."

"All she said was hi." Claudette stepped in front of her girlfriend. "If you're that twitchy, you've got no business toting around that gun."

"True enough." I had to agree. "He almost shot my kitchen table."

Derek turned to gape at me and my treachery. "I also shot a *bear* in the face, so you're welcome!"

"For what?" I asked. "Blowing its jaw all over the Harrises' corn?"

"Okay, give it here." Claudette held out her hand.

Derek stuck the pistol back in his waistband, barring his chest with his arms. "It's my gun."

"It was *Dad's* gun," Claudette said, "and *I* let you have it in the first place."

"My dad. Your *step*dad. And you don't get to gatekeep his stuff."

True, Derek was a Pewter-Flores, while Claudette was technically only a Pewter. Her delinquent birth father, Mrs. P's first husband, had come and gone, leaving Claudette with his washed-out complexion—and nothing else. Mr. Flores was her dad in every other way, as far as everyone was concerned. Even Derek—unless he was pissed.

Angie sucked in a pained hiss on Claudette's behalf, dropping a calming hand on her shoulder.

But I guess it wasn't calming enough.

"Say that again and I'll deck you." Claudette's voice didn't get hot. It got cold.

Derek found somewhere else to look.

"That's what I thought." Claudette smudged out her cigarette against the porch post and dropped it where it fell.

"Come on. That's dangerous," Derek mumbled, seeking it out to stamp it down.

Claudette coughed out a sound between a laugh and a snarl. "Wouldn't want to do anything dangerous." She swept her arm toward the front door. "Well then, why don't you get your night-wandering, suicidal asses inside?"

Despite that pointedly lukewarm welcome, it was good to be back in what I'd considered my second home. Even a couple months away felt like a long time. I understood now, the way Derek had looked around my kitchen, smiling a smidge at anything that hadn't changed, frowning at anything that had.

The butter-yellow wallpaper and old-fashioned furniture. The walls hugging each room a little too tight. Pink florals warring against blue plaids and decorative camo.

It was the complete opposite of my spartan house. I can't explain why I found its gentle chaos so soothing.

We tracked down Mrs. P in the kitchen. She looked mostly the same—like an older, softer-edged Claudette—blond, pale, tall, and skinny. A little gaunter than usual. It felt good to wrap myself in her arms and breathe in that spearminty perfume she always used too much of. Most of us smelled like sweaty dirt about 70 percent of the time. I appreciated her efforts to be an exception.

She let me use their landline to call home. I tucked into the kitchen corner, pretending there was such a thing as privacy in a room this small.

Maybe, just maybe, my parents had somehow made it back.

The phone rang and rang as Derek and Mrs. P pretended not to watch.

Then Mom answered, in her characteristic bouncy tone, "Heya, it's the Warrens! We're out chasing rainbows, but leave us a message and . . ."

A deep, sharp dread twisted through me again.

I shook my head at Derek and Mrs. P, and left a message to tell my parents where I was, just in case. I did the same on their cell phone voicemails.

I tried the Murphys next. Their truck had been at the Harrises', too.

No one answered there, either.

"I'm sure they'll find you tomorrow, Wren," Mrs. P said, even though she knew no such thing. Still, it felt good to be lied to in that nonwavering voice parents always seem to master.

I slumped into a rounded chair at their square table, dragging my finger over the swirls of the wood grain.

"Here." Derek set a glass in front of me, barely a quarter full of sloshing pale-blue juice. "I'm sorry it's not more."

Ghost melonade.

I looked up at him in surprise. We'd run out at my house ages ago. The entire Hollow's End supply was melting away, but of course, the Pewter-Flores family had some stocked.

Like our rainbow wheat, ghost melons had their own cult following—folks who swore they calmed the nervous system, soothed anxiety. Mrs. P believed that. Any time I came over to study with Derek for a test, she'd set a freshly sliced plate of ghost melon down on the coffee table, with a little wink. Derek believed it, too. After his dad disappeared, he'd inhaled whole melons in a sitting.

Now, anxiety in Hollow's End had never been higher, and here was Derek, sharing their dwindling supply.

"Derek, no." I pushed the glass back toward him. "Please, you take it." He'd had the same heart-racing night I'd had. "Or save it."

"No, no, hon. Don't worry about us," Mrs. P said. "You drink that up."

After thanking them both profusely, I took a guilty, precious sip—musky sweet, chased by that citrusy zing of a finish. I never knew if the effect was purely psychological, but with every taste, a relaxing heaviness tugged at my limbs. Inviting them to lay down their burdens.

But no amount of melonade could calm the deep-set panic rooting into my bones. The headache hounding me all night had crawled from my forehead, deeper and deeper, to throb at the back of my brain. And my ears rang with a strange new frequency, a low buzz that bit at my eardrums.

"If that sounds good to you, Wren?" Mrs. P said.

I looked up, blinking her into focus. "Huh?" Was that the end of some sentence I was supposed to have processed?

"I said I could toast you up some unicorn braid, too, if you want. You look a little pale, sweetie." Mrs. P's tight lips twisted into a grimace as she scanned me over.

She probably figured I was sick over my missing parents, and I was. But did she suspect it could also be more than that? That I might've been exposed to the blight? Derek had said not to tell her or Claudette. I didn't know what they'd do to me if they knew. Send me to the emergency triage clinic, where anyone who went in blighted never came back out?

"I feel okay," I said again. Every time I said it, it meant a little less.

Mrs. P kept staring at me. And now Derek was, too.

Was the burning in my face only in my sinuses, or was it showing in my cheeks, too?

"Excuse me," I said. "I have to use the bathroom."

I didn't really. I just needed a minute to lock myself behind a door. I pressed my back against the cool tile of the pink bathroom wall and slid to the ground, sinking my forehead against my knees.

It's the advice Mom had given me since I was a little girl, when bad things happened and I didn't know what to do. To hold myself in, close my eyes, and breathe. I'd been doing it an awful lot lately, since early March, that horrible day when I realized where the blight had come from: our very own farm.

If I could've gone back, I would've done so much differently. Ever since, it'd all felt like a straight downhill line, one that led here—to me cowering on the bathroom floor, head huddled into my knees.

The government responders had just passed out their first flyers, describing the blight's appearance in depth. It sounded so close to something I'd seen before that, in spite of my parents' ban of contaminated areas, I drove all the way to the Murphys' farm to see for myself.

And yes.

That dripping silver oozing over their crops. The deep, sour stench of unforgiving rot.

I did recognize it.

It was everything I'd been afraid of.

So I drove straight back to Rainbow Fields and crashed my way into Dad's study.

Dad had actually jumped in his chair, a seismic startle, since his reactions were usually a matter of millimeters. "Wren!" He was at his big walnut-wooded desk, writing in a gray journal I'd never seen before. Instantly, he clapped it shut and slid it into the top drawer.

For Dad, privacy meant respect—so he must not have appreciated how my eyes tracked that gesture. When I came back to check for it later, it was gone.

"You're home late from school," he said. "Where have you . . . ?" He trailed off as he watched me.

My chest was heaving as I caught my breath. I hovered a couple steps past the doorway, wavering on his worn oriental rug. "Dad," I finally blurted out. "What if the blight came from our farm?"

Dad peered at me carefully. Every line on his face was crisp, like a fresh-pressed shirt. He always did his best to appear unsullied by the world around him, even though I knew that wasn't true. "Why?" he said. "You haven't seen it on the wheat, have you?"

"No. Not on the wheat."

"Then where on our farm would it have come from, Wren?" His eyes, gray and guarded like mine, gleamed like steel.

He'd been edgier than ever with the responders sniffing around. On the surface, Dad seemed like the type who would've cooperated when they asked for soil samples and wheat to analyze. After all, this was a man who kept a periodic table above his desk. The towering bookshelves lining the walls around us were stuffed with tomes on soil salinity and chemistry.

But I knew why he'd sent them away empty-handed. And why he was trying to freeze me out now.

"You know where," I said.

That spot at the center of our field, where the emerald-winking wheat grew a little too tall. Our farm's best-kept secret, the truth behind our miracle wheat.

We never, *ever* talked about it. I'd been thirteen before Dad had granted me a glimpse, leading me out to the field at night. He dug down into the blackened earth until it came into sight—a clear stone long as half my arm, craggy and cloudy pale. Like a crumpled ghost, curled up, nestled in the soil.

At the slightest glint from Dad's flashlight, it flared to life. Every color in our field danced inside its rough-ridged crystal planes. I'd reached out and laid my hand on it, gently, as if it was a newborn's head. The stone was cool as fresh wind. It felt almost alive under my touch, humming and vibrating with its own quiet glow.

I'd known right away what it was: the heart of our farm.

Rainbow quartz.

Dad had trusted me, by sharing that secret. He'd put faith in me. And there in his study, I had to confess just how much I hadn't deserved that.

I forced myself forward, to stand behind the chair across from his desk. I had to clench the top of it tight to hold myself steady. "Why didn't you tell me?" I asked. "That the blight was inside our quartz."

"How would you know . . . ?" His voice drifted off as he realized the only way I could possibly know.

That I had broken our farm's rainbow quartz.

"I was trying to help," I squeezed out, in the tiniest, feeblest voice.

The worst part was how proud of myself I'd been for dreaming up the idea, the one that had led to me lopping off a chunk of the quartz. I'd never felt more like a competent heir, like I had big new ideas about how to save our farm and rescue Mom and Dad from all their financial miseries.

But when I'd chiseled into the quartz, something came out.

Shining like silver, stinking like rot.

Now that I'd seen it on the Murphys' farm, I knew—it was the exact same substance.

Dad squeezed his eyes shut, but not before I saw his utter horror. He leaned back so far in his chair that the old wood let out a painful groan. "Wren. You have no idea what you've done."

But I did now, actually.

That's why it felt like Dad's study, Rainbow Fields, all of Hollow's End was caving in on my chest. Like I had to push through all that weight to fight for breath.

My legs got so weak I had to sit down. As soon as I saw the blight at the Murphys', I knew it was probably my fault. The timing alone was damning. I'd broken the quartz in December. The blight showed up in January. It didn't seem like a coincidence.

Still, there'd been some tiny, desperate part of me that hoped I was wrong, that hoped Dad would tell me, *No, no, it's not what you thought.*

I peeked up through my lashes to find him rubbing the bridge of his nose, so hard that blood was rushing to the surface of his freckled skin, leaving angry red marks.

"Could you at least tell me . . . ? I don't understand," I said. "Why would the blight be inside the quartz? What *is* it? If you know, can't you help stop it?"

"What do you think I've been trying to do?" Dad's voice picked up that hot, hard edge.

"Well, if you told me, maybe I could help—"

"Wren, stop. Please." Dad's jaw cranked so tight a muscle clenched in his temple. "Your job is to keep yourself safe, and you will leave the rest to me. You will do nothing. You will *say* nothing. To anyone. Not even to Derek, and I mean that. This can't get back to Mrs. Pewter."

My mouth opened and closed like a fish drowning on air.

Then I started to argue. If *we'd* done this to Hollow's End, if *I* had done it, then wasn't this my responsibility to help fix?

And more and more slipped out—like that forbidden trip I'd just taken to the Murphys' blighted farm.

That's when Dad stood up from behind his desk. All his careful words and careful gestures vanished into the fear that wrinkled his forehead, the tight fury as he made me swear not to tell anyone. Swear to do nothing as Hollow's End crumbled apart around us. "If you insist on acting like a child," he said, "I will treat you like one."

I'd thought I couldn't feel any more helpless. He'd proven me wrong that day, when he shut me out of his study and left me sobbing. I slid down to the hallway floor, hugging my knees.

All I could do was what Mom had taught me: cocoon. Remind myself that, no matter who else was there to help, I had everything I needed within myself.

But on the Pewter-Floreses' bathroom floor, in the echo chamber of my own breath, it bounced back to me—that pervasive rotting-mold stench.

Mom and I hadn't covered this. What if I really was blighted? What if I didn't even have myself to count on anymore?

I pulled my head up, before I choked on my own rot. My eyes caught on something that wasn't quite right. A part of *me* that wasn't quite right.

The beds of my nails—they were gray. Just a tinge of silver mold arcing up from under my cuticles.

Oh God. Oh no, oh shit.

I held them as far from me as I could, blinking wide, then pulled them close, an inch in front of my nose, and squinted.

No matter how near or far, there it was.

Those quicksilver-blight flyers may not have been right about everything, but I'd practically memorized their list of symptoms, and this was one of them: "discolored or shedding nails, skin, or teeth."

This was worse than some nasty taste in my mouth, a cough, a twitch, a headache. There was no way to write this off.

Now all I could think about was the other advancing symptoms, those still left to come: silvering veins; loss of motor control; impaired vision and whitening eyes; hallucinations and delirium. Psychotic reactions. Homicidal tendencies.

I had no idea how much time I had.

The flyers said how fast the blight set in depended on the amount of exposure. If my infection came from breathing it only this afternoon, how long did that give me? A week? Three days? Two?

If I could see the proof right here on my fingers, Mrs. P, Claudette, and Angie could see it, too.

Cursing on loop, I fumbled into the medicine cabinet and rattled past bottles of ibuprofen and chalky antacids.

Bingo. Claudette's nail polish. Only a couple bottles. She'd never given much of a crap about dolling up the tips of her fingers. She usually wound up smearing them in some kind of mechanical grease anyway.

One was granite-colored. A little too close to the truth.

I snatched a peaceful sky blue. Resting my hands on the edge of the sink, I lacquered over my rotting nails, though my quivering fingers made a slashy mess of it.

I did my best to clean up with nail polish remover, which had the bonus of being so chemically noxious that it drowned out the mold in my mouth. Temporarily.

I just had to get through tonight. I had to get back to my parents tomorrow. Maybe they'd hoped that holding back secrets about the blight and our farm, and who knew what else, would protect me, but the least they could do now was tell me the truth. The worst had already happened.

I was blighted.

And I didn't know how to do this without them.

CHAPTER 5

Mrs. P said I could sleep in Derek's room, as long as he slept on the floor.

"Keep the door open, you two." She left a two-foot crack and wedged a doorstop into place.

"Yeah, Mom, we're not even . . ." Derek shook his head and then held up his hands in surrender. "Sure, fine."

She tossed a sleeping bag in after us.

Derek unfurled it, unleashing a visible wave of dust, and crawled into it.

If anyone should've been sleeping down in the dust, it definitely should've been me. I'd offered, multiple times, and of course, Derek wouldn't hear of it.

I sighed as I nestled under his puffy comforter. It embraced me with a hug of Derek's woodsy body spray. I pretended not to notice the old, faint drool spots when I flipped the pillow over.

I don't know what it was—the smell of something that felt close to home?—but the tears I'd been holding back all night started leaking out. They slipped onto the clean side of his pillowcase, dampening it against my cheek.

"Wren?" Derek's voice came soft from the floor.

My sniffling gave me away. "I'm fi-ine," I squeaked out, voice cracking.

Great. Real convincing.

I was too afraid to look over at Derek, to find the pity that must've been all over his face, because then I'd really lose it.

"Do you want me to . . . ?" he started to ask. "Should I . . . ?"

I did turn to him then.

He chewed on his lower lip as he nodded to the bed. "I just thought, if you wanted somebody . . ."

At this point, being close to someone was less of a want and more of a desperate need. Derek and I had never slept in the same bed. We'd drifted off a couple times bingeing shows on his couch—and woken up to Mrs. P's throat clearing. I remembered the warmth of his arms, though.

I could go to him now. Or let him come to me. Bury my head against his chest, and he'd do that thing he always did, tucking down his chin to shelter me. He'd stroke my back, his callused hands pouring over my aching muscles like a slow and steady current. Sweeping away the deepest aches, leaving me loose and shivering. He'd tell me it would be okay.

But under my secretly rotting nails, the skin ached with a very different kind of promise.

I couldn't risk it, any of it.

"No," I said, "that's okay." The words came out sounding far from my body. Detached and hollow.

"Right," he mumbled. "Sorry."

"Don't be sorry."

Derek just sighed. "Well, Wren, I can't help it."

I understood what he meant, so much better than he knew.

My thousand-pound eyelids eventually drifted shut. Derek's eggshell ceiling and his monster truck posters from that unfortunate preteen phase faded away, and I lost even the sound of his rhythmic breathing—the reassurance that, if nothing else, someone still cared enough to be here with me.

I saw the forest.

Towering trees loomed over my head. Between the cracks of their gnarled bark, gooey sap welled and bubbled, like something that had oozed out of a cauldron. It stank like dead meat. Roadkill on summer-scorched pavement.

It wasn't sap at all.

It was the same dripping quicksilver I'd dug out of my soil this morning.

I leaned closer. Within those dripping swirls, there were flecks of gold, as bright as Murphy yams; snowy blue, as pale as ghost melons; and auburn, like the smoldering shade of Buckwheat's coat.

And violet. Violet that sparkled like diamond dust. Like the last rows of our glinting wheat.

I reached out to touch it, but the liquid squirted out into beads, dodging my fingers. If I wanted to hold it, I'd have to cup it, like something precious.

I took only a tiny handful, but it dipped my wrist like it

weighed pounds. Viscous and thick, it settled into the lines of my palm—clammy. Almost warm.

How could it be warm when the trees had no warmth to give it?

"*Wren.*" The voice came from behind me.

The nape of my neck seized at the low, slithering sound of it.

My legs twitched, ready to fly from this forest, fast. But something was lapping at my ankles, that same tepid kiss of wet, seeping up from the moss to sink my feet into the earth.

"*Follow me.*"

The hiss of the voice drew closer, but there were no footsteps behind me. Just the slurp of sucking tar, like the tar that had swallowed the dinosaurs. Slugged them down and stripped the flesh from their bones.

It started to laugh, the same laugh I'd heard this morning when I spat back at the trees, defiant, as if I'd had any power.

I got it now—why it was so funny I'd thought that, even for a second.

"*This way, this way . . .*"

The tar swiveled my legs, turning me around.

I didn't want to see. I squeezed my eyelids shut until they ached.

"I don't want to go," I said.

"*Not yet,*" the voice said. "*But you will.*"

Liquid seeped from my closed eyes, no matter how tight I tried to seal the cracks. Maybe I'd squeezed so hard my eyeballs had burst. Maybe that's what was gushing down my cheeks.

"Wren?" A new voice.

A hand grabbed my shoulder from behind, and I screamed my eyes open.

This wasn't the forest. This was . . .

The rickety posts of Derek's porch. The ghostly glow of the melon field and trees beyond. Something wet ran down my cheeks, but it came back clear on my fingertips. There was no purple-flecked quicksilver on my hands.

That pressure on my shoulder, however, stayed strong and solid.

I turned to find Claudette staring at me.

Maybe I'd jumped from one nightmare to another.

When I was a kid, she'd reminded me of a scarecrow, with those overlong limbs, the flat sheen of her cornflower-blue eyes. Throw in her straw-pale hair and the dusty denim she always wore, and she was a walking vision of Halloween gone wrong.

"What are you doing out here?" she asked in her husky smoker's voice.

I wasn't dreaming anymore, was I? The back of my skull burned, like needles poking from my brain, stabbing up into my scalp. "I don't . . . I'm not sure."

"Sleepwalking," Angie diagnosed, stepping up from a rocking chair to lean against Claudette's shoulder. "My little sister does it all the time." She smiled warmly, probably trying to steady my quivering chin.

Yes, I had been sleepwalking. On a trajectory that would've taken me straight into the forest.

The blight always seemed to make people wander away and vanish into the trees. Is this how it got you? In your sleep?

I shook my head, backing away from the front of the porch. From the forest looming beyond the field.

"Why don't you sit with us?" Angie led me over to the rocking chairs.

I slid down into one and leaned into the soothing lull.

Claudette watched us for a long cricket-chirping minute before she sat down on my other side, hemming me in.

"Is it late?" I asked, rubbing my eyes and glancing up at the moon-drunk sky. "It looks late."

"It's late." Angie dug out a blanket from under her. "Here, take this."

"Won't you get cold?" My back teeth were chattering, and Claudette was already wrapping her skinny frame back up.

Angie smiled, like that was adorable. "Girl, I'm from Maine. This is nothing."

Right. Of course. She and Claudette had met at the University of Maine, Angie's choice for in-state tuition, and Claudette's out-of-state choice for its forestry program. Claudette had grumbled on loop about how she'd rather be getting her certificate in agricultural machinery, but her dad had insisted on four-year college. Then she met Angie and, according to Derek, the grumbling suddenly stopped.

"Well, thanks." I wrapped Angie's offering around my shoulders, sagging into its fuzzy plaid embrace.

"You'll want this, too." Claudette passed me a hot mug of . . . something.

The smoky booze of it smacked me up the nose.

I'd only had alcohol a couple times before. The first time when Dad was traveling and Mom let me share her cider. We ate popcorn together and watched *Gone with the Wind*. She'd been on about it for ages, how it was a classic. When we finally watched it, we spent the first part wincing, and clicked it off halfway through. "You know," she'd said, "that was less romantic than I remembered, and also, totally racist."

"An American film from the 1930s? About the South? During the *Civil War*?" I feigned a dropped jaw.

Mom sighed. "Maybe, from now on, we stick to modern classics . . ."

A smile tickled my lip.

And then the truth flooded back: My parents still hadn't called. They hadn't found their way home. Maybe they were holed up at someone else's place and just hadn't gotten my message. Maybe they'd even called Rainbow Fields, but I wasn't there to answer.

Maybe.

Or . . .

I gulped down the booze in my mug. It hit my throat, fiery and bitter, a hint of lemon at the end. I drank it all, so no one could sip after my blighted lips.

Claudette's chair creaked to a stop. Both she and Angie stared at me.

A rush of heat hit my cheeks, and I wasn't sure if it was the drink or the embarrassment or both. "Sorry. Thanks," I mumbled, and passed the mug back.

Claudette tipped it upside down to see if any drops would come out.

Nope.

She grinned at me. "Atta girl. Looks like someone just graduated." She dug a pack and a lighter from her faded jeans with their huge legs and huger pockets, and sparked up the night with a new cigarette.

After two or three billowing exhales, she said, "Sounds like some wild shit went down tonight. Nothing got hold of you or my trigger-happy brother, did it? No bites? Scratches, even . . . ?"

I shook my head.

"You'd tell us, though? If it did?" Claudette tilted her cigarette until the hot end leered—like a third eye, burning red. "That's really something we should know."

Remembering Derek's warning, I shook my head again. It was just for tonight. Tomorrow, I'd be back to my own house, empty or not.

"Let me see your arms." Claudette held out an impatient hand.

"Claud, stop." Angie leaned forward in her rocker to cast her a warning look.

"I don't mind . . . ," I mumbled, holding them out. If she was looking for silver veins, like the flyer mentioned, I didn't have them. There was nothing to hide on my arms.

Except—oh no—my nail polish.

Claudette paused at the tips of my fingers.

She smiled. "I used to have a color just like that."

Must've been a while since she checked in the cabinet.

"All right." Claudette drew back. "Good. Because once someone gets bit, there's nothing to do but chuck 'em at the triage clinic before they become an even bigger problem."

Hot whiskey ate at my roiling stomach.

"Anyway," she drawled, "we'll be ready tomorrow morning, first thing, to head back to the Harrises with you."

It was bad enough I'd dragged Derek into this. "You don't have to come," I said.

"We can't stay long," Claudette said. "We've got work of our own here." She grimaced out at the fields, where sparkling blue glinted in scattered constellations. Whole swaths sat dark. "It's everywhere now. Every goddamn patch."

It wasn't just plants. Those fields represented countless weeks, months, years, *decades,* of work. The farm was a triumph, their whole family's legacy—which went back as long as mine had, one hundred and fifty years.

I was afraid to see those melons by the light of day.

"I'm sorry," I murmured. Inadequate words, but at least they were heavy with understanding.

Claudette nodded, curt. "We're not giving up yet."

Angie nodded, too.

"How long are you staying, Angie?" I asked.

"As long as it takes. They need the extra hands. Besides, if I leave Claud alone, she'll smoke herself dead before fall semester." Angie flicked a pointed glare to the cigarette in Claudette's hand.

Claudette fought back a scowl. "Yeah, yeah." She stabbed out the butt on the arm of the porch chair. Instead of lighting another, she went back to rocking.

I'd seen her come to blows with Derek over subtler digs. But Angie clearly knew how to get through Claudette's thick skull. She was the first gal Claudette had ever brought home. At Christmas break, no less, so it was obviously serious. At the end of the countdown at the Murphys' New Year's party, Angie threw her arms around Claudette's neck and kissed her so hard that Claudette stumbled backward and sloshed the sparkling wine from her glass. When they broke apart, Claudette was beaming like I'd never seen. I'd had no idea that her eyes could light up. That her skin could flush that pink.

And now, here Angie was again—showing up in a crisis, so Claudette didn't have to face it alone.

"Your parents really don't mind?" I asked. "I mean, the quarantine . . ."

"I've been here since early May, before all that. Sure, Claud and Mrs. P tried to get me to leave when they announced it, but . . ." She shrugged. Like they were being silly. "If I wanna leave, I just go to the bridge and let them hold me a few days, make sure I'm not some blight zombie—and then I can go, right?"

Yeah, in theory, that was still an option. For anyone not infected.

I managed a nod.

"To be honest, when I told my parents Claud needed help, I may have left out a few key facts about the blight . . ." Angie's shoulders caved with a wince. Her parents must've had no idea how dangerous it was. "They're not happy I haven't been home this summer, but campus is ten minutes from their place. We see them all the time."

"You *both* see them?" The idea of Claudette dressing up nice to meet Angie's parents welled up a laugh in my chest, one I barely managed to swallow. I hope she at least swapped out her self-imposed uniform of white ribbed tank top.

Claudette's eyes narrowed, like she knew exactly where that incredulous tone came from.

But Angie laughed. "My dad hurt his back, so she's been helping out in our brewery on the weekends. Hauling crates for us."

"Free beer and all," Claudette muttered, like she wouldn't have done it anyway. She never shied away from a job that required rolling up her sleeves, especially not if someone needed her help.

"Plus, de facto babysitting. Because my little sister is obsessed with her. Bri thinks Claud is, like, the coolest." Angie's brown eyes glittered. "Even made her a bracelet." She was clearly getting a kick out of exposing Claudette's softer underbelly.

"A bracelet?" I asked.

Claudette pulled back her army-green jacket cuff with a long-suffering sigh. A woven twist bracelet in blue and pink was tied around her wrist.

She hadn't seen this kid in months, and she was still wearing her bracelet? She could act as grumpy as she wanted, but that mushy kind of dedication spoke an awful lot louder. "My parents really like her, too," Angie told me, "believe it or not."

"Fooled 'em pretty good, then, didn't I?" Claudette asked Angie.

"Nah." A smile crooked into the corner of her mouth. "You don't really fool anybody."

Claudette's face got caught between grin and grimace.

She cleared her throat, running a hand through her butt-length Barbie-blond hair.

"Speaking of not fooling anyone . . ." Angie turned to me. "Wren, are you and Derek actually still fighting? Because you seem to be sleeping in his room."

"We're . . ." I sank in my chair. "I don't know what we are anymore."

"What happened anyway?" Angie asked. "Derek wouldn't say. But you've been close since you were kids, right? The way Claud tells it, everyone knew you two were in love by the time you hit twelve. We've been wondering, what could be bad enough to ruin something like that?"

I knew what she meant. When Derek and I finally got together this past New Year's, it was *long* overdue. The kind of love we had, it was meant to last. Instead, we got three months. Three months before it imploded.

But, you know, I'd been wondering something myself—how someone as salty as Claudette snagged someone as sweet as Angie. Her easy smiles, her bubble-gum-pink sweatshirts. Berry blush shimmered across her dark brown cheeks. The puff of her natural hair was smoothed back from her face with a cat-patterned sweatband. But maybe Angie wasn't quite as sweet as I'd thought. At least, when it came to personal questions, she sure went for the throat.

"Ange, you can't just . . ." Claudette shook her head. "Christ, they're in high school. It could've been nothing. The wrong comment on Insta—who knows."

Seriously? Like she and Angie were so much more mature at the ripe old age of nineteen?

"It wasn't nothing," I said, more hotly than was wise to direct at someone as scary as Claudette.

She turned, customary snarl even deeper than usual. "Oh, really?"

I couldn't tell them everything. Things between Derek and me had been falling apart in slow motion for weeks before I ended it. But the breaking point . . .

I sighed. "Listen," I said.

It was Teddy.

Derek and I had just come back from school when we found her in the backyard with the blighted bird. Before I could stop her, she'd gulped the whole rotting carcass down, licking her chops like she'd just finished Thanksgiving dinner. She was so damn pleased with herself.

Derek had assisted with a couple cleanup efforts by then, so he knew a thing or two about the blight. He told me then and there that my dog was infected. There was no help for her.

But Teddy looked fine. Happy even.

"Maybe I can help her," I said. People said there wasn't a treatment, but I hoped we just hadn't figured it out yet. I had to at least try. "I just need some time with her."

I moved toward her, but Derek blocked my path. "There is no time," he said. "She's contagious."

He didn't get it. I'd raised her from that sickly pup the Harrises were ready to give up on. I'd had to feed her by hand, one artificially bacon-flavored pellet at a time. At night, she'd slept on my chest, next to my heart. When I went to school, Mom said Teddy would sit at the front door and howl like a baby wolf. And when I came home, she tumbled over her stubby legs to meet me at the door. She curled up in my lap while I did homework on the couch. She tripped after me all over the farm when I did chores. She was my puppy-shaped shadow.

I snuck unicorn braid to her under the table at dinner.

She grew up bigger and stronger than her sisters, even most of her brothers.

She was only seven years old. In my book, she had at least another seven to go.

I knew Derek was right: she was blighted. But I couldn't accept that it was over. That my dog couldn't be my dog anymore. Especially not as she ran to my side, gazing up with trusting eyes and a wagging tail, a playful pant.

"You have to tell your parents," Derek said.

If Dad heard Teddy had eaten an infected bird, he'd get rid of her. No question. I'd be lucky if he didn't shoot her in the head.

"Just let me handle it," I told Derek.

He didn't. He wouldn't. He was worried about my safety. I promised I wouldn't let her infect me, but he marched right inside anyway. And he told my parents.

I get why he did it. I honestly do.

But I didn't fucking care. What got burned into my brain was Dad charging out of the house, screaming at me, screaming at Teddy, like she'd have any idea what that scary shit was about. That's how it was with Dad—his feelings were tiny, careful, until they *weren't*.

He had her leash in his hand. He was going to put her down. He had to, he said; you don't let a rabid animal run free.

Except it was Teddy he was talking about. Teddy. She leaned against my leg and gave her nose a nervous lick. She knew I'd protect her. I always had.

It wasn't a choice I made. It was the only thing to do.

I took off as fast as I could, calling Teddy as I raced for the forest. She bounded after me.

Dad and Derek chased after us, and Teddy thought maybe we were playing, but she didn't seem sure. She kept looking back at them and up at me, and I kept calling her on.

Dad tried calling her, too, of course. So did Derek.

Ha. *My* dog.

It was me she trusted. Me she followed.

I ran her so deep into the woods that Derek and Dad lost us. Then she caught sight of a rabbit, and, hyped up by our running frenzy, she took off after it.

I watched her go, my dog vanishing between the dead-ened trees. *Good,* I thought. *She'll need to find her own food now.*

And that's when I started to cry.

When I came back from the woods, Dad was still yelling, but this time I screamed right over top of him that if he *ever* hurt my dog, I would pack up my stuff and run away where he'd never find me. That I'd never forgive him. I'd never come back.

That kind of thunder had never come from my throat before.

Dad stared at me like the devil had taken over my whole body. He stepped back. Like he was scared.

I charged past him, slapping tears from my burning cheeks. My whole body steamed with unquenchable rage.

Over the next two months, Derek had reached out every way he could. He kept saying how sorry he was that this had happened. Sorry I felt this way.

Not sorry for what he did.

He would've done it again. He would've done anything to keep me safe.

Every time I saw his name or heard his voice, I couldn't see our history anymore; I saw Teddy. When she came back the following morning, and I had to chase her into the woods again. And the next day when she *still* returned. And the day after that.

She didn't understand. Her head hung, and her tail sagged. She whined. She lowered all the way to the ground and put her chin on her paws. She rolled on her back and showed her belly.

Every time she came back, her eyes were just a little whiter.

Then she vanished. For weeks.

After that, she only came back at night. Smelling of rot, with eyes that weren't hers. No longer my dog.

Teddy's begging whimpers, her living decay—that's what I saw when I looked at Derek.

I hated him for it, no matter how hard I tried not to.

Claudette turned to Angie. "So, there you have it. Over some mangy dog." She dropped her hand like she was resting her case.

I knew she wouldn't get it, either. Claudette gave even

less of a shit about animals than anyone in Derek's family. Her bedroom wall was lined with her own hunting trophies, rows and rows of antlers, and she'd never cared for pets.

Angie, though, she nodded at me. "That's awful."

"How is that awful?" Claudette demanded. "He did what had to be done."

"But it was *her* dog! It should've been *her* decision." Angie held firm on my behalf. "She would've figured something out. She clearly has a brain."

"She wasn't acting like it," Claudette said. "Wren, you know he was only trying to help you."

"I know," I said.

If there'd been any doubt, he'd proven it earlier tonight when he didn't shoot Teddy. In the way he'd taken me in, even though he knew I'd been exposed to the blight myself.

Claudette raised hard eyebrows. "Well then, get the hell over it. Some things are more important than grudges." Her thin lips quirked to the side. "Not a lot of things, mind you. But some."

"Wow," I said, "that means a lot coming from the biggest asshole I know."

Then I sucked in a sharp breath, shocked at what had come from my mouth.

Claudette froze.

Oh my God, she was gonna deck me. I winced pre-emptively.

But she only barked out a laugh. "Look at the cojones on this one tonight." She clapped me on the arm. "I don't know what's gotten into you, but I like it."

Yeah. Nothing like a mug of whiskey and a death sentence to get me speaking my mind.

God, and Angie was worried about Claudette dying young from smoking. Derek didn't know how little time we had. We'd wasted too much of it before, dancing around each other for years. In love, but too scared to admit it.

Maybe Claudette, white wolf though she was, was right—some things were more important than grudges. Especially now.

I padded back to Derek's room, the hall rug tickling my bare feet. I tried to walk softly, to let Derek have the sleep we both so sorely needed. It was a skill of mine that had come in handy, tiptoeing down the hall in my own house—slipping in and out of the bathroom—before my parents realized that I was out of bed. That the sharp edges of their voices through my bedroom vent had jostled me from sleep yet again. I knew they were trying to keep their fighting private, like if I couldn't see it or hear it, it wasn't really happening.

Tonight, though, my ankles were lead. I tripped, just a little, as I slipped through the crack in Derek's door. Was it an uneven floorboard, the whiskey, the blight eating away at my muscles already? No way to tell. But I winced at the door's moan. And the tiny yawn of light that spilled in from the hall, across Derek's sleeping bag.

Luckily, he was a deep sleeper. His eyes were sealed, his long black lashes brushing his cheeks. He'd bunched the sleeping bag under his chin to clutch as he slept.

I couldn't help my smile. It was the same way he'd slept as a kid. He'd used that same sleeping bag, *Toy Story* characters and all, back when things were still innocent and our parents didn't bat an eye at us spending the night together. The last time I'd seen it was six years ago.

My tenth birthday. I was born on the Fourth of July. Derek used to say that felt exactly right—of course I was born the day that the sky lit up, the day that night was brightest. Even as a kid, Derek said a lot of things like that, but never in some cheesy way, like he was trying to compose a sonnet on the spot. It wasn't poetry to him, just simple truth.

The Fourth was also the last day of the summer harvest festival, and the town always set aside a primo spot, a grassy patch by the community center, for the founding families to watch the fireworks together—a sort of thank-you for all our work. For making these festivals possible in the first place. Derek's family and mine always set up together, with overlapping blankets.

Afterward, Derek came back to my house for cake and presents. Once we were done licking the frosting from our fingers, we would take my birthday spoils—whatever new flashy gadgets or toys or candy—out to the tent Dad had set up for us in the wheat field.

Nature wasn't scary then. It was home. I'd never felt safer, sitting cross-legged with Derek, bundled in sleeping bags. A flashlight sat between us, its light bouncing our shadows so big we seemed to take up the whole tent. Derek liked to leave the flap open, so we could watch the moonlight catch the opaline stalks, glimmering rose red.

That year, Derek's family had the bright idea of partnering with a candy shop across the bridge to make ghost melon–flavored *everything*. He'd basically given me a year's supply of their brand-new ghost melon popping candy. We burned through bags, in contest after contest, pouring sour, glowing fistfuls of crackling candy onto our tongues and seeing who could make them pop the loudest.

Derek insisted he won. I insisted I did. Guess we never settled that score.

Hyped up on melonade and cake and candy, Derek was way too twitchy to sleep. I lay down first, surrendering to the hug of my sleeping bag while he sat up on his. He watched the shadows of moths flutter on the tent walls, chattering about dreams and the future and whatever burst into his buzzing brain.

That was the night he asked me what names I liked.

"I dunno." I fought to keep my sleep-scratchy eyes open. "Daisy, Delilah . . ."

He nodded thoughtfully, swiping a finger inside the empty popping candy bag, seeking out phosphorescent sugar dust. "What about for a boy?"

"Huh?" I'd thought he was asking about names I wished I had.

"Do you like Luis?" he asked. "Dad says it means 'brave.'"

"I guess?"

"I like Delilah. So there it is: Luis and Delilah." He crumpled up the now extra-empty bag and hugged his knees. "Do you just want two?"

"Two what? What are you talking about?" I mumbled, squishing down farther in my sleeping bag.

"Kids. Duh."

That got my eyes open. "Kids?" I sat up on my elbow, barely registering the sting of a scab. Those days, my elbows and knees were always covered in scabs, from adventuring with Derek through the woods, rolling in the grass with Teddy, playing tag through the wheat . . .

"Yeah. For after we get married." He seemed surprised by my own surprise—like, how could I not have thought this through? "Dad says it's good to be at least eighteen. Mom says twenty-two. So I know we have to wait awhile, but what do you think?"

"Um . . ." I was weirdly shy all of a sudden, like my freckles were popping out of my face. Like I was turning purple. I wanted to lie back down and pull the sleeping bag over my head, but Derek was smiling at me, so maybe I looked okay.

The other kids would make fun of us if they found out this was the kind of thing we talked about. Claudette *definitely* would. She teased us enough as it was, always calling me Derek's girlfriend. But in our tent, held in the field's palm, sheltered by a wall of our wheat, none of that mattered, did it? The wheat's gentle ripples drowned out our words, hid them from anyone else, kept them all just for ourselves.

So I smiled and I nodded. If we were being honest, that's what I wanted, too.

"Just so you know," I said, "I want a lot of dogs."

"That's okay—there's a lot of room here." He waved at the tent walls, to the wheat all around us, hugging us in.

"You'd stay here?" I asked. "What about your farm?"

"Claud's farm." Derek shrugged. "There's only one of you. You have to stay here, so I will, too."

The next day, after Derek and I rolled up the tent, when I hauled my sleeping bag back into the house—Mom caught my flushed cheeks, red as windswept rose wheat. Something about it made her look twice. And that's when she said no more sleepovers with Derek.

As I hovered in his bedroom doorway now, watching the rise and fall of his chest, I thought about how he'd hung his head at my kitchen table. How he'd mumbled that if anything would be safe from the blight, it would be the wheat . . . Was he sad for more than just me and my family? He had always worked on my farm like it was his own. Was it possible he hadn't given up—that he still had any kind of hope for our shared future?

Even now?

A sob left me in a gasp.

The floor creaked as Derek shifted.

"Wren?" His voice was so much lower and deeper, more grounded than it had been once upon a time, camping in my field. "You okay?"

He sat up, so quick to leave his own sleep behind. So quick to check on me.

I sucked the sobs back down my throat, into the shallow heave of my chest.

"Yeah, I—" The lie was right there on my tongue. It'd be so easy to tell him I'd gone to the bathroom. That everything was fine.

But I was stuck there: a step past the doorway, shoulders sagging.

Derek clicked on the flashlight he'd been keeping beside his pillow. He set it upright, like we used to do camping, so the light bounced up. Not against small and friendly tent walls this time. Against his pale ceiling, where our shadows didn't make a dent, swallowed by the larger darkness of his bedroom.

He was only half-awake, rubbing sleep from his eyes with his palm. He didn't say anything, just waved me down beside him.

I sank to my knees, his familiar yellow rug rubbing through the way-too-baggy sweatpants he'd loaned me.

"I'm sorry." My voice scraped against my constricting throat. "I'm so, so sorry."

There it was. I'd finally said it.

We sat together in the quiet dark, crickets crying through the outside wall. The house sleepy around us. The flashlight's beam glowing across the underside of his cheek.

His throat bobbed with a swallow.

"I don't understand," he said. "I spent so much time trying to figure out why you did it. I know why you got so angry about Teddy, but I thought after I apologized . . ."

He shook his head, bleak and grim.

I had to stiffen my neck into metal, to stay there with him. To not look away.

"But even before it happened, things weren't right with us," he said. "I don't get it. I needed you, Wren. I *really* needed you. I'm sorry if me being depressed was too much for you to handle, but my dad is *gone.*"

Like my parents were now.

The worst part was, he still thought it was because I

couldn't handle him. That I didn't understand how deeply it hurt, his dad's disappearance.

From the day Mr. Flores disappeared, I'd been by Derek's side, comforting him. I'd stayed up nights to chat, read aloud, anything to keep him company. Those gloom-stained hours were when Mrs. P's excuses wore thinnest. When Derek couldn't help asking the question: Did his dad run away like his mom claimed, or was his dad *taken* away—attacked that lonely January night by some blighted animal and dragged off into the forest?

I was there for him for all of January, February. Then came the day when I saw the quicksilver blight on the Murphys' farm for myself. When I recognized that molten ooze from the quartz I'd broken on my own farm.

A toxic cloud of debilitating horror had plagued me ever since. Because I knew the blight had escaped thanks to me.

And Mr. Flores's disappearance . . . I knew in my gut, he had to be out there in the forest.

The worst thing that had happened in Derek's entire life: I'd done it to him.

I couldn't forgive myself for one single bit of what the blight had done, but that—*that* ate at me more than any-thing. From that day on, every time I looked Derek in the eye, it felt like I was lying to him. But how could I tell him? If Derek realized the person he trusted most had done this to him, how much more would he hurt?

I tried to keep going like nothing had changed. I tried and tried and tried until April.

Until Teddy.

Derek was the one who said it was too late for her, even when she still looked okay on the surface. He was the one who said once something was blighted, it was dead.

And yet, he didn't see that was true for us, too. Our relationship was poisoned. I'd hurt him. He'd hurt me. All that pain would fester under the surface. Incurable.

I'd seen all this before, with my parents. The way Dad shut down every time Mom yelled at him—his distant stare—and the hurt in Mom's eyes as she went overlooked, underconsidered. They went round and round, and their hurts only rotted deeper.

All they could do was cling to the scraps of what they once had, until they hit that inevitable tipping point.

I'd tried to delay mine and Derek's, but after Teddy, I knew—we'd reached it.

I told Derek I never wanted to speak to him again. And I didn't. I walked past him in the halls at school. I switched my desk from the middle, where we'd sat together, to the back of the room. I ignored call after call. I deleted text after text unread.

And I cried every single night.

I honestly thought it would hurt us less in the long run.

But I'd been wrong about that, because I'd been hurting more than ever, and judging by the slump of his spine, Derek had, too.

Now, in the dark of his room, all I could do was keep saying it: "I'm sorry. I'm sorry, I'm sorry, I'm sorry." It burst out of me—the million times that I'd thought it, lain awake in bed and prayed the air would carry it to Derek's ear.

I was trembling, nose running, eyes watering. My fingers clutched the rug to stop myself from grabbing him. I couldn't promise I wouldn't leave him again. The blight would force me to, sooner or later. I just needed him to know, before it was over.

"Okay, Wren. Shh. It's okay." He believed me. Even if I couldn't explain myself, at least he knew that I cared.

"You should sleep," he said gently. "We both should."

I glanced to the bed behind us, the naked skin of my neck shivering.

He tracked my hesitation, and he just seemed to know—I wanted him to offer again.

"Should I come with you?" he asked.

My head drooped with gratitude. "I-if you don't mind. If you still want to. It's just . . ."

As far as we knew, the blight was only airborne once it collected in plant roots. And I'd always heard people exclusively passed it by biting or breaking skin, swapping fluids.

But to sleep beside him all night, it wasn't a risk I was willing to take. For my breath to be so close to his.

"Maybe you could face the other way?"

Derek blinked. "You want my feet in your face? That's gonna make you feel better?"

"I dunno." I shrank into my oversized loaner clothes, the ones that smelled like him. "Maybe."

"Well." He shrugged. "Okay."

He left behind his giant dust bunny of a sleeping bag and followed me back to his bed. He let me get in first. As he lifted the covers at the opposite end, he moved turtle-slow, not chancing that his body would brush against mine. It was a twin bed, though. Even with me sliding up against the cold wall, he was only a couple inches away. The heat of him flickered just out of reach.

This was all wrong. I wanted to curl up against him, feel the solid reassurance of his broad chest. Or better yet, to yank off his shirt and trace his skin with my fingertips. Feel his breath heat and quicken, his smile under my kiss. Everything with Derek was sunshine-warm.

And we couldn't have that now, no matter how much I wanted it.

Somehow, this was even lonelier. If it hurt this much to have him inches away, how was it gonna feel when I couldn't be near him at all? Near anyone?

My eyes flooded all over again, even hotter.

"Wren . . ." How was he supposed to have the words for this?

Derek didn't talk anymore, though. Instead, his hand wrapped around my ankle.

I reached my own out and wrapped it around his.

We just lay there, holding each other's ankles, like this was some kind of hug.

Funnily enough, it really did feel like one.

CHAPTER 6

My dreams were marrow-chilling, but I still hated when morning washed in past Derek's blinds, bleaching the room with its white rays. Time to get up. Time to stop hiding.

Time to find out what really happened to my parents.

We dragged ourselves awake, and Derek flashed a shy little smile when he changed his shirt. Like I hadn't seen the bare skin of his chest and abs a thousand times, back when we'd go swimming in the bay as kids. And then that handful of times, earlier this year after we'd started dating, when our parents weren't home.

Great. Now *I* was smiling shyly, too.

My sweet sentiments faded the second I sat up in bed. My arms itched with a writhing squirminess. I scratched my forearm, and I swear something wriggled away from my fingers, like a worm burrowing deeper under my skin.

I stifled my shriek.

I glanced at Derek, but he was busy fussing over his hair in the mirror. While he was distracted, I ripped back my sleeve.

All I found was my usual spray of freckles.

Maybe my mind was playing horrible tricks. I couldn't tell what was real. One thing was for sure, though: something awful must've been happening to my nails under their polish. Just scratching at my arm made them ache.

"Wren?"

I looked up—to find Derek watching me in the mirror.

"Your arm okay?" he asked.

I froze, clutching my arm. I should tell him what was happening to me. I'd almost done it last night, but as we were brushing our teeth, I saw how he was looking at my nail polish. He'd opened his mouth as if to ask why I'd put it on.

Then, instead, he chose to close it. To smile at me, like he needed nothing to be wrong.

But this was only going to get worse.

I chewed my chapped lip, working up the guts to tell him the last thing he wanted to hear. The last thing I wanted to say. "Derek, I . . . I think I'm . . ."

He broke the gaze we'd held in the mirror. His shoulders hunched.

He didn't want to know. He desperately, desperately, didn't want to know.

The second I told him the truth, so much hurt was going to crash in on those soft brown eyes. And I'd hurt him so much already. The idea of wrecking, so soon, that small respite we'd found for ourselves last night . . .

The resolve I'd been building crumbled around me. I managed the flimsiest of smiles. "Never mind. It's nothing."

Derek nodded, the tension disappearing from his shoulders. He turned and leaned against his dresser to face me. "So, um, should I ask Mom for some extra clothes for you? I'm sure she'd have something, if you're tired of my stuff."

I hugged my arms across my chest, clutching at his baggy shirt. I had the same one from eighth-grade gym class, but mine was three times smaller. "No, that's okay."

Derek smiled at me again, like he had yesterday on my porch. Like I was cute.

And maybe this time I wouldn't have minded—if my heart wasn't still pounding from whatever had just happened to my arm.

"Well then, I'll go make sure the coffee's on," he said. "You want any?"

I shook my head.

"Right. You don't drink coffee." He winced. To be fair, breakfast was the one meal we hadn't really eaten with each other in recent years. "Just the bread, then?"

"Thanks."

"No prob. So . . ." He pointed an awkward finger to the door and then shuffled out through it.

The second it clicked shut behind him, I looked back at my sore fingertips.

I pressed lightly on my thumbnail.

A sharp sting. The nail jiggled in a way it shouldn't. A thin line of blood pricked up from under the bed, peeking at me through the sky-blue polish.

Oh my God, my nails were going to rot off, weren't they?

My stomach lurched with a rolling nausea, one I couldn't get to settle.

I couldn't be alone with my body, not for a second longer. I pulled the long sleeves of Derek's shirt over my hands, so I didn't have to see my nails, and jumped out of bed. I caught up with Derek in the kitchen, cramming in alongside Angie and Claudette and Mrs. P. Everyone else ate eggs and toast at the breakfast table, but I could barely choke down the unicorn braid Derek had set aside for me. Even that made me gag.

Once I ate, though, I did feel a smidge better. My stomach settled just a little. The buzzing in my head, and the headache that came with it, dampened.

Maybe there was a good reason customers snatched up so much unicorn braid during flu season.

Teddy, come to think of it, who I'd been feeding our bread to for months, was holding up better than those other Harris dogs who'd chased us and Buckwheat last night.

It was only a theory, but also the only hope I had to cling to.

So I crammed down another slice before Derek and I ran out to feed the goats. We soothed Buckwheat with an extra couple of well-earned apples, and I made Mrs. P promise to check on her again later. She was staying behind to work on their own farm's catastrophe, while the rest of us squeezed into Claudette's pickup. It was too many bodies, too tight a space. We might've fit better if I'd overlapped my leg more with Derek's, but my thigh squeezed against his was about as much as I could handle. He wedged against the passenger door, and I wedged between him and Angie's hip. Somehow, Claudette found the steering wheel past Angie's body.

As we drove by the ghost melon patch, I saw it—the oil-thick blight dripping from the vines and their withered buds, the silver-veined globes caved in and rotting.

This was supposed to be peak ghost melon season, when the Pewter-Flores family went all out: harvesting, stocking up, freezing and grinding pulp to have on hand for the winter. It was supposed to generate the income that carried them through the rest of the year.

Claudette and Derek stared straight ahead at the road, refusing to look at the patches any more than they had to.

I looked away, too. And tried not to wonder how far the blight had eaten into Rainbow Fields overnight.

It was easier once we were out on the road. By the sun-dappled light of morning, the drive to the Harrises' almost seemed normal. Even the birds were out, though their song was thinner than usual. The animal population in Hollow's End had been dwindling for a while, at least the ones that still came out by day. I closed my eyes and strained to catch the faint melody.

As we reached the Harrises' winding driveway, the illusion shattered.

There, in the hard-packed dirt, was a mad mob of tracks. So many they swallowed the hoofprints Buckwheat had left behind. The blighted horde must've chased us all the way to the end of the driveway last night. Thank God we weren't there when they'd arrived.

We pulled up next to my abandoned truck.

Under the morning's sun, I got too good of a look at the Teddy-sized dent in my driver's-side door—at the flecks of molting fur and skin she'd left behind. The impact hadn't even fazed her. How much did she feel at all anymore?

The other cars still sat abandoned. There were no new tire tracks. No one had come back.

"The police sure are taking their time," I grumbled, peering through Claudette's empty rear window. Mrs. P had called them last night. Apparently, they said they'd visit the Harris farm "first thing in the morning."

"They'll come," Derek assured me.

In the meantime, it was down to us to investigate, because we sure appeared to be the only living souls out here. The house still stood dark. The barn doors hung open, creaking in the wind.

Cicadas buzzed lazily from the tree where the blighted owl had stared out the night before. No owl now. Just the occasional crow dipping down, searching for unspoiled corn.

We fanned out into the field, heading toward the forest, combing for any scrap of our missing neighbors. My missing parents.

Everyone knew the blighted didn't come out by day, but each time the wind twisted the corn by my side, I whipped my head around. Snapped stalks were littered everywhere, sloughed with foul streaks from the blighted as they'd slithered and surged through the crops.

Every sparkle on the ground clutched at my chest—Dad's watch? Mom's ring?

No. Just rocks. Just blight.

My guilt was in overdrive. Nothing about the blight was fair, but it seemed extra-cruel that Mom could've gotten caught in its cross fire last night. A thousand times, she'd tried to get me and Dad to leave Hollow's End before it was too late.

Even before the blight.

"What do you think about taking a trip with me, baby?" she'd asked me in December.

That morning, I'd found her on the porch swing, huddled small in the afghan her own mom had made her. Her lips must've been nearly blue under her red lipstick, the way she was clutching her tea to her chest. My teeth clacked with cold the second I stepped outside, and who knew how long she'd been sitting out there, staring distantly at our wheat, its young leaves gleaming low to the frosty ground. Normal winter wheat would've gone dormant by now, but ours would grow awhile yet before pausing until spring.

Mom coolly regarded our miracle.

All I could see was Texas in her eyes—the home she'd left behind. The home she gave up for Dad, after they met in college. In their first married photo album, I'd seen how happy they were together, the smiles and hand-holding and bear hugs. But slowly, somehow, all that had crumbled away, especially the last few years. Until it felt like I was just watching her, each and every day, weigh the life she'd given up against the one she'd chosen with Dad at Rainbow Fields—always another tally closer to admitting the trade wasn't worth it.

I hadn't heard her and Dad fight the previous night.

I thought it'd been a good night—and we needed one. At the start of December, they'd let one of our farmhands go so they could siphon off more money for my college fund. Since then, it'd been extra-tense, and Mom and Dad were exhausted from working longer hours. But we'd set all of that aside the night before. We carried in our sap-sticky Christmas tree, decked it with twisting ornaments. Then Dad brought Mom and me hot chocolate and sat back to watch us, the blues and greens of string lights glowing in his gray eyes. Afterward, he wrapped his arms around us both and sighed.

I'd thought it was a happy sigh.

But finding Mom on the porch the next morning, freezing and alone, I had to wonder.

"Wouldn't you like to come visit Texas?" She dragged her gaze away from the wheat, her eyes probing deep into mine.

I wasn't sure she really meant "visit." The way she said it, it didn't sound like she was talking about something temporary.

I sat beside her, and she draped the blanket over me like a giant wing, snuggling me into her side.

"You'd love it there," she said. "It's got magic of its own. Not like Hollow's End maybe, but you haven't seen the sun until you've seen it there. Those wide-open fields, sky so big you'll swear it can eat you whole."

Thanks, but no thanks. I didn't want the sky to eat me whole.

And I could never leave Rainbow Fields. I'd learned to

walk in those fields, taking my first steps to reach a stalk of flickering sun-orange wheat. Since then, I'd traipsed barefoot through that soil so often the farm was now the bottom of my feet. Sometimes I was afraid if I left Hollow's End I'd forget how to walk. Or maybe I never actually knew how to walk in the first place. Maybe all this time, it had only been the magic of Hollow's End holding me up.

Mom knew well enough what my silence meant. She rubbed a little too hard at the perpetual knot under my right shoulder. "I hope you'll go away for college, baby. I think it'd be good for you."

Maybe it would be. Maybe some secret part of me even wanted to. To prove to myself that I was more than I thought. But Derek wasn't planning to leave. If there truly was a better home for me, I wasn't sure I wanted to know. I wasn't sure Dad wanted me to know, either.

"Let's see what happens," she said. "Let's see about those SAT scores."

She smiled that condescending smile—the one she thinks I don't notice—and passed me the warm mug of tea. As I sipped the bitter, oversteeped brew, I saw her, under the blanket, twisting the silver ring on her middle finger. The one Grandma Peg had given her when she and Dad took over Rainbow Fields, some kind of welcome-to-the-farm gesture. She twisted and twisted, like she could screw the whole thing off—ring and finger and all.

She'd come to Hollow's End for Dad. She'd only stayed for me.

And now . . .

Standing on the Harrises' ransacked farm, I hated how the corn swayed around me, caging me in until I lost all sense of the horizon. I scrubbed a sleeve across my forehead. On my next step, my boot squished too far into the earth.

Into a pool of quicksilver, squirming away from my sole in little beads.

"Jesus Christ!" I yanked my foot back.

"What? What is it?" Derek's call came from several feet to my right, stalks cracking as he pushed toward me.

"No, don't come any closer!" I answered through the muffling mask of my bandana. "It's blight. Just more blight."

I cursed and wiped my boot against cleaner dirt.

The blight balled up and trickled back to its pool, sucked together almost magnetically. It gleamed with a sparkle—violet, there in the silver.

Like in my nightmare.

It looked exactly like the glittering flecks you'd find in a loaf of unicorn braid. It couldn't be a coincidence that yesterday it had broken into the violet wheat. But how could that possibly affect the blight here? Rainbow Fields was thirty minutes away, by car.

Then again, peering closely, I noticed there were other tiny specks: gold and pale blue and coppery auburn. All the colors I'd seen in my dream. And the blight had eaten the Murphys' yams, the Pewter-Floreses' ghost melons, the Harrises' animals . . .

Now, there was dark blue, too.

It couldn't have eaten that much, not all the way into the indigo wheat, could it?

Claudette called out from the tree line, "Hey, I found something." Her voice was always flat, but this sounded outright bleak.

I broke into a breathless dash, coughing the congestion back from my throat as I pushed out of the swaying corn.

There, at the edge of the forest.

A mess of abandoned steel shovels glinted in the sun. Some lay dead flat, like they'd been dropped. Others had shattered handles, or had been flung aside a good distance from the rest, like they'd been used as weapons. Really ineffective weapons.

The dirt was a tangle of hoof- and paw- and footprints. What stood out most of all, though, were the ragged scratches in the ground. So many. In sets of five or ten— finger marks clawing, snatching at the soil when there was nothing left to cling to.

All of them led back into the trees.

"Wren, wait!" Derek cried.

I was already twenty feet deep into the forest. My legs flew. The raw panic exploding in my gut carried me deeper and deeper.

"Mom! Dad!" The scream snagged against the ache in my throat, the stickiness clinging at the bottom of my lungs.

All the birds cut silent. Only my tattered voice echoed

back, bouncing off trunk after trunk. The writhing trails in the dirt were harder to follow among the roots, but all the chaos led in one direction—toward the heart of the forest.

Through my bandana, the stench of rot squirmed thick into my nose.

A cool whisper fluttered like moth's wings inside my ear. *"Wren. Welcome home."*

Icy prickles stung under the skin of my shoulders. Frantic, I searched for the source—that same voice that had visited in my nightmare.

No one in sight. Not even Derek. His footsteps still crashed after me, trying to catch up.

It had to be one of the blighted, whispering at me. Some person who'd lost their mind. It's just . . . it had sounded so close. Like it was inside my ear.

"Who's there?" I peered through rows of trees. Suddenly, they all looked like teeth, like this forest was the mouth of some titanic beast, and I'd stumbled right into it.

"Follow me."

The ground softened, shifting as droplets of blighted mercury seeped up from the soil. They trickled together into one unified line—a thin quicksilver river winding into the woods. Along the same path as those stampeding tracks.

A pale fog crept across my vision. It rolled in fast, faster than any natural fog ever could.

Impossible or not, it hung in front of my eyes, masking the world behind a cushy cobweb gauze.

"Wren?" Something brushed my arm.

I shrieked. The fog vanished instantly.

Revealing Derek by my side.

"Sorry, I . . ." I clutched my hands to my chest to stop my heart from bursting through my ribs. My eyes searched the forest floor for that metallic trickle in the moss, but it was gone, reabsorbed into the earth as fast as it had emerged.

It had felt so real. The voice, the quicksilver river, the fog. But I must've been hallucinating. Another blight symptom from the flyer.

God, maybe I had less time than I'd thought.

I shook my head, trying to clear the static out of my brain, and refocused on Derek.

"I don't know if you noticed, but . . ." Derek pointed in a half-halting gesture—off to the right, where a set of tracks broke off from the rest.

Human tracks.

We followed the footprints as they stumbled off the path, past the nearest trees. From Rainbow Fields, I'd seen quicksilver glinting behind tree bark at the edge of the forest, but I hadn't realized just how much had grown this deep in the woods. Fungus climbed tree trunks, and blight welled over the cupped edges like some grotesque mercury fountain. It dribbled down to lie low at the trees' roots.

We stayed light on our feet. Careful. Tiptoed around the puddles.

My breath came shallow. If we could find a survivor, any survivor, maybe they could tell us where everyone went. What horrible thing had happened.

At a rock at the top of a hill, the tracks floundered and turned into large swipes in the dirt. Someone had tripped and tumbled.

It was a long way to roll. I scanned every passing rock and root for blood, for any indication a person might've smashed their head.

No blood, but . . . All the way down by the creek, there was a flutter of faded red plaid.

A body sprawled.

My shoe skidded against pebbles. I grabbed for Derek so I didn't lose my balance and roll all the way down the embankment.

"Mom," I choked out.

That was the shirt she'd been wearing yesterday morning.

"*Mom!*" I staggered down the hillside faster than I could find footholds, sliding and catching myself each step of the way.

The body at the bottom lay in a limp hump of ripped jeans and tattered plaid. Boots slick with dripping blight. Blood seeped into her jeans from her torn-up knees. Her face was smashed sideways into the earth, her golden-brown hair spilling over her outstretched arms like she'd tried to catch herself—and failed.

"Mom, Mom, *Mom!*" I grabbed her shoulder.

"Wait!" Derek cried after me. "You don't know if she's—"

She moaned, low and scratchy.

"Mom . . . ?" My finger slipped through the torn shoulder of her shirt, grazing her skin. It was sticky with blood. Clammy.

She hacked a ragged cough into the dirt and dragged herself up on raw fingertips, cracked nails.

"Wren, get back!" Derek held out a hand to yank me away.

But I didn't take it. I'd frozen solid. I couldn't move. I could barely breathe.

She rattled out a wheeze—"Wren"—and turned to face me.

Gashes oozed on her left cheek, her jaw, her forehead, the skin rubbed bloody. My own face stung just looking at it.

My heart stuttered when I saw her eyes. Her hazel irises fogged white around the edges. Where she'd coughed on the ground, she'd left behind a quicksilver froth.

Blighted. She was already half-gone.

"Get away from me," she croaked, and pulled back.

I kneeled, paralyzed, touching the empty space she'd left behind. This was all wrong. Mom was the one who never got sick. She was the one with the bouncy ponytail and too-wide eyes. The bright-red lipstick, even in her rattiest patched-up overalls. She had the kind of energy that left everyone in her wake exhausted.

She wasn't supposed to look like this—torn skin and moth-eaten eyes. Lipstick raked down her chin in an undignified scarlet smear. Mold blooming from the inside of her lips.

"Mom, what happened . . . ?"

"We were working." She sat in the slack mud of the creek bank, not bothering to pull herself up. Just letting the blighted earth seep through her jeans. "It was still light out, but it didn't matter. They came out of the woods, all at once."

No wonder they hadn't seen it coming.

"We ran. I bashed one with my shovel, but . . . they got us all, I think. Your dad . . ." Her foggy eyes gazed out through the trees, deeper into the woods.

Another knife stab to my heart. Dad was lying out there somewhere, maybe in even worse shape.

"Where?" I demanded.

"I'm sorry, Wren." She wasn't even listening, busy shaking her head. "It's all our fault."

I blinked. "What happened yesterday? How is that your—"

"Not yesterday. *This*." She waved a trembling hand at the toxic forest walling us in. "All of this."

Their fault? She had no idea what I'd done.

"Mom, no." I clasped my hands together hard, pressing against my own guilty tremors. "It wasn't you."

I flicked a glance back at Derek. He watched warily from the corner of his eye but stood aside to give us privacy.

I dropped into the tiniest whisper: "It was me, Mom. I broke it. The quartz."

And Mom was the reason why. I dug it up in December, the same day I'd found her on the porch swing, after I'd watched her twist and twist that ring on her finger.

She was going to leave, I'd known then. With or without me.

I couldn't fix things between her and Dad, not completely. But the one thing they fought about more than anything was money. Our farm. The advantage to a novelty product like our rainbow wheat was that we could charge an arm and a leg and a firstborn for it. But we only had so much to sell. Rainbow Fields was confined by the range of our rainbow quartz.

I thought if I chiseled off a chunk, if I planted it farther out, I could spread its impact—that we could plant more rainbow wheat. Earn more money. Then Mom and Dad could afford the help we actually needed. They wouldn't have to set their alarm clocks blaring an hour before the sun even thought about coming up. They wouldn't have to put away their tools after it had gone down. Maybe they'd even smile again.

For the record, I'd been right. I'd buried my splintered-off quartz behind the silo, back near the forest where no one would spot it. And the new test wheat I'd secretly planted on top of it had been growing in just as I'd hoped.

But, of course, I hadn't realized the cost of breaking that stone—that I would unleash the quicksilver blight on us all. After Dad made me swear not to tell another soul what I'd done, I hadn't. I hadn't spoken another word about it.

Until now, staring into Mom's blighted eyes.

"You broke the quartz?" she asked. Slowly. Uncomprehendingly. "How big of a piece?"

I held up my hand, fingers spread, to estimate the size. "I'm so, so sorry, Mom." I sucked back a sob. "It's all my fault. I ruined everything."

A low, guttural retching came from Mom's throat. Like she was about to throw up.

Except it wasn't that at all. She was laughing at me.

"M-mom?" Had she lost her mind entirely?

"Baby, we've broken that rock a hundred times."

Something icy and dreadful lurched in my stomach.

"You . . . ? And Dad?" My jaw hung. Dad had neglected to share that little tidbit of information. I'd been so proud, at first, of my bright idea to expand our planting area, but in reality, he and Mom had already had that idea.

And it wasn't a bright idea at all.

It was a colossal screwup. Of epic, disastrous proportions.

"The blight got out every time?" I asked Mom.

"We took much smaller pieces. But, yes, some did get out. Every time." Her head drooped on her neck. "Maybe it's true that the chunk you took started the leak in our quartz, but—"

"The quartz is *still* leaking?" I'd had no idea that was even possible. "Under *our* field? Then why is it the Murphys' where it first showed up?"

"I don't know. Your dad said something about the rainbow quartz being special, that it gives us more protection than the other farms, but . . ." She frowned, like the very topic exhausted her. "What you need to understand is, it was only a matter of time before some straw broke the back of Hollow's End. You didn't know, baby. Blame me. Blame your dad. Just don't blame yourself."

Derek. His dad. Teddy. All the pain and suffering and disappearances. Even this latest catastrophe, the one that had taken my parents . . .

It wasn't completely my fault?

How much it had cost me, believing it was. How much it had cost Derek.

I was replaying my conversation with Dad in his study

now, sifting and searching and digging back through. I guess he'd never said, point-blank, "This is your fault and yours alone, Wren." But he had to be able to tell that's what I thought, and he just let me think it.

Because he hoped it would shame me into keeping farther away from the blight? Into staying silent?

I dug my fingertips into my palms, hard enough that my nails twinged. Hard enough that I had to stop myself before they did anything worse.

"Mom, how *could* you?" I'd only broken the quartz because I'd had no idea the foul rot was inside it.

"A little extra leakage wasn't supposed to hurt," Mom said. "Even what you did, it wouldn't have been enough. Not if we were the only ones doing it."

She looked over my shoulder to find Derek. "What's your mom been up to, Derek?" Mom asked. "How is it you have more melons to sell every year?"

His neck stiffened. "I don't know what you're talking about, Mrs. Warren."

"That so?" She grinned at him.

A nasty grin—that didn't look like hers at all. It looked like someone else was playing with the muscles of her face. *"Too late now,"* she said. *"Either way."*

All at once, her mouth fell slack and she winced.

"Oh, it hurts." She clutched a hand to her head, leaving half a thumbnail behind in her hair. "The buzzing. It's getting so much louder."

I knew exactly what she meant. The low-frequency hum at the back of my brain, the one that had started yesterday—it was louder today.

Mom looked a lot worse than I did, though. She shook her head, still recoiling from the static. "Your dad keeps everything in our basement. Behind the shelves."

Derek and I shared a slow, horrified look.

"Dad keeps *what* in our basement?" I asked.

"Take it, baby. Take this." She slid Grandma Peg's ring from her trembling finger and held it out to me. The pure silver band, its center stamped with a strange symbol: a triangle intersected by a horizontal line through the top. The sides carved with little crescent moons.

"Mom . . ." I could barely speak past my locking jaw. "Don't give me your stuff."

She'd promised Grandma Peg not to take it off. And here she was, doling it out like it was time to distribute the assets from her will.

Tears ran from Mom's eyes, stained gray, like they were running through mascara, even though she wasn't wearing any. "I told your dad none of this was right. It's not natural. Of course, he felt he owed it to his family, to the whole town, and now . . ." Her muttering trailed off into another headshake. "'Our black earth is a fertile earth.' What a sick joke."

That phrase sounded some bell in my head, like I'd heard it before. But I couldn't place it. She was making less and less sense.

"What's not natural?" I asked. "What's—"

Her hand shot out and grabbed mine, grinding the ring into my palm before I had time to jump back.

I gasped, and Derek leapt forward to help.

Mom held up a hand to still us both. "Listen to me,

Wren. You, too, Derek. Get out of Hollow's End. We should've gone months ago." She sighed through heavy lungs. "Go. Take Derek's family with you."

Of course, blighted as I was, I'd never make it past quarantine at the bridge.

It didn't matter. "I'm not leaving you and Dad. And the farm, the blight finally reached it yesterday. The violet. Maybe the indigo, too. It'll get the rest unless I—"

"Forget the farm. Let it die."

The lump in my throat swelled to choking size. She couldn't mean that. I knew she dreamed of leaving. Rainbow Fields wasn't magic to her, not the way it was to me and Dad. But she knew how much it meant to him, to me. That farm was our family's life together.

I stared at her from across a chasm.

"You don't understand," she said. "It's a lie, this idea of a free miracle. There's too much we never told you, and now . . ."

A prickle lit across my neck, as if a centipede was crawling across my spine. Seeking a way into my skull.

I slapped at it, like I could smash it out of me.

This way. Follow me.

Mom and I glanced in the same direction, back through the trees.

That voice again. Mom and I *both* looked, but Derek didn't. So whatever it was, only the blighted could hear it?

I turned back to Mom and saw that a little more of the hazel in her eyes had vanished into white. The skin of her forehead was rippling by her hairline, squirming in a way skin shouldn't. The blight was already in her head.

She pulled herself first into a crouch and then all the way up to stand, swaying and hunched.

"Don't follow it," I begged her, giving myself away. She would know that I could hear it, too. That I was blighted, just like her, and there was no sense giving me her stuff because I wouldn't be here to use it, either.

But she didn't even react. Didn't process. She wasn't really here. "Be good, Wren," she mumbled, lurching away. "Be better than us."

Was that really the last thing my mother was going to say to me, sixteen years of life and parenting distilled into "Be good"?

How was she this far gone? We must've been infected around the same time. Maybe it was the level of exposure—I'd only inhaled the blight, while she'd been slashed by blighted animals and laid in puddles. But then again . . .

There was another difference between us—I'd been eating the unicorn braid. And so had Teddy.

"Mom, wait!" I cried. "I can bring you the bread. I think maybe it slows down the infection."

"No," she said. She didn't even turn around.

"If I bring it here, will you eat it?" I could leave it out for her and Dad each day, like I did for Teddy. Maybe it would keep the blight from getting worse until we figured out how to cure it. Maybe—

She did turn now, hair whipping her ears. Her silvering lips pulled back from her teeth in a snarl. "I told you, *never* come back here."

In spite of myself, I stepped back. From my own mom. A hollow ache opened up behind my heart.

My voice came out small. "At the house then. I could leave it on the porch."

"If I ever come to the house, if your dad ever comes," she said, "don't answer the door."

She turned and staggered away through the trees in the exact direction the voice in my head had pointed me before.

I watched her until she disappeared. Until the forest of Hollow's End swallowed her whole. The Texas sky never got its chance.

CHAPTER 7

Derek and I pushed our way back out of the forest to the dying edge of the Harrises' farm. Angie and Claudette straightened up from examining a bush. Maybe they'd found something, but I'd seen enough.

Angie gasped when she saw me. At whatever soul-sucked expression I must've been wearing.

"What did you see?" Claudette demanded.

I kept walking past them. I couldn't handle questions right now. The bandana tied around my neck felt too tight, like it was cutting into my throat. Talking would hurt anyway.

"Wren!" Derek called. "Don't leave without me, okay?"

I nodded dully.

He turned back to Claudette and Angie, and I shuffled toward my Teddy-dented truck.

After the darkness of the forest, the fields felt double bright. I squinted against the glaring haze, because it almost looked like, among the trucks ahead . . .

No, it wasn't an optical illusion. A new vehicle—a big white van—clogged the driveway.

Doors banged as three people climbed out. They were covered top to bottom in white hazmat suits, pure, like untouched snow. Their faces masked by cloudy shields.

The emergency responders.

I stumbled over my hitching step. My skipping heart.

It was what I'd wanted, wasn't it? Someone had come. But it wasn't the police. It was the folks locking up the blighted, and I had to look at least half the sick mess I felt.

My truck was past their van.

I could turn back, but if they'd already spotted me, how was that gonna look?

Maybe I could make it to my truck before they could stop me. I forced my stiffening legs forward, quicker than before, but not *too* quick.

The responders weren't looking my way. They hauled open the van's doors and rustled around, equipment clinking as they gathered it up. A voice crackled out, tinny, like it was filtered through a microphone, one suit talking to another. "—doesn't make any sense. We're talking about some impossible recipe from the 1600s, and you really think the ones who cracked it were these backcountry hicks?"

I wasn't sure what they were talking about, but the "backcountry hicks" part sure got my attention.

One of the responders turned at the sight of me. "Excuse me. Miss?"

Shit. I'd slowed unintentionally to listen. I tried keeping my expression neutral—like it was remotely plausible I hadn't heard that—and focused on my truck. Tried not to quicken my pace.

"Miss!" the responder called, following me.

I had to stop. I tugged down the long sleeves of Derek's shirt and clenched my hands into fists inside, just in case my veins had started to silver. In case my nail polish had chipped. In case something started wriggling again, under the skin of my arm.

With a face as blank as I could manage, I turned. "Yes?"

The suit closed the distance between us, stiff and awkward, plastic rubbing with every step. "Do you live on this farm?" That mechanical crackle droned out at me.

I shook my head. "I'm from Rainbow Fields. I was just heading back—"

"The wheat." The face mask regarded me, bouncing back the sun, reflecting a distorted picture of my own wild eyes. "You're a Warren?"

Something changed under that mechanized fuzzy tone, a sharpening of interest.

Which I didn't like at all.

I wiped the sweat from my hairline and pointed quickly to the woods. "People were attacked here last night. Where are the police?"

"They're coming."

I stared, waiting for more, but I guess that was all I was getting. "Okay, well . . ." The triage clinic didn't have the best reputation, so I wasn't exactly eager to sic them on anyone, least of all my parents. But, given the state Mom was already in, what choice did I have? "Look, people are in the forest. My parents."

"I'm sorry to hear that. We'd like to find a cure to help them. You know, Miss Warren, this quicksilver blight seems quite unique to Hollow's End. But that's not the only unique thing about Hollow's End, is it? There are four very special farms here. Our research might go more quickly if you could tell us a little more about them."

I blinked.

The suit stared into my silence, with a slight tilt of its head. "Maybe there's something you could share about your wheat? The soil? Any unconventional farming practices . . . ?"

They'd already questioned Dad and the rest of the farmers about our miracle crops. As much as Dad wanted to protect our farm, if he'd believed there was any chance confessing about our quartz would help find a cure faster, he would've done it. But he hadn't. None of the farmers had.

So I guess when they saw a kid here, alone and trembling, they saw an opportunity.

I eyed the white suit from top to bottom for any ID, badge, insignia.

Nothing. Zilch.

I sucked in a breath, slow and steady as I could manage. "Do you mind sharing," I asked carefully, "which agency you're with again?"

"US government, miss. We're here to help."

My tongue went numb in my mouth.

"If you're here to help, then what about the people in the woods?" I asked. "The people who need your help right now?"

The suit stood there, staring. For what felt like minutes. Finally, it turned away. "You shouldn't be here." As if that was an answer.

No. I shouldn't. Every second I stood here was another second that whoever was in that suit might notice my paling skin, the chilled, sweaty sheen over my face and neck—see them for the symptoms they were.

If they were done with me, I was more than done with them.

As the suit returned to the van, I beelined for my truck. The second I was inside, I slammed the door behind me. I watched through the windshield as the suits gathered their bags—slowly, methodically—and tromped into the field. They didn't even give me a second glance. All three stooped down to admire a single silver-smeared cornstalk. One took out a vial and began to scrape the blight in, one microbead at a time.

They weren't going to step foot in the forest, were they?

No. Of course not.

I sat in the driver's seat, dead as dust, and stared at the ring in my palm.

I wasn't taking it from Mom. I was just looking after it for her. I tried it on my own thumb, which was barely thick enough to hold it in place. Right above it sat that nasty mark I'd gotten ages ago, learning the hard way not to play tug-of-war with a dog as sharp-toothed as Teddy. To this day, the burst vein pooled purple under the surface of my skin. I'd asked the school nurse about it once, why it'd never healed. "You have circulation in your thumb?" she'd asked. At my nod, she'd said, "Then it's healed."

Back then, I'd still expected things to return to their original setting. To heal all the way. I knew that was a fairy tale now. I'd known since the day I had to run my own dog into the woods and leave her to rot.

Broken things didn't get all the way better. They just got a little bit worse, or a hell of a lot worse, and you had to make do. Until you couldn't anymore.

My mouth was dank, like a swamp.

I didn't want to know—I didn't—but I had to check. I flipped down the visor. My truck was so old there wasn't even a built-in vanity mirror, but the one I'd clipped on did the trick.

No wonder Angie had gasped. The suit's face mask had done me a favor by distorting my reflection. In a clear mirror, I was waxy and trembling, eyes sinking into my skull.

I pulled down my inner lip and searched for mold, like the rot creeping out from my own mother's lips, clouding over the pink.

No mold yet.

But under my gumline, there was a graying tinge, blossoming like a bruise toward my teeth. I lifted my tongue. There, nestled in my saliva, were three silver beads.

I shoved open my door and spat, wretched.

Acid burned the back of my throat, but I clapped my hands over my mouth and swallowed against the vise of my bandana. I'd eaten unicorn braid this morning. It was still in my stomach. If I was right, even by a fraction, that the bread could be slowing my symptoms, I needed to keep it there.

How much longer would this body even be mine?

Before I turned into some rabid wild animal, tearing into my neighbors and dragging them through the woods to God knows where.

"Wren?" Derek called. He was jogging toward me, giving the suits a wide berth. They didn't bother to look up from their science experiment. Guess they figured if I was a lost cause, the other Hollow's End kids were, too. "Are you okay?"

All I could do was shake my head.

I leaned against my seat, pressing my palms over my eyes. I needed dark. Quiet. Just for a moment.

Dry grass crunched under Derek's work boots as he trekked around the front of the truck.

The passenger door creaked.

When I opened my eyes, there he was. I took in the tenderness of his face—the kind eyes and heavy brows, that pale curve of the scar in his upper lip. That scar was nothing like my thumb. A reminder that things didn't always get worse.

Sometimes—just *sometimes*—people knew how to make them better.

I was pretty sure this wasn't one of those times, though.

"When you're ready," he said, "I think we should go."

But where was there to go? My whole body felt so heavy, so utterly exhausted.

He frowned at my silence. "We have to find out what your mom meant about your basement, right? If we're going to figure out how to save them."

Save them . . .

Mom had said to let the farm die. She'd essentially said to let her and Dad die, too. Although they wouldn't really, not all the way. The blighted might seem like zombies, but they weren't—because they weren't dead.

They were alive. Rotting alive.

Maybe they could still be saved.

Unfortunately, I was the last person on earth who should be trusted to help. "Derek, what are we supposed to do?" I thumbed out my window toward the massive trees. "You saw the size of the horde last night. Half of Hollow's End has been swallowed into the forest, my parents included. And the last time I tried to help anyone, I did the complete opposite. Didn't you hear what I told Mom? I broke the quartz. I let the blight slip out."

Derek's face barely changed. So he *had* heard.

"You thought all this was your fault." He glanced out the window, toward the Harrises' empty house. Another ruined Hollow's End home. "How long have you thought that?"

He was finally putting it together, wasn't he? What had happened to us.

I looked down at my lap. Derek's borrowed sweatpants were still the only thing keeping me warm. "Since March."

"March." Derek rubbed at the bristles of his short black hair. "I see."

Exactly when things started going downhill between us. When I stopped honestly answering his questions: "How are you?" and "Is everything okay?" and "Wren, what's going on?"

"I wish you'd told me," he said.

The dry scoff left my throat before I could stop it. Easy for him to say now, after he heard Mom let me off the hook.

"You would've hated me," I said.

"Maybe," Derek admitted. "Maybe not. Do you hate your parents, now that your mom told you they did it, too?"

Angry heat welled in my stomach, my chest, the back of my throat, behind my eyes. But I shook my head. "I don't have any right to hate them. The only difference is that they did it again and again. Who knows? If I'd had time, maybe I would've, too."

"No. You only did it the first time because you didn't know the risks. You were just trying to help your family, weren't you?"

I saw it again behind my closed eyes: Mom on that swing, twisting and twisting the ring on her finger.

With a sniff, a sucking shudder, I nodded.

"Anyway, it's not like it's all on you and your folks. She said my mom had something to do with it, too." Derek's hands clenched beside his legs as he shook his head. "Look, just because you made a mistake one time doesn't mean you have to keep making it. We don't have to be like your parents or mine."

I lifted my eyes to his.

"But if we even want the chance to be better, I guess we're going to have to clean up their shitty mess first," Derek said. "Looks like no one else is going to do it."

He nodded through the windshield to the suits. All three had moved on—to another cornstalk. Another sample.

Mom's parting words flashed back to me. *Be better than us.*

"You're right," I said to Derek. "It has to be us."

He smiled, just a little, and laid his hand on mine, where it rested on the steering wheel.

I gave him a smile back, even if it was a sad one.

"You must be freezing. You're shaking." Derek scooted closer. His hand shifted against mine.

And my pinky nail slid, hard.

A sharp pain shot through my finger, and I shrieked and jerked back, clutching my hand against my racing heart.

Something had uprooted. Like when I'd yanked the violet wheat from the soil, those naked roots trembling in the air they were never meant to touch.

The outer edge of my nail seared, and I looked down at it. Hot blood seeped up and dribbled down the side of my finger.

I pressed the nail into the bed, like I could glue it back into place.

I had to look away.

"Oh my God, sorry!" Derek tugged the bandana from his neck. "Take this."

It was too big, but it was something. I clutched it against the blood, my nail. I fumbled to wrap it around my whole finger again and again. If I pressed hard enough, I could numb some of the sting.

"I'm so sorry," Derek said. "Did you snag it on something in the forest?"

I just stared at him from out of my rotting body.

For God's sake. He had to know by now.

He looked away.

Right. He didn't want to know. Maybe he couldn't handle knowing yet. Maybe I couldn't handle telling him.

"I can drive," he mumbled, nodding to my wrapped hand—the kiss of red already seeping through the blue of his bandana.

"No." My voice came back harder and hotter than I meant. "I can do it."

I just had to turn the key in the ignition. Drive the car. I just had to move one action, one step at a time. I just had to save my parents.

Before I joined them.

If something awful was lurking in my house, it'd be no surprise that it was in the basement. I unlatched the cellar door and stared down at the gray stone walls, the dingy wooden stairs and floor.

"Jesus," Derek said from behind me, "I forgot how scary your basement is."

Yeah. It had always been dank and gloomy, littered with sticky bug traps that caught way too many roaches for my peace of mind.

After what Mom had said, I had the feeling it was about to get a hell of a lot scarier.

"Well, down we go," I muttered to Derek.

I led the way into the cool, damp air, the stairs moaning under our footfalls.

At the bottom, I reached up and yanked the cord of

the first light bulb. Naked and dangling, it flickered to life in the dusty, sour air. The pale rays fell on open wooden crates of produce, lining either side of the stone walls.

"Oh God!" Derek made a spitting noise behind me.

I whipped around.

To find him swatting a bundle of dried rosemary and sage away from his face. "You guys couldn't have hung these a little higher?"

Since all that extra acorn squash had rotted away down here, we'd been hanging herb bundles from a beam in the ceiling to dampen the stench. "Usually, it's not an issue."

"Because you're pocket-sized?" Derek teased, an old jab.

"Because we don't go walking into things face-first," I replied. I yanked on the other light-bulb cords, illuminating the back wall, the one blocked by shelves, stocked with cans and jars of pickled vegetables and homemade strawberry preserves.

Mom had said we had to look behind the shelves.

I forced myself forward as Derek trailed after me, nearly tripping on the back of my boots. "What do you think it could be?" he asked. "That your parents have been hiding?"

"No idea. And I'm extremely unexcited to find out."

I tugged on the shelves, but they didn't budge. I frowned at the rows and rows of pickled cabbage.

"Here." Derek tugged on the shelves, too.

This time, they moved out just enough—to reveal the heavy wood of a small door, about a foot higher than the normal basement floor.

A door in the wall.

"There's a room back there?" Derek gaped.

Just how many secrets had my parents been keeping? A whole secret room's worth?

We dragged the shelves out farther to reach it. Then I slid the old leaden latch and shoved at the door.

An ancient groan, a punch of stale air and decay. Derek reeled back. "Christ, that's rancid."

The rest of the basement was a little mildewy, but nothing like this. It smelled like someone had stuffed ten mummies into a walk-in closet and sealed the door. Maybe the old acorn-squash funk wasn't all those herb bundles were meant to mask.

Even I had to duck as we climbed in. It was a tight room, only a little bigger than our dining room table, though, thank God, the ceiling was several feet higher than the cramped doorway. It was made of the same gray stone as the walls in the rest of the basement, which meant it must've been an original part of the house. I felt the cool, rough-hewn walls by the doorway for a light switch. No such luck. I dug out my phone and turned on the flashlight.

The beam found benches carved into the walls. An empty stone pedestal. Not much else.

But that smell had to be coming from somewhere. I raised the beam higher, illuminating a series of shelves lining the walls.

The light caught and gleamed off row after row of mason jars. All of them contained something liquid, silver—lapping against the glass like it was alive and trying to eat its way out.

Blight. Bottled blight. Bottled death.

Everything went black as my phone dropped from my startled fingers, cracking against the stone floor. I rescued it in a scramble. The screen was half-shattered, but at least the flashlight still worked. I couldn't bear another second in the dark, smothered by the looming stench.

"Wh-what is that?" Derek stood huddled by the door.

I swept the light up to the jars, heart pulsing through my fingers. They were the same jars we used for pickling and preserves, each labeled with Scotch tape and a number. The blight inside sparkled, glinting with tiny flecks like smashed jewels: gold and silver-blue and auburn, violet, indigo, and . . . oh my God, was that a brighter blue, too? Shining like sapphire.

Could these colors really be from the wheat? The jars were sealed. No way the blight in here could access nutrients from our field—not unless all the blight was somehow connected. But that was impossible, wasn't it?

If the blight really had stretched into indigo overnight, if it had crept into blue now . . .

My stomach swirled with a noxious mix of fear and nausea—the queasiness that had haunted me since this morning. I forced my flashlight forward, to step in for a closer look.

What on God's green earth had Dad been doing down here?

Derek had stepped up beside me. We shared a glance, his rounding eyes reflecting every bit of my own horror.

On the shelves to our right, my light found something else. Books. Some looked old, older than the ones Dad kept in his study, with peeling bindings and faded gold lettering down the spines. I squinted to read the titles. *The Hermetic Arcanum. Fasciculus Chemicus, or Chymical Collections. A Discourse of Fire and Salt: Discovering Many Secret Mysteries* . . . A few I couldn't read. They were in other languages, mostly French and Latin. There were unmarked books, too—thin and gray and nondescript.

Like that journal I'd seen Dad writing in back in March—the one he'd slid out of sight as soon as I walked in the room.

I reached for the one at the end, pulled it down, and flipped it open, finding page after page scrawled with Dad's scratchy writing.

January 31

1 p.m. I don't tend to come down here during the day. Now I wonder if I've been missing key behavior. Vial 4 is doing something strange. I'd expected to find a dry jar and the mouse blighted, as I left it last night. Instead, the jar is full of liquid argent vive. The mouse is floating inside. Alive. How can it breathe while entirely submerged? Why, after the blight had been absorbed into the mouse's body, would it come back out? I'll see what happens tonight.

11:30 p.m. Vial 4 has reverted to the state I'd expected earlier: dry jar, blighted mouse. No liquid argent vive. So the mouse has reabsorbed it? Very strange.

February 1

12 p.m. Vial 4 is liquid again. Mouse is floating inside the argent vive. What can this mean?

"Argent vive?" Derek read over my shoulder. "Is that what he's calling the blight?"

As if I had any answers. Whatever he was calling it, Dad hadn't even mentioned it was inside the rainbow quartz. I'd had the joyful discovery of finding that out all by myself.

In the journal, I flipped ahead, skimming for more about Vial 4.

February 27

10:30 p.m. Vial 4's mouse is gone, entirely dissolved. Only argent vive remains. Shocking, though, when I checked the jar's final weight. It should've been 3,566 grams—a sum of the jar, the mouse's weight, and the initial argent vive I added. Instead, the weight is 3,624.

An unexplained 58-gram addition.

It's physically impossible, a violation of the law of conservation of mass. Nothing comes from nothing.

And yet, I am positive I've measured correctly.

There's more to the argent vive than even I realized. It has taken the mouse, consumed it, and grown. I wonder now if I've witnessed its process of *digestion, internal to the mouse by night and external to the mouse by day?*

Is the argent vive eating? Could it actually be alive?

Eating. Is that what the blight was doing? Eating our crops, our animals, our own bodies?

I had wondered how much blight there could possibly be in Hollow's End. Even if every last drop had escaped from our quartz—which I don't think it had—it couldn't be more than a couple gallons. And yet, blight festered on every farm. It surged through the veins of an amassing infected horde. In the woods, it overflowed from behind the bark of blighted trees, pooled on the ground beside dead leaves and pine needles.

This is how: It was *growing*. It grew with every creature it consumed.

So now, it was eating me alive, from the inside out.

But Dad theorized that the digestion process was only internal by night? *External* by day? So far, there was no blight seeping from my pores to gnaw away at me. But maybe I just hadn't reached that point yet. Maybe, first, it had to build up enough of itself inside me.

A shiver crawled under my skin. As if it wanted to wriggle away from the rest of me while it still had the chance.

Derek didn't say a word. He reached up and grabbed another book—this one musty and golden. The words weren't English, but it was mostly pictures. Old black-and-white drawings of the sun and the moon. Angels hovered over blossoming fields. People in long dresses and tunics mixed potions in jars.

Actually, it was a little like the mural on the Cormac Murphy Community Center. The sun and moon hanging in the same sky. There was even a cornucopia.

In the back, there was an entire index of symbols. Planets and elements were depicted by circles and triangles, straight and squiggly lines.

"What the hell is any of this?" Derek muttered.

My thoughts exactly.

I stood on the closest bench to see the books better, and my light caught a different gleam. Not blight in a jar this time. It was a silver chest.

Small, about the size of a shoebox, but as I pulled it down, I battled to hold it steady. It was shockingly heavy. I winced as I set it on the bench below, knocking it against my bandaged finger.

There was something written on the top. I ran my thumb across the ridged lettering, carved straight into the metal: NOW IS THE HOUR OF SILVER AND GOLD.

Silver and gold. I stiffened.

It was like something Dad had once said. Back when I was thirteen, that night after he showed me the quartz, I couldn't sleep, lying up thinking about it. I went down to his study and asked him how it worked, what it was doing to our wheat.

He'd let out the quietest chuckle. "Wren, what if I told you a story? One your very-great-granddad Thomas used to tell."

By "very-great," he meant "several-generations-great." Thomas Warren, our farm's founder.

With slow and measured words, Dad continued, "Once,

the whole world was silver and gold, your very-great-granddad said. Deep down, everything still is. However, with time, most things have veered off track, picking up grime and debris, slipping further from their pure nature. Can you imagine there might be a way—a special kind of chemistry—to bring them back?"

I'd honestly had no idea what he was talking about, let alone how it related to the quartz. "A way to bring things back to silver and gold?" I said. "You . . . believe that?"

He just kept staring at me, fingers steepled, resting against his lips. He was never one to overexplain things. He believed I should work them out for myself.

As my awkward silence stretched, he finally said, "I'll tell you what. I'm not sure what I believe anymore. Someday, you might find that's true for you, too."

Well, about that much, he'd definitely been right. I had no idea what to believe anymore.

I tilted the silver box, hoping further examination might make some sense of this thing. On the front, there was a lock unlike any I'd ever seen. A keyhole in a strange shape: a triangle pointed up, a horizontal line intersecting the top.

"Hey, wait." Derek flipped to the back of the faded golden book, to the index of symbols. "That's in here." He tapped the page. "See? Air."

Air, huh?

That index wasn't the only place I'd seen it. That triangle was the exact shape on Mom's ring. In fact . . .

I kneeled before the box, pulled the ring off my thumb, and pushed it into the lock.

Click. A perfect fit.

I turned the ring.

Click. Again.

I pulled at the heavy lid.

And it wouldn't budge.

"Dammit!" Maybe it was stuck. I turned the ring to the left and to the right. It clicked and unclicked, and nothing happened at all.

"Uh, Wren?" Derek moved the flashlight's beam from the keyhole to the area below.

There were three other keyholes, arranged so that the one my ring fit sat at the top of a diamond. In the bottom center was the inverse of my ring, an upside-down triangle with a line intersecting the bottom. On the right, there was a plain triangle facing up. On the left, a plain triangle facing down.

"Those are all in here." He double-checked the book, pointing to each, clockwise from air at the top: "Fire, earth, water."

I shook the box in frustration. "But this is the only ring like this I've seen."

"I've seen one." Derek reached into his pocket. With a small clang, he deposited something onto the chest's lid.

It was a silver ring, the same size and shape as mine. This one, though, was stamped in the center with a plain right-side-up triangle. Fire.

"Angie found it," he said. "At the Harrises', in a bush by the edge of the forest. She and Claud wanted me to show you in case . . . Well, they think someone chucked it there deliberately. Maybe, you know, as they were being . . ."

Dragged screaming into the forest?

I inspected the ring. "I don't think this belonged to my dad." Then again, apparently Dad was up to all sorts of secret things. "At least, I never saw him wear it."

"Now I'm actually starting to wonder if it might belong to the Harrises," Derek said. "There are four slots. Four families. And the thing is . . ." He tapped the leftmost symbol on the lock—water, the triangle facing upside down. "My mom wears *that* ring."

I'd noticed before that Mrs. P wore rings, but I'd never looked closely. "She has it on now?"

"Every day. She was wearing it this morning."

To be sure, I pressed the one Claudette found against its matching piece of the lock.

Another click.

Definitely the right ring. Odds were good Mrs. P's was a match, too.

So we were only missing one: the Murphys'.

CHAPTER 8

Unsurprisingly, the Murphys didn't answer their phones. We loaded up my big backpack with as many creepy old books as we could fit, including Dad's journals, and of course, the silver box. And in the little time we had, I did what I could to take care of my wilting body. I grabbed an entire loaf of unicorn braid from the breadbox and crammed down as much as I could stomach. I changed into fresh clothes and swapped my pinky's clumsy bandage for a real Band-Aid. Even though I was trying not to look, I caught a glimpse of the dangling sky-blue nail, and the red underneath, as crusty as rust.

As we walked from the porch to Derek's truck, I glanced back at the field. From here, all I could see were the front rows, rippling crimson in the breeze like a red sea. But the fresh malty scent that hung over Rainbow Fields was beginning to sour.

Little wonder if the blight really had eaten all the way

into the blue. Our miracle was rotting into the dirt, and there was no time to save it.

The back of my neck burned as I turned away. I kept walking.

After what I'd seen in the basement, I couldn't help wondering what Mom meant when she'd said that the idea of a free miracle was a lie.

I was more and more afraid she was right. Like I was about to stumble backstage after the most spectacular magic show and discover there was no magic at all—just trick wires and mirrors. Polished fraud.

I snuck one last look at the field. The sun gleamed rose-gold over the wheat's bushy tips. Waving goodbye in the wind. I climbed into Derek's truck, and we drove to the Murphys'.

We found the Murphys' farm as quiet as we feared: no lights on in the house, no one working in the fields. Just row after row of plastic sheeting, stray edges blowing loose in the wind.

Even on a good day, the Murphys' farm had always been the least flashy. All you could see of the golden yams was their heart-shaped greens, rising in bushy clumps to coat the field like ivy. The tops of the leaves were smooth, glossy green. The undersides were peach-fuzz soft, gilded with the tiniest golden hairs.

The yams themselves came out of the ground strangely warm to the touch, like rocks that had been baking in the sun. The more you scrubbed away the caked dirt, the more those sunny flecks glinted through its skin. The inside was yellow as butter, and just as smooth and creamy.

Eating them warmed you from the inside like hot mulled cider. They were supposedly way more nutritionally dense and filling than normal yams. One was a meal. Two would keep you full all day. So folks watching their weight always swarmed the Murphys' booth at the farmer's market. And yams were a staple of every farmer and farmhand's diet in Hollow's End.

Or, well, they had been.

The Murphys' protective plastic sheeting couldn't hide the swampy stench of mold. Or the shriveled remains of green that peeked out, eaten alive by quicksilver.

Mom had told me weeks ago that the Murphys had lost every one of their golden yams, their miracle crop deader than the dirt around them. From the looks of their fields now, though, they'd lost *everything,* even their normal insurance crops—the carrots, parsnips, radishes, beets . . .

This farm was a graveyard.

Ice dripped down my spine. Soon, this would be Rainbow Fields. Derek's farm, too.

He stood beside me, grim. "You don't think we're too late, do you?" His voice was muffled through his new army-green bandana, courtesy of Dad and my hall closet, since I'd bled all over his last one.

I followed his gaze to the heart of the Murphys' field, where a foot-wide, foot-deep crater jutted into the earth— an empty hole someone had dug. Roughly. Maybe with claws.

"I don't know. That pit's probably too big to have been

for the *ring* . . ." I said, even as my stomach opened into its own sinkhole. I couldn't help picturing the rainbow quartz on our farm, in the center of our field.

The Murphys must've had their own special something, like our quartz, that made their yams grow the way they did. But why would the blighted horde dig it up? What could they possibly want with it?

And maybe that wasn't the only digging they'd been doing on this farm. If the Murphys' ring was where I suspected, they might've already found it, too.

We still had to try.

We made our way to the old barn at the back of their property, with its pitched roof and the big doors in the side. It was too ancient for actual farm business, but every year the Murphys hosted a New Year's party here, a small one—just for the founding families and their guests.

And thank God for that.

Don't get me wrong, I did love the fluster and bluster of the mid-December winter festival, when the Murphys sold their spiced golden yam pies by the dozen. Their pie-eating contest was always a spectacle. Every year, Derek was *convinced* he would win, even as he slumped in his chair, eyes glazed and glassy. By the end, he'd just about face-plant into his plate. And still, he always staggered to his feet, banging the table with a cry of "Next year!" At least he'd outgrown the part where he threw up in the bushes. So, progress.

They served yam-flavored everything. Yam curly fries, dusted in smoked paprika. Salt-and-pepper deep-fried yam balls. There were also ghost melon–striped candy canes, and the Harrises hitched jingle-belled horses up to their antique carriage to cart couples around town. My family set up a photo booth and wove wintry backdrops from blue- and indigo-tinged wheat. Teddy was on call to pose with fuzzy antlers strapped under her chin and a flashing Rudolph nose she tolerated in exchange for bites of roast turkey.

Sometimes, if we got really lucky, it snowed the perfect amount—enough to glaze the glowing lampposts and spike everyone's holiday cheer.

But it was a relief when the tourists finally cleared out. When the streets and shops emptied, and everyone could exhale. Take down the mistletoe and scrub the carols out of our ears.

Drop the perfect Hollow's End act.

After all that, a quiet New Year's get-together in the Murphys' old barn, just founders and invited guests, was actually pretty peachy.

Today, though, without the string lights and golden party banners, the barn looked sad and abandoned. Its crooked boards were beginning to break away.

Derek went to check inside while I circled around to the back.

I stopped when I saw it. By the edge of the forest, a thin rectangular block poked up from the grass.

Every year, before the New Year's party started, our parents dragged us all to this crumbling stone marker. We mounded up a tiny pile of magic before it: golden yams, silver-veined ghost melons, a stalk of wheat in every iridescent shade. A lock of mane from the Harrises' highest-earning stallion, cinched with a blood-red ribbon.

We'd pile it all up, and then we'd leave it there. It always felt like a funeral. If anyone coughed, they whispered, "Sorry." We'd been doing it since before we even thought to ask why.

When I got a little older, I finally did ask, "What is this? Some kind of grave?"

Mom pursed her red lips real tight. "There's no body under there."

"It's just to give thanks," Dad told me. "Pay our respects for all that's been given to us."

When I opened my mouth again, he cut me off. "It's tradition," he said.

Like that was beyond questioning.

I approached the marker. Our offerings from this past December were still there—though eaten away by frost after frost, thawed and frozen and rethawed, now nothing more than a monument to mold and decay. The marker itself was so old it was practically part of the earth, worn by years of rain and the steady creep of moss.

It bore a simple inscription: OUR BLACK EARTH IS A FERTILE EARTH.

This was where I'd heard that phrase before—what Mom, in the forest, had called some sick joke.

I had a hunch the ring might be close. I just had to retrace my steps from this past New Year's, when I was out here with Derek.

I wandered over to where we'd sat six months ago, against the back of the barn, giggling and shushing each other. Trying not to spill the beer I'd stolen from the party.

It's still hard to pinpoint exactly when we'd fallen in

love with each other. All those years ago, when ten-year-old Derek asked ten-year-old me what I wanted to name our kids, it felt harmless enough. Less so, in the year or two after, when Derek's voice went low instead of high, and Mom suggested I start wearing a bra. That was around the time I started noticing how if any part of us brushed, Derek jerked away like I was a venomous copperhead. It had stung, until I felt the same. Suddenly, his skin might as well have carried an electric charge. We turned into total cowards, dodging around each other for years.

This past New Year's Eve was different, though. Derek, at least, had decided enough was enough. He asked me to dance. At first, I thought he meant in our usual goofy foot-apart way, but this time, he held his hand out for mine. His other hand, trembling a little with nerves, wrapped around my lower back.

At the end of the countdown, we were going to kiss. I was sure of it. As the clock ticked from ten to one, I stayed close, my arm brushing his as we stood side by side.

Three . . .

Our glances kept meeting and ducking away as we shouted each number.

Two . . .

My belly tightened. Something below my belly tightened.

One!

The room exploded into cheers and kissing couples. Angie grabbed Claudette and laid one on her so good I thought Claudette's head might pop off.

Derek and I looked to each other, mouths parted, bodies paralyzed.

In awkward unison, we said, "Cheers," and clinked our glasses.

As we both drank our private sips of cider, I recognized that look on Derek's face—eyes cast down, eyebrows scrunched. He was disappointed. Angry at himself. Same as when he missed the mark during Claudette's shooting lessons.

I knew it then, too: enough was enough. It was a new year, and I'd learned to create my own hope. I'd dug up the quartz a couple weeks earlier. New rainbow wheat was already sprouting behind the silo where I'd planted the hunk I'd chiseled off. I'd wait for it to come all the way in before I told my parents, but it would help them. It had to.

I didn't know yet what was coming. That everything was about to be ruined.

"Wait here," I'd said.

For the winter festival, Rainbow Fields had tried partnering with a nearby brewery that had been begging us to let them make unicorn beer. The cans and labels were gorgeous.

The taste, apparently . . . not so much.

Probably why we had so much left over for the Murphy party and why Angie, from her family of brewers, had taken one sip and squealed, "*No*. That is *not* beer. That is a travesty. Okay, they need to let my parents partner with them, because . . ." The rant went on. But she'd left her nearly full can on a table nearby.

It had been easy enough to swipe it. A perk of being small and stranger-shy and overlooked. No one suspected me, not even my parents, who were off chatting with the Harrises in a corner. Mrs. P and Mr. Flores were busy dancing, though they probably only would've laughed if they'd seen.

I took Derek's hand and led him out into the fresh January dark. Even as my breath blew clouds in the air, I was lit with a steadily growing warmth, a joy that turned my cheeks pinker than the cold could.

I led him here, to the back of the barn. We just needed somewhere quiet, that's all. The town was small, people were bored, and news traveled fast. Everyone had been teasing us about each other for years. If they found out about us now, we'd never hear the end of it.

We had to be sure first.

The unicorn beer was . . . Well, I'd have to take Angie's word for it being a travesty against beer. But I could personally attest that it was a travesty against our wheat. A flat, sour shadow of its seven naturally vibrant flavors.

Regardless, I knew then and there I'd forever love the taste. I played with the cuff of Derek's jacket, running my fingers along the inside lining, letting the tips of my nails graze the skin of his wrist, his pulse thudding under them.

He swallowed, and his brown eyes were so very open, tracking every flick of my pupils.

I told myself what I did next was because of the beer. To be honest, it had nothing to do with it.

I pushed up my chin and, for the very first time, touched my lips to his.

Instant relief. A warm bath on a winter's day. Cider's steam against frozen cheeks. The green pine in a dead, white forest. That's what Derek was to me—evergreen, the piece of summer not even winter could strip away.

His hands found the waves of my hair, and before I knew it, I'd turned to face him, straddling his lap.

Music beat away inside the barn, pulsing through the cracks between the vertical planks, warm little slivers of light along with it. One of my favorite songs—about golden skies and buzzing bees. "Oh, thank heavens," said the chorus, over and over.

It's all I could think, too.

Afterward, we stumbled back to the barn, our noses red from the icy air, my chin pink from rubbing against Derek's stubble. We were so busy staring at each other we weren't watching the ground, and I tripped on something in the grass.

Near the stone marker.

We both paused, joy frozen. The marker wasn't something you messed with. If I'd knocked something out of place and the Murphys noticed . . .

It wasn't an offering. It was a small wooden box, covered in dirt, that I'd accidentally kicked free from the ground. When I picked it up, something rattled inside, but I shoved it back into its hole as fast as possible and stamped the grass down flat over top of it.

If we weren't going to get caught, we didn't even care what it was. We just traipsed our way back to the barn, snickering to each other like it was another part of our secret. All I could see then, clear as crystal quartz, was that Derek and I were finally where we were meant to be.

Then the blight came. His dad went missing. My parents fell further and further apart. Teddy.

Now I stood at the back of the barn, staring into a

night so very far away. My arms had wrapped around themselves. I hugged my own shoulders.

Maybe that mound in the dirt wasn't what I was hoping. But *something* was buried there, out of the way, a place no one really should've been walking, not unless they were sneaking around like Derek and I were. It was about the right size. It had made the right sound . . .

I retraced our path, combing the grass near the stone, pressing down to test the earth. The toe of my boot poked around a withered ghost melon rind, carved up by squirrel teeth.

And I found it—a spot that was a little harder than the rest.

I dropped to my knees, damp dirt soaking through my jeans. Slowly, very conscious of my aching nails, I dug my uninjured hand into the earth.

Only a couple inches down, I scraped against a hard surface.

A wooden box about the size of my palm. Right where we'd left it on New Year's.

Please, I silently begged, *don't let this thing be covered in four locks or a passcode or—*

I pulled it out, and there were no locks at all. The Murphys hadn't guarded this like it was something they wanted to protect. They'd shoved it behind the barn like they wanted to forget it existed.

I lifted the lid. Inside, rattling alone in its empty nest, was a silver ring. An upside-down triangle stamped at its center, with a horizontal line near the bottom. Like the symbol from the book: earth.

"I should thank you, Wren."

That voice.

That slithering, shifting voice.

It echoed in my head. Was it echoing in my ears, too—out in the world, aloud? It seemed to come from everywhere.

Mom had said the blighted came just before nightfall yesterday, but the midafternoon sun was still burning in the sky. It wasn't remotely close to sunset. I was supposed to be safe.

At the back of my neck, the hair bristled.

I looked up from the Murphys' silver ring to face the forest. In December, the woods had been a scenic show of snow-dusted pines. Still and silent in that sleepy winter way, saying all is well, time for peace and rest.

Peace and rest. God, it was laughable.

Now the only white from the trees came from the icy wink of eyes. Rot rode the wind's breath, seeping out from those trees that had never regained their leaves. Never found spring.

Thirty feet from the forest's edge, the shadows stood.

Some on four legs, low to the ground, some just the right height to be human.

Clutching the ring to my thudding chest, I backed up.

"I've been looking for that."

Whether or not it was also in my head, those words *were* coming out loud from the tree line. From every human mouth. All those blighted vocal cords sounded out the whispering words in unison.

And yet, they didn't say, "We've been looking for that." They said "*I*." "I've been looking for that."

The blight itself.

The blight was talking. All these bodies, like bees or ants, were just drones following orders.

How was that possible? That couldn't be possible.

"Come give me that ring, Wren." The blight spoke again through its horde in the tree line.

This time, my own mouth moved along, the whispering voice rasping from between my lips. I was talking with them.

No. My stomach plunged with pooling horror. Those weren't my words.

I clutched at my throat, like I could choke the blight out of me. A pale sheen washed over my vision—the fog from the forest, rolling in.

Muscles squirmed in my bicep, my shoulder. My arm lifted.

I didn't give my arm that order, did I?

Before I could stop it, my body hauled back and hurled the silver ring into the forest, far out of sight.

"No!" I seized my arm, clutching the offending wrist.

So the blight could control me, too. I was shaking, trembling, with the wild urge to outrun my own self. My body served two masters now. I couldn't trust it to do my bidding.

One of the tall, shadowy shapes broke away from the rest, stalking toward where I'd thrown the ring. Already retrieving it.

"You're hurting, aren't you?" the shadows asked me. And the blight made me ask myself right along with them. *"Let me help. Follow me."*

Of course I was hurting. I was rotting from the inside out.

I tried to shake my head. I was doing so in my mind. In reality, though, I fired the order, again and again—but my body ignored me. It lurched one foot forward, then the other. Stumbling toward the forest.

Oh my God, it was happening. I was losing control of myself. And it wasn't like I'd thought it would be at all. Fog was clouding over my vision, and it was getting harder to see, harder to feel. That awful buzz at the back of my brain was screaming louder and louder, like it could drown out my thoughts. But even through all that, I wasn't rabid or crazed; I was still myself. My mind was all here, and it didn't matter, because the blight had control over my body.

My left hand reached for my right thumb. For my own ring.

It was going to make me throw that, too.

No, no, no.

I couldn't stop. My hand twisted the ring on my thumb, sliding it forward. I couldn't stop, I couldn't—

A loud crack rang out. A gunshot.

"Wren!" Derek shouted, running around the side of the barn. "Get back!"

The startle from the shot disintegrated the fog, snapped me back into control of my body.

I didn't wait to find out for how long. I ran.

Derek ran with me, brandishing his gun at the tree line, like that'd be enough to hold them off.

I flung a frenzied glance over my shoulder, checking if the creatures had followed. I'd counted at least fifteen, far more than we could fight.

But they weren't following at all. They just stood there, crowding the crooked gaps between trees, blinking dull white eyes as they watched us retreat.

Somehow, that scared me way worse.

We made it back to Derek's truck. It may have been a false sense of security, but it was still reassuring to put a wall of metal between us and those creatures.

"The ring?" Derek asked. "Did you—?"

He must've seen the wooden box dropped by my feet, the dirt on my hands.

Still gasping after our frantic dash, I uncurled my fingers and revealed my empty palms. At least I still had my own ring. I'd held on to that much.

Derek swallowed. "It was a long shot anyway. Let's get you home."

Home? He started the truck and rumbled out of the Murphys' driveway, taking the turn not to my house, but to his own. Honestly, it was more like home than my place could be, hollowed out like it was—the wheat dripping with blight and the tree line waiting for me with open teeth.

But Derek was still talking like nothing had changed. As if I deserved somewhere safe to hide from those monsters in the forest.

As if I was any better than they were.

I stared down at my jittery hands, shivering with dread. At the now smudged, dirty bandage covering my throbbing pinky. It stung, and it had to be because my nail was coming more and more unhinged.

If Derek hadn't startled me back into control of my body, that would've been it. I would've wandered away into the forest. Joined that reeking, rotting horde. When the blight did win the war for my body—and I knew now, it *would* win—what would happen to my mind? Would I be trapped inside, feeling every ache and pain as my body rotted apart— watching through fog as I bit into screaming flesh?

All those people I'd been staggering toward in the forest, were they still themselves, too? Unwilling prisoners in their own decaying bodies?

Oh my God, that would be so much worse than if they'd truly lost their senses.

And I was about to be one of them.

I didn't want to say anything. It'd be a moment before I could anyway. It wasn't just the running. My breath really was coming up thicker from my lungs, with the slightest rattling wheeze.

Finally, I managed it. "Derek, you shouldn't take me with you."

"What's that supposed to mean?" he asked, eyes fixed on the road.

"The horde came for me for a reason." I leaned my pounding head against the headrest, sticky where it touched through my hair to my neck. "I am blighted."

His face registered absolutely nothing for three full seconds.

And then, he shook his head.

"You're not. You can't be," he said, walling up behind that same shield against reality. "Your mom couldn't have been exposed much before you, and she looked . . . Well, you could see . . ."

He landed on safer words. "You're not showing symptoms."

"I am."

"You're not. You're—"

This was going to take forever, and I was already tired of talking about it. I was tired before I brought it up.

"Derek." I waited until he glanced to me. Then I pulled down my lower lip to reveal the moldy splotch climbing my gums.

The wheel spun out from Derek's hands. The whole truck swerved with a nasty lurch, tossing my queasy stomach into a burn at the back of my throat.

Derek's breaths came even shallower than mine. He clutched the wheel with fists tight enough to pop the blue veins under his brown skin.

"The truth is," I told him carefully, "I found the ring. The blight made me throw it into the forest. It moved my body for me. It made me talk." Every bit squeezed out of me like a knife inching out of a wound. I was killing the only home I still had.

"Do you understand what I'm saying?" I asked.

His driving slowed. The trees rolled one at a time past the windows.

He was thinking very hard about something.

"I know you have to take me back to my place," I said. "You should. That's why I told you."

He jerked his eyes to me, already forgetting that he'd

nearly run us off the road a second ago. "What? And leave you there alone?"

"Well . . ." Maybe it'd make him feel better if I didn't agree out loud. But of course, yes, that's all there was left to do.

"No," Derek said. Flat and final.

It wasn't like him at all. He was always the one who wanted to keep talking. I was the one who wanted to cut the tough stuff short.

But I couldn't let that stand. "What do you mean, 'no'? I'm—"

"Wren, we're just starting to get answers. Even if we don't have the Murphys' ring, we can go through your dad's stuff. We can talk to my mom. She has to at least know more than we do." He was practically begging me.

I had to shake my head. "It would be good to do those things, but you'd be better off doing them without me. Derek, this thing we're all calling the quicksilver blight . . . it's more than mindless rot. It can talk."

"The *blight* can talk?" Derek gave me a good hard side-long look, like he was reassessing my sanity levels. "You mean, the blighted can talk?"

That's what I'd thought at first, too.

But no. And how had no one else realized?

Then again, maybe others *had* realized. Too late, when the blight was already swallowing them deep into the forest. Without Derek, it would've been too late for me, too.

"Derek. Look." I gathered a deep, moldy breath. "I know how it sounds, but I'm telling you, this thing made me throw away the Murphys' ring, and it tried to get me to throw mine away, too. Who knows what else it could make me do? What if I tear up Dad's journals? I can only hurt more than—"

"Bullshit!" Derek slapped the steering wheel, jolting me with the sound. "You're the one who found the box. The ring! Even if you lost it, I wouldn't have found it in the first place! You're the one who rescued that random horse who wound up saving our asses. So don't talk like you're good for nothing. You're yourself *now*, aren't you?"

I licked my drying lips, recognizing too well that look in his eye, that rigid set in his shoulders. I'd worn it myself two months ago.

"It's just like you said with Teddy," I told him. "I'm out of time. Even if it doesn't look that way."

Derek hit the brakes.

With a world-weary squeal, the truck ground to a halt.

"Wren." He turned to me, full on, and held out his hand for mine—gently, open-palmed. Both of us far too aware what had happened last time we'd touched hands. My pinky still throbbed under its Band-Aid.

But this could be the last time anyone asked to hold my hand, to touch me.

I gave it to him, trembling dirt-smudged fingers and all.

He curled his fingers around my palm with care and squeezed.

"No," he said again.

I opened my mouth, hoping the words would come to fill it.

"Not yet." His voice choked out past a thousand tiny fissures and cracks, a feather's touch from shattering. "You can't just let it take you apart. Please. What happened to 'It has to be us'? If no one else is going to help, what happened to you and me at least doing this together?"

The blight happened, of course. Like it happened to everything else.

"I could be dangerous," I said softly. "To you. Your family."

He didn't look at me. He looked out at the road. "You are my family."

It was involuntary, the way my fingers squeezed against his.

Unfortunately, he took it for an answer.

He nodded, turned, and revved the truck back to life.

He was right that I needed him. If he hadn't been there a few minutes ago, the blight would've vanished me into the forest then and there. If I slunk off to my house, alone, who knew how long I'd have?

But all our plans for the future, our plans to be family—that could never happen now.

How much was it going to cost Derek, that he wouldn't let himself understand that?

Maybe I could give him just a little longer. Take at least one more step toward untangling the mess of the blight. Before . . .

I leaned my forehead against the window. The cold glass rattled against every dip and bump, sloshing my brain.

I left it there. I wanted the headache.

It was an easier kind of pain.

CHAPTER 9

By the time we pulled up at Derek's farm, the sky was fading—the sweet pink clouds graying as the sun melted behind the trees. The darkening horizon brought strange relief to my eyes. The sun on our ride back had seemed so much harsher than usual, stabbing into my retinas. But twilight meant all sorts of other trouble.

Mrs. P, Claudette, and Angie had already barricaded themselves inside.

We closed the doors to Derek's truck as softly as possible. So softly, in fact, mine didn't latch. I had to bump it shut with my hip. At the thud, Derek and I both darted our eyes around, scanning for any shapes that might be running in our direction.

Nothing.

But high up in a tree near the driveway, a barn owl clung to a crooked branch—wings hunched, head askew on its putty-loose neck, eyes whiter than the snowy down of its face. Watching us, like the one at the Harrises'.

Sloppy dread tugged at my gut as Derek and I darted inside.

"Welcome back," Angie greeted us. She was lighting candles in the living room to prep for the coming dark.

Mrs. P had a fondness for the scented kind, so that's what they had stockpiled. A tangle of competing fragrances wafted our way—pea blossoms and pumpkin-apple spice and campfire smoke and pine.

Like spring and autumn had crashed a Christmas campout.

"Jesus, that's some kinda mood." Derek blinked, his eyes watering.

I followed as he ducked into the dining room, which acted as a holding area for all the hastily packed boxes of his dad's stuff that nobody wanted to deal with. Mr. Flores had always liked the dining room. He'd installed the needlessly fancy French doors himself, though it only made it harder to carry plates in and out from the kitchen. Especially since he'd accidentally installed them backward on their hinges. They didn't swing into the dining room, where there was plenty of space, but into the kitchen, where there was none.

Derek shoved them open, banging into the kitchen table.

Mrs. P jumped back from the stove, hands pressed to her heart. "Derek! What have I told you about those doors?"

The kitchen was a fresh assault on my senses. From the stove, tomato sauce and garlic butter. From the candle Claudette bitterly plunked on the table, tropical pineapple coconut?

Before the blight, if Mrs. P knew I was coming for dinner,

she often tried to make my favorite—quesadillas stuffed with roasted rounds of fresh golden yams, along with onions and jalapeños and gobs of stringy white cheese. But now, the yams were dead, and that tomato sauce smelled like the metal can it probably came in.

No way I'd be able to choke down dinner.

My stomach cringed even at the thought of unicorn braid. But it had started to gnaw at me, too—the first stirring of hunger since before I'd found my blighted wheat. I had no idea how my stomach expected me to fill it.

"Oh, Wren. Oh, honey . . ." Mrs. P reached out with a willowy arm, stepping toward us and wincing a little on her bad foot. An old injury, ever exacerbated by farm labor. "Claud told me what happened. I'm so sorry—"

She saw the silver box in Derek's hands, and her words died. The pity in her eyes faded to a far-off haze.

Slowly, she asked, "What are you doing with that?"

In all the time I'd known Mrs. P, I'd never heard her voice come out like that, hard-scaled and steely.

Derek deposited the box at the center of the kitchen table and planted himself in a chair. "Why don't you sit down, Mom?"

Mrs. P regarded her son, the coolness he bounced right back at her. Sixteen years of Claudette had prepared him, after all, to be at home in wolf dens.

She pursed her thin lips and snapped the burner dials to OFF.

"Uh . . ." Claudette looked back and forth between the box and the stovetop. "Is dinner not happening? Angie and I are pretty damn hungry."

"Sit down, Claud," Derek said. "I'm betting you'll wanna hear this, too."

"Really? Betting I won't," she grumbled.

There were five places at the crowded table. They'd set one for me, too, with a folded napkin and everything. As I took my seat beside Derek, a pang hit me deep, that even the small respite of family dinner was off the table. I might never be part of one again. Not with my parents, and not even with this family ready to welcome me with open arms. The blight corrupted everything—even private moments like these.

A creak came from the French doors. Angie hovered in the entryway, glancing back toward the aggressively perfumed living room, which I bet was suddenly seeming more appealing. The strings of her sweatshirt ended in little felt strawberries, and she twisted one uncomfortably. "Um, should I give you all a Hollow's End family moment or . . . ?" she asked Mrs. P.

But it was Claudette who answered, with a hard head shake. "Whatever it is, I'm going to tell you anyway. And I don't give a shit if anyone has a problem with that." The last part she said straight to Mrs. P.

Mrs. P swallowed a grimace. She looked more like she'd rather leap out a window than have this conversation, period, let alone have it with any more witnesses. But she gave Angie a limp nod.

"O-okay then . . ." Angie flushed, tucking her head to hide an anxious smile, as she squeezed into the seat beside me.

Claudette leaned against a counter behind her, mouth

turned down. She fished some half-cooked spaghetti out of the pot and crunched on it.

The Pewter-Floreses' kitchen usually felt cozy, despite the seasick-green accents, the loud floral wallpaper. But now, by candlelight, it felt cavelike. Downright claustrophobic.

Mrs. P lowered stiffly into her customary chair. A silver ring encircled the middle finger of her right hand. Funny the things you see only if you're looking for them. There it was in plain sight: an upside-down triangle stamped right in the center. Water.

As I stared at her hand, she stared at mine. At the new ring on my finger. Air.

The box's metallic sheen glared up at all of us.

Mrs. P glared back, like it was a snake she'd found in her basement and carried outside on the tip of a stick. Something she'd hoped never to deal with again, now coiled in the middle of her kitchen table, framed by a candle and a bowl of venom-green apples.

"Mom," Derek said, "I don't know how much Claud told you about what happened today, but we . . . we found Mrs. Warren in the forest." He glanced at me guiltily, like just saying it aloud was enough to freshly wound.

And, well, I guess it was—my stomach dropped. I saw it all over again—her moth-eaten eyes, her cracked, bloody nails. The undignified smear of crimson lipstick that I'd longed to wipe from her chin.

Mrs. P nodded grimly. "I know, honey." She glanced at me, too, in the same protective way Derek did. "We don't need to say too much about that right now."

"Well, a little bit we do. She told us some things," Derek said. "About the blight being the Warrens' fault—and ours."

Angie blinked, stunned.

Claudette stopped crunching on half-raw pasta. "No way that's true."

Mrs. P sat woodenly. She usually handled herself more gently than Claudette, with a grace that softened the sharpness of her long limbs. Even though she had the same long straw-colored hair and stonewashed eyes, I'd never been scared of Mrs. P. Never thought she looked like a scarecrow.

Not until now.

I wasn't sure she was even breathing.

Angie must've seen it, too. She was leaning farther back from the table, intentionally or not.

"Mom?" Claudette didn't get closer. She asked from where she stood.

"No," Mrs. P said finally. "I can't agree with that."

Well, hell. At least my family was taking responsibility. The fact that she wouldn't . . .

Heat flared into the hollow parts of my chest, itched against my ribs. I fought to keep it out of my voice. "But you have something like we do. Something in the soil, that makes your melons grow."

Mrs. P swiveled those flat eyes to me. "I didn't ask to inherit this. None of us did. All we can do is be grateful, and leave it at that." Her tone came sharp.

Sharp enough to inch that angry heat up my throat. "Grateful?" I said. She was going to lecture me about gratitude the same day I'd had to watch my own mom stagger away, get swallowed whole by the forest. As blight crept unseen from the roots of my painted nails. *"Grateful?"*

"Wren." Derek tried to pacify me with a gesture.

He was right. I wasn't helping. And this, after all, was his family. I nodded down at my clenched hands.

"Mom," he continued, "Mrs. Warren said the blight was inside their stone. That each time they broke it, they let some out."

Mrs. P nodded. "Maybe if they hadn't broken theirs so much—"

"Stop. Stop right there," Claudette said.

She stood directly behind her mom's chair, looming over her in the flickering candlelight. "That's what's in the agate?" she asked. *"Blight?* You told me it was nothing to worry about."

So, Mrs. P wasn't the only one on this farm who knew something.

"Claud?" Angie's brow furrowed.

Claudette sighed, running an agitated hand through her long hair. "Ange, I knew about the rock, but I didn't know—"

"Hold on," Derek said, "Claud knew about our stone? You told her and you didn't tell me?"

"She's older," Mrs. P said, like that settled it. "I was going to tell you about the agate, too, when you turned eighteen. One of you had to know in case something happened to me, especially now that your dad . . ."

She caught herself, eyes flicking to my slumped shoulders, maybe remembering my missing parents.

"Wren, there's a contract to cover how much leakage each farm is allowed. We didn't break it." Mrs. P tried to make that sound final.

But it clearly wasn't. She reluctantly added, "Not by much. I only did it because I knew there was a buffer. It shouldn't have mattered that we went a small fraction over our limit."

"Except," I said, "that everyone went over their limit?"

Mrs. P nodded, a grudging dip of her sharp chin. "I'm not sure about the Murphys. They've always been more cautious. We did have to call the Harrises on it. It wasn't so bad back when they were sticking to the horses, but they've been using more and more of their cinnabar on those dogs, too. When I was a girl, they had an ordinary pack. German shepherd and beagle mixes. Floppy ears. Cute. Now they're just about red wolves."

Is that why they were all that same eerie auburn—the horses and the dogs? From the Harrises' own stone, deep-red cinnabar.

"And I'm not saying it was right that we stretched the ghost melons, either!" Mrs. P rushed to clarify. "But you have to understand . . ." She looked down at her ring, straightened it on her finger.

Then she looked up at me. "Wren. Do you even know what that is? That ring you're wearing." Something about the intensity of her stare knocked the wind right out of me.

She seemed to take my silence for an answer.

With a knowing nod, she held hers up for us to admire. The proud triangle stamp. The crescents lining the gleaming band. "These were hand-forged in the late 1800s by Andrew Harris. One of our founders," she added for Angie, even though Angie was already nodding. She'd been staying in Hollow's End for less than two months, but I was sure by now she'd heard about our founders a million times.

Mrs. P continued, "Andrew Harris used to make his own horseshoes, you know—all sorts of metalwork. Well, he made this box." She gestured down at the table. "And he made these rings, from the first silver dollars our four farms ever earned, melted down. I don't know if you can imagine the accomplishment that would've been—to earn this kind of money from farming back in those days, when so many farms were going under. It's the American dream our families built for us . . . It's . . ."

She shook her head. Bit her lip.

"It's the dream our families built for all of Hollow's End," she said. "Take, for instance, the shop owners. They need the harvest festivals maybe even more than we do. The simple reality is, Hollow's End can't grow if our farms can't. Back then, the soil here, it wasn't workable. They had no choice. What they did saved us all—took us from starving to thriving."

I met eyes with Derek; we were both confused.

"But what exactly did our families do?" I finally asked. "They . . . what? Found the blight and stuffed it inside magic rocks, like that was somehow supposed to help?"

"No." Mrs. P frowned at me. "The stones weren't magic. And the blight . . . that substance didn't used to be toxic. The founders called it *argent vive*. That means 'living silver'. I don't know quite how it works, but, yes, putting it inside the stones—the quartz, the agate, the cinnabar, the geode—*did* help. It's the core of our farms. Without the argent vive, there are no miracle crops. There is no Hollow's End."

Suddenly, the ring on my thumb felt extra-heavy. I had to quash the urge to yank it off and hurl it across the room. "Does the town know that?" I asked. "Do they know about our farms?"

The locals never asked. *Never.* How our farm worked. Tourists did, the customers from over the bridge, visiting farmers. But the locals?

A fair number were offshoots of our four families, so maybe they were in on the secret. But that didn't account for everyone.

Mrs. P swatted that question off, as if it was so much as empty air. "Oh, they know enough. At least, they know enough not to ask."

Derek had been sitting quiet, taking all this in. "Then what's in here?" he asked, pointing at the silver box. "What is this 'Now is the hour of silver and gold' crap supposed to mean?" He gestured toward the carved saying. "And what could be so important that it needs all four families to open it?"

Mrs. P sealed her mouth so tight her lips disappeared.

At last, she said, "I don't expect you to understand this, but it's better that some things remain in the past."

"In the past . . . ?" Derek glanced through the window of the back door, at the view out into the night. Where a certain hardship lurked very much in the present.

If Mrs. P heard the accusation in his voice, she sure did

ignore it. "Yes." She reached out and pressed his hand, moving it away from the box. "We need to respect the sacrifice our families made for us. It was a terrible price to pay, but we paid it, and that's the end of it."

Static fizzed across my brain. A numbing bite pierced my skull like a slick, strong knife.

"Liar!" The word flared across my mind, hot and strange.

The candle fire infuriated me, the way it assaulted my eyes.

The solid ceramic of the fruit bowl sat right in front of me. It would feel good, something heavy in my hand. It would feel good to dash it to the floor, send those apples rolling like heads.

It would feel even better to tear skin. To sink my teeth deep.

My arm, the one closest to Mrs. P, spasmed with an awful urge.

God, what was I thinking? *Was* I thinking? Were these even my own thoughts? Maybe I was going to lose my mind after all.

I yanked my arm back by the wrist and clutched it under the table.

Derek touched my arm. "Wren?"

That sharp static sting faded. Enough for me to wince. I clutched at my scalp and rubbed back the pain.

All their stares burned into me.

My face steamed up. They'd all seen that, my sudden spasm and recoil. Did they suspect . . . ?

Derek rubbed at my shoulder, the same knot Mom

always worked at. "Are you . . . okay?" he whispered. As if everyone couldn't hear him.

I didn't say that aloud, did I? Call Mrs. P a liar?

She was frozen. Ice in her chair.

"That's very unlike you, Wren," she said quietly.

Shit. I did, didn't I?

I withered into myself. I shouldn't be here. One more outburst like that and, at best, they'd realize I was blighted. Send me away.

At worst, I'd hurt someone.

"I'm sorry," I muttered. "I'm angry, I guess."

At least that much was true. I was furious. Even if I had no right to be. I'd done the exact same thing that Mrs. P had done, that my parents had done. Our ancestors had done before us. All we wanted was to take care of our families: More crops. Money. Stability. We all knew, for our own reasons, that we needed more, but we hadn't realized the cost.

And those who did realize, they didn't care.

Besides, I was the one lying. To all of them. Even to Derek and myself.

I needed to get out of here. The second I got the chance.

"Well," Claudette broke in, "she's right, isn't she?" She stepped closer to her mother, bony hands on bony hips. Leering. "You tricked me into helping you carve up that agate. You told me it was fine. You lied then, and you're lying now."

"Lying about what?" Mrs. P locked scowls with her daughter. "You can't open that box anyway, not without all four rings. And the Murphys buried theirs a long time ago."

There was another silence.

Beside me, Angie had stopped breathing, glancing back and forth between Claudette and Mrs. P.

Then Claudette said, "Screw this. Let's just cut it open."

"You can't!" Mrs. P said. "It's lined with argent vive— blight! Either you'll break your saw, or you'll cut through the silver casing and let it out."

"I'll wear gloves." Claudette reached past her and grabbed the box from the table.

"Claudette, wait!" Mrs. P reached after her, but Claudette stomped out of the kitchen, moving toward the living room. The front door.

The shop with Claudette's tools was past the goat shed, out there in the dark.

"Wait! Not now!" Mrs. P charged after her. The rest of us did the same.

Claudette banged out onto the porch with a hard shove, sending a burst of cool air back to slap us all in the face.

Mrs. P caught up and snagged her by the arm. "At least wait until morning. It's not safe—"

"Well, excuse me, Mom, but I'm not feeling too safe under your roof now, either." Claudette ripped free and headed for the stairs.

This was my chance. Claudette and Mrs. P were moving toward some kind of family showdown, and maybe I could just slip away. Run off before I did something awful that I couldn't undo. But we'd come in Derek's truck, not mine. I still needed his help to get home. Or maybe I could take Buckwheat. Ride her back to—

"Holy hell." Claudette stopped on the first step.

Mrs. P froze too, a pace behind her.

Like maybe if they stood very still, they'd go invisible. Like maybe it could keep them safe.

I followed their stares past the blue-dotted fields toward the forest.

Rows of paired-off fireflies.

Eyes. Eyes and eyes and eyes. Shuffling this way.

It was too late for me to run. I didn't stand a chance against that horde.

Mrs. P pulled Claudette back and ushered the rest of us into the house. "Blow out the candles!" she said. "No flashlights!"

Angie and I wasted no time blowing out the candles by the front door, in a whiff of sugary and pine-scented smoke.

I'd only seen the blighted in a pack like this at the Harrises' last night, and at the Murphys' this afternoon. Before, at my place, it was usually one or two aimless wanderers that stumbled out of the forest. Most often, it was just Teddy.

It couldn't have been Claudette's door slam that lured them over. They were too close. They'd already been coming. It couldn't have been the lights. No overheads had been on. No lamps even. There were a couple flashlights in strategic locations, but no way that would've been enough. Not to draw a crowd like this.

Claudette shoved the silver box into my chest, hard enough to jostle my clogging lungs.

"Take this. Don't let Mom near it," she said.

Before I got the breath to respond, she snagged Derek by the wrist. "We need weapons."

Claudette the drill sergeant.

Honestly, it was calming. Her narrow focus. Her tight, clipped plan of attack.

She unlocked the metal cabinet in the corner where they stored their guns. Handed Derek a long-nosed hunting rifle and took one for herself. She clicked a massive magazine of bullets into place and passed another to him. "I've been stocking up," she said, fondly patting her ammo-stuffed chest pack and tightening the strap into place. "Don't go wild and waste them."

Derek nodded.

She nodded back and clapped him on the shoulder. "You got this."

I swear he grew a full inch on the spot.

I hoped all her past lessons with Derek paid off. Lord knows, I'd be no help in the weapons department, but there was at least something I could do—the backpack.

I scampered back into the kitchen. Dad's notes, those strange precious books, they were in my bag. I shoved the silver box in, too, and zipped it tight. It weighed me down, and sharp edges were digging into my back, but someone had to carry it.

We all met in the dark dining room, wedging in between the chairs and table and boxes.

"Let's not draw them any closer," Mrs. P said. "Angie, hon, get back from that window." She tugged her away with the familiarity of a family member. I guess she was getting used to playing mom for other people's kids.

"I've never seen so many at once," Angie said.

"It doesn't matter how many there are. They'll pass, like they always do. As long as we stay quiet and out of sight," Mrs. P said. "Everyone, just hunker down."

Same as when she'd told me last night that my parents would come back, it sounded steady enough. But she'd been wrong about my parents.

The pit in my stomach told me she was lying now, too.

I crowded in between Mrs. P and Derek as we huddled under the table. It was bigger than the one in the kitchen, but not by much.

Claudette sniffed. "It smells like mold," she whispered. "Why does it already smell like mold in here?"

It had to be me. The candles and their thousand scents were dissipating around us. Stripping away my cover.

Derek positioned himself even closer to me, blocking me from Claudette. "I don't smell anything."

"Shh!" Mrs. P turned back to them.

At the front window, the one across from us, a shape moved in the dark.

Two white eyes stared in. Human height. Glowing roundly.

I squeezed Derek's arm so hard he winced. But then he turned, and he saw, too.

Angie gasped.

The eyes swiveled toward the sound.

Could it see us under the table?

My whole body locked rigid. All of us froze, a knot of unbreathing tension, curled tight as a fist. Under my grip on Derek's arm, his pulse hammered away.

Outside, the porch groaned with the weight of bodies. Claws scratched against floorboards, like Teddy's did on ours. But there were more this time, and they were louder. Heavier bodies. Bigger animals.

I should unfreeze. I should do something. Anything. What should I do?

A thump came from the window, spiking my heart into my throat. A hand, a palm pressed flat against the glass. Streaking it with a sludgy smear. Its finger tapped, like it was poking at fish in a tank, seeing if it could get them to move.

It saw us. It had to see us.

At the corner of my eye, Claudette creaked into motion, slow, like she was moving frame by frame. She inched out the chair beside her, leaning over to ease up the barrel of her rifle. She was used to hunting in the forest, hiding in bushes, waiting for her shot. Her barrel was tight and steady, locked between the shadow's eyes.

Derek raised his gun, too. His was shaking.

My mouth dried up. That thing was person-shaped. It could be Mom. Dad.

I tugged at Derek and shook my head.

Whatever he saw in my eyes, he lowered the gun immediately, shamefully.

Claudette was still aiming, though. I couldn't stop her without making a ruckus, and if I did, this whole thing was gonna blow up. The blighted could hear our whispers. They'd sure as hell hear that. Who knew how many were on the porch by now.

Another floating pair of orbs appeared behind the first. Beastly eyes big as fists. They looked in the window, too.

So did another pair. Taller. A human maybe. Probably.

God, I couldn't even tell.

All the shapes stopped moving. Just stood there and held.

Mrs. P reached out with hesitant fingers and grabbed the bat she'd laid by her feet.

They were going to smash through the window, weren't they? They were waiting until enough of them gathered before bursting in all at once. We'd be trapped under this table, hemmed in. The odds of all five of us getting out before somebody got caught . . . The blighted were sickeningly fast when they wanted to be.

"Why would you run from us, Wren?" A whisper squirmed in my ear.

Everything got gauzier, as if fog had crept inside the house, right in front of my nose. It was knitting together, boxing me in.

I fell back farther and farther from my own eyes.

Suddenly, my body was doing something. My arms and legs moving.

Someone pulled at my arm, but from far away, like they couldn't reach my skin. I was wrapped in a suit made of soft white pillows. That was reassuring, actually, because nothing could hurt me in here.

Strange, though, this distant tug, like someone was yanking at something attached to me, but also not attached to me.

"Let me go. I have to check something." Did I say that? It came out in my voice. My own mouth moved.

The distant tugging stopped. My legs were moving again.

Something touched the palm of my hand. Smooth, cool. A faint clicking sounded.

My right hand turned.

"Wren? What are you doing?" Derek's voice filtered through. "Don't—*oh my God, Wren!*"

All at once, the fog blinked out of my sight.

I was in the kitchen. Derek stood in the doorway, hand outstretched. Behind him, Mrs. P and Claudette and Angie stared at me, kneeling frozen under the dining room table.

What was I doing here? I was . . .

I looked down at my right hand to find it on the doorknob.

Of the open back door.

I blinked, as if the open back door might clear away like the fog. But it didn't. The night air blew in past me.

"Oh my God. Oh my God, no!" I shoved the door to close it.

It thudded hard against something already in the doorway. A stumbling stag with gnarled antlers thrashing its way through—a horde of the blighted clamoring behind it.

"Thank you, Wren."

I'd let them all in.

CHAPTER 10

They poured into the house, a tangled mass of bodies from the porch—charging hooves and stomping shoes. The claustrophobic crush of their stinking hides threw me back from the door.

Derek stood, shell-shocked, in the kitchen doorway. It was all over his wide eyes and dropped jaw, how he saw me now: traitor.

He ran.

"Derek, wait!" I cried after him.

Uselessly. Of course he shouldn't wait. It was too late to stop the incoming flood. Definitely too late to help me, surrounded by them all, even if he'd wanted to.

I ran, too. Panic blared inside my scrambled brain. I shoved my way through bodies. Pushed at sticky, wet fur, and skin that slipped under my touch.

The blighted staggered on with eroded tendons, rotting muscles. I rammed the stag so roughly he kicked in a raccoon's head with his hoof. He clanged into the oven, antlers crashing against hanging pans.

Behind me, wood cracked at the open back door. A furious roar rang out.

The black bear, our friend without a jaw, was wedged up to its shoulders, straining against the tight fit. Human hands, gray-tipped and waxy, reached around it, swiping at the air. The rest of the horde couldn't get past, not with the bear stuck like that.

But too many were already inside.

I hurtled into the dining room, gasping in my first lungful of fresh air, and slammed the French doors shut behind me. A flimsy barrier, but Mr. Flores had done us an accidental favor by installing the doors backward. I sure hoped that'd buy us a little extra time.

I pushed my way through his old boxes, tearing them down behind me. The contents spilled, fragile things shattering.

Anything to slow the blighted. Every second counted.

From ahead came frantic whispers and scrambled footsteps. My adopted family was retreating into the living room.

Blond hair flashed. Claudette or Mrs. P, I couldn't tell, but she swung the door to close it behind them.

Fear spiked up my spine. "Wait, wait, don't leave me here!" I pulled the same move the blighted had used on me in the kitchen—wedging my desperate body into the gap.

The door crunched with a bang, against my shoe, my

ankle, my arm. I winced against the red-hot slashes of pain. But I flashed back to those gouges my parents and the Harrises and their friends had carved with their fingers into the dirt, clutching the earth as they were dragged into the forest.

I couldn't get left behind. Not here, not like this.

I pushed back. And the door yielded by one fraction. Then another. My corrupted muscles were reshaping, growing stronger.

"Please, please let me in!" I gasped against the pain. "You can tie my hands, whatever you want! Just please!"

An uncertain quiet fell in the living room. Behind me, thrashing beat against splintering glass, buckling wood. The French doors wouldn't last much longer.

"Why?" Claudette's husky voice snapped in my ear. "So you can open *this* door for them, too?"

"Let her in," Derek said. "She has the box in her backpack, Claud!"

"So what! Then let's take her backpack—"

Mrs. P cut off Claudette. "Let her in." She spoke, grave and irrefutable, in the ultimate authoritative mom voice.

Claudette released the door with a snarl. "You're lucky I don't put a bullet between your eyes right now."

My breath whooshed in relief as I squeezed into the room, putting one more barrier between me and the bowing French doors.

Claudette slammed the door after me. Then she and Angie screeched furniture across the floor to block it— a bookshelf, the armchair.

Derek stood, stunned, by the sofa. "Wren. What was that?"

I'd tried to warn him. As much as he needed me or I needed him, terrified as I was to lose my mind and body all alone in my abandoned house, I shouldn't have let him bring me here.

"It got ahold of my body. I didn't do it on purpose, but I might . . . You should tie my hands." Escaping the blighted horde with my hands tied behind my back would be a nightmare, but it'd be even worse to betray them all again. "Take the backpack, too. So I don't run away with it." I started to shrug it off.

"Oh, no," Claudette said. "If you're coming with us, you'll do at least one thing that's useful. Keep it on." Her shadow yanked a cord from the TV and came at me. "Don't worry. You're not going anywhere without us."

I held my arms out in front of me. She wound the smooth plastic around my wrists with expert speed and knotted it. The cord bit into the tender skin.

"You watch her," Claudette hissed at Derek, shoving me toward him. "You brought her here. She's your problem."

I stumbled on the rug and instinctively held out my hands to catch myself, which, of course, I couldn't.

Derek caught me by the shoulders. "You gonna be trouble, Claud?"

"No more than your blighted girlfriend," Claudette returned coldly.

A horrible splitting cracked out behind us—the French doors slamming to the ground.

Crashes came from the obstacle course I'd left behind, but it didn't hold them back long. The pounding advanced to the door of the living room. Scratching and tearing, growls, eager snorts.

We all jumped back.

The bookshelf rattled. The armchair inched out. Claudette and her dad's hunting trophies jostled on the walls above our heads. Glassy-eyed and dead, the deer heads still looked more natural than the slavering creatures battering at the door.

Bile stung the back of my throat. They'd be through in no time.

"Over here!" Mrs. P waved us to the window. "From here to the driveway, it's clear."

It was maybe a six-foot drop to the sharply sloped grass below. Then a hundred-yard dash to the driveway, where the heaped shadows of trucks sat idle.

Of course, if anyone stepped outside and the blighted spotted them, it wouldn't stay so quiet.

"One of us should get a truck." Mrs. P maintained an impressive sort of deadness in her low voice. Every once in a while, when I did something really reckless, I'd heard the same fearsome determination from my own parents: *protect.* "Drive it back here, and the rest of us can hop in the bed."

A better idea than anyone else had come up with.

Unfortunately, it was still incredibly dangerous.

"We can take mine." Derek pulled his keys from his pocket.

Claudette held out her hand for them.

"No." Mrs. P shook her head. "You're the best shot we have. You stay here at the window and help cover."

That made good sense. Claudette started to nod.

Then Mrs. P said, "I'll go."

"*No.*" Derek and Claudette hit that note in unison. With her limp, Mrs. P wasn't the fastest.

No way I could be trusted to do it. The blight could make me drive away with their truck or slash all the tires.

"I can—" Angie started.

But Claudette touched a hand to Angie's lower back and shook her head. This wasn't Angie's farm. Even if she was an honorary Hollow's Ender, the last thing she needed to do was to risk her life.

We'd eliminated our options, all except—

"I'll do it," Derek said.

My heart sank into the acid of my stomach.

Derek looked to me, but Mrs. P's skinny hand fell on my shoulder. "I'll look after her."

"Right." Derek turned to the window, trying to set his shoulders straight. "Right . . ."

He passed his rifle to Angie. "You've been practicing, yeah?" he asked.

"Yeah . . ." Angie darted her uncertain gaze to Claudette. "But cans on the fence aren't exactly moving targets."

Claudette adjusted Angie's shaky grip. "Even if you miss, the extra shots could scare them." More quietly, she added, "Just back me up, that's all."

Angie nodded.

Mrs. P turned to Derek. "Run fast. Be careful." Her rock-solid voice wavered. She had no choice but to send her sixteen-year-old into a night plagued by infectious creatures, who would maul him the first chance they got.

With my teeth, I tore at the inside of my cheek to stop myself from pleading with him not to go. The living room door shook behind us, a death sentence for everyone if we did nothing.

"Ready?" Mrs. P asked.

By the scrap of moonlight from the window, Derek's face looked paler than his usual sun gold. He peered straight ahead, setting his sights on the dark hill of his truck. And he nodded.

Mrs. P hauled the window up in one squealing scrape.

So much for a covert op. Speed was the only chance Derek had now.

He leapt from the opening.

Six feet wasn't the easiest drop, and Derek wasn't an action hero. He landed with a thud, staggering to one knee.

Inside, we stopped breathing, waiting to see if he could get all the way up. If he was uninjured.

In a squeak of boot rubber against dewy grass, he lurched to his feet and took off through the yard.

Right as several sets of eyes crept out from the back of the house.

They blurred into a writhing mass of motion—lumbering after him with savage snorts and shrieks.

The thrill of the hunt.

Something lithe and lean broke out from the pack and swam through the grass, gaining faster than Derek could pump his legs. A fox, given away by its white-tipped tail.

Derek spared a backward glance to see it lunging after him at top speed. Looking slowed him down even more.

The fox leapt for his calf.

I wanted to scream. I reached out with tied hands, but I couldn't do a thing.

A shot clapped by my ears so loud I staggered back.

The fox was laid low in the grass.

Claudette had dropped to her knees at the window, arms resting against the ledge to steady her rifle. She swung the barrel, tracking the shadows streaming across the yard. Aiming at whichever pulled into the lead.

Angie kept her gun pointed behind us, at the trembling, nearly bursting door. Thirty, fifty yards by moonlight had to be a nearly impossible shot for her. The twelve feet across this room was more on par for a beginner.

The blighted bore down on Derek faster and faster, converging on his retreating back. Claudette swung her gun left and right, cracking out shots. But there were more and more at the front of the pack now, and it was harder and harder to tell just how close they were to Derek.

Down went a deer. Down went something doglike I hoped to God wasn't Teddy. Probably too small for Teddy. Maybe a coyote.

The humans were never the fastest in the blighted pack. And thank God for that, because Claudette might not have cared what kind of creature she was aiming at, if it was after her brother.

Something big, maybe a moose, charged toward Derek from the side.

Claudette sighted it instantly, pulled the trigger.

Click.

"Shit!" Claudette scrambled in her chest pack for another magazine.

Derek was almost to the truck, but the moose was almost to him, too. It lowered its head, aiming antlers at his stomach.

Claudette looked up and down. "Shitshitshit—"

Bang. She fired.

The moose stumbled to the ground.

When the truck door creaked, out there in the night, the tendons in my knees went slack.

He'd made it.

The door slammed shut behind him with a furious bang, and I nearly crumpled to the floor with relief. Louder than the growls, the engine revved.

Much closer, though, wood splintered at the living room door.

"Oh my God," Angie breathed. The barrel of her rifle trembled as she took aim at cracking wood, the imminent promise of catastrophe. "Claud. *Claud!*"

Claudette whirled around. She kicked the coffee table onto its side and kneeled to sight against it, waving Angie down beside her. "Just a minute more. Just till the truck pulls up," she whispered.

Mrs. P stuck fast to the window, clutching the sill like a life jacket.

Derek's white truck blazed across the yard, flinging mud and grass.

A blighted mob chased behind him.

Something leapt up and caught the lip of the truck bed, but Derek swiveled into a turn so sharp that the creature flung off with a beastly yelp.

"Get ready!" he hollered from his open window to ours.

Mrs. P stayed crouched at the opening, but she was smart not to chance getting a head start with one leg out. The truck bashed into the side of the house with a cringe-worthy crunch. Mrs. P swore as she scrambled through the window.

She was halfway out when the living room door burst like an overrun dam.

A surge of fur and fangs and people. But they didn't act like people. They barely looked like them, with their cracking yellow teeth, fingers curled like claws.

The closest one had sludgy gunk clinging to the gingery frizz that framed her gaunt face, her sunken eyes. Her striped shirt was stained with gore; her shoes were moldering. But even now, I knew those freckles, those sneakers with the glittery check marks and different-colored laces.

"Amber." It came out in a hoarse gasp.

Amber Murphy.

Swap out some superficial features, and it was my future reflection staring back at me.

Foamy, gray spittle dribbled down her chin.

Claudette knew her, too. She looked up from her gun. "Holy shit."

"Come on! Angie!" Mrs. P called.

Angie, in a daze, tried to hand me her gun. Of course, I had no available hands to take it.

"Take it with you!" Claudette said. She moved her skinny body to block the window, covering Angie and Mrs. P's escape best as she could. She clapped out two shots—one at the doe charging for us, one at the possum scrambling up the bookshelf, poised to leap. The blighted tripped over each other in their surge to cram past the door.

Mrs. P helped Angie down, metal scraping under their desperate feet.

"Hurry!" Derek shouted from the driver's seat.

A clang at the truck warned that the blighted inside weren't our only problem. A stag lowered its head and charged the truck bed.

Angie aimed. She fired. But she wasn't Claudette. Her shot went wild, and the stag pounded the truck hard enough to get an antler caught in the metal.

Over the back, dirt-crusted human hands caught the edge.

Mrs. P stomped them with the heel of her shoe. "Wren!" She raced back to the window, reaching up to me.

But, already, more fingers were hooking over the edges of the truck bed. Frantic, Angie swung from danger to danger. Not knowing where to aim, where to shoot.

With my hands tied, I couldn't get down there quick enough. Even Claudette would cost them more time than they had.

"Go!" I shouted. "We'll meet you at my place! I know a way!"

Derek flung a desperate look back at me, through his open window. Choked with panic.

Yes, they'd be leaving Claudette and me against very

bad odds. We'd have a chance, though, even if it was slim. If they idled any longer, everyone would be lost.

It was the ugliest kind of calculation, but we all knew how to do it.

The truck peeled away from the house with a whipping turn, snapping the neck of the stag that hadn't been able to free itself. It dragged along behind them, until its carcass tore free, left behind in the grass.

The rest of the horde chased the truck all the way down the driveway, to the road, disappearing into the dark behind them.

Now it was just me and Claudette, and a farmhouse overrun with the horrors I'd let in.

CHAPTER 11

Claudette hadn't stopped shooting that whole time, her jaw clenched, a muscle straining in her temple. No way she hadn't heard the whole desperate business with the truck, but she didn't turn to look. If she had, we'd both have died right there.

Amber crawled over the corpses Claudette had shot down. She stumbled on their silver blood, hands reaching for something to grab, like she needed someone to catch her.

Probably not what she actually had in mind. Not with her jaw unhinged, her teeth gnashing, her iridescent tongue, wrapped in blight, stretching toward Claudette.

Claudette turned the gun on her.

I strained desperately against my tied wrists and grappled with the tips of my fingers for the framed portrait of Claudette and Derek's parents on the wall beside me. They were sitting on the porch, a younger Mrs. P in a tight cotton dress, laughing on the arm of Mr. Flores's rocking chair. Derek loved this picture. So did I.

But I had no choice. I grabbed the frame with both hands, twisted to one side, and hurled it like a Frisbee—dead-on at Amber's head. It spiked against her scalp, and she let out a gurgling yelp as the glass shattered.

Less deadly than a bullet, though enough to incapacitate her.

Claudette re-aimed and shot the ram that was at Amber's back. Harris livestock, no doubt, caught up in this awful mess like the rest of us.

From the kitchen came the sound of cracking wood. The foundation shook.

"What was that?" Claudette said through clenched teeth.

If I had to bet, the trapped bear finally breaking free.

We needed a way out. Now.

At least the horde in the yard was off chasing the truck. Outside the window, if only for a moment, it was quiet.

"Claudette," I said. "We have to jump out the window."

Claudette chanced a single-second glance to see what I meant.

And then she hip-checked me with her bony pelvis, knocking me through the opening. "Go!"

I thrust my tied hands out, hoping to catch anything and slow myself down. But I only scraped my knuckles against the window ledge, and the weight of all Dad's secrets and silver and bullshit stuffed into my backpack toppled me out.

The ground greeted me with a ruthless whump. I choked, hacking up a foul lump, something tangled and mossy. It slimed my tongue with the stink of decay, and I spat. Beads of blight sprayed the grass, dribbled from my lips. My lungs rattled, promising plenty more where that came from.

Claudette's jeans scuffed against the window ledge above. I shoved hard to roll out of her landing path.

She hit with a grunt and pushed to her feet. "We don't have truck keys. Are we supposed to run?"

"The horse," I wheezed, inching my way up beside her, bracing my body against the battered house siding. "She's in the goat house."

Claudette's entrenched scowl grew even deeper. I hadn't seen her on a horse since we were kids, when she'd taken lessons in the age group above mine. At her first show, with all the parents watching, she botched a jump—a low one, not even a hard one—and her mare threw her off headfirst. She made a horrendous squeak as she pitched through the air and crunched down onto her helmet. No one laughed, but her sunburned cheeks still flushed a furious red. She stormed out of the ring, and never came back for lessons again.

She didn't argue with me now, though. She scoured the yard from right to left, glanced back at the moon-white eyes staring out the window above us—and took off at full speed.

I clutched my tied wrists against my aching chest and charged after her.

Blighted creatures jumped through the window, bounding after us.

Adrenaline didn't let our desperate bodies down. We terrified the goats and Buckwheat into wild-eyed snorts when we banged our way into the small barn.

We didn't even have time for a saddle.

Claudette was stronger than her skinny arms let on. She hauled me onto Buckwheat, backpack and all, and flung herself up in front of me. She didn't trust me enough to cut my hands free. Instead, she wriggled under my tied arms and grabbed hold of Buckwheat's mane. All I could do was clench Claudette's waist for dear life.

Her whole body tensed when I touched her.

"Barebacking it with a zombie," she muttered. "Just how I wanted to spend my Saturday night."

I glared into the back of her grass-stained tank top. "I'm not a—"

"Whatever you are, *behave*."

The hard heel of her boot thudded into Buckwheat's side, and we burst out of the barn, ducking our heads through the doorway.

The poor goats were on their own.

We charged for the empty driveway. Buckwheat knew what to do this time. Thank God she was a Harris horse. She galloped into the wind, punishing the earth with her hooves. I gripped my thighs against her bouncing sides so tight it felt like my muscles might tear.

White eyes followed in our wake, but Claudette didn't shoot. At least she had enough sense to realize Buckwheat couldn't handle a sound like that.

And then the eyes began to fade.

At last, the empty road embraced us with a black velvet hug. The unbroken dark promising that we were, at least for this moment, free. Alone.

Claudette whooped so loud that I nearly jolted from my perch behind her.

"Shh! They're still out there!" I said.

"Come on, dead girl. Live a little." She patted my hand where it clutched at her shirt, quivering against her wiry abs. "Someone's watching over us tonight."

Right. That's exactly what I was afraid of.

"Just keep Buckwheat going," I told her. "We'll celebrate when we meet up with everyone at Rainbow Fields."

She grunted in reply.

Our conversation faded as Claudette's giddiness dissolved like vapor into the cold night.

I kept scanning the woods for eyes. We still didn't know how many were out there, even if we'd gotten a head start. I strained my ears, past the clop of Buckwheat's hooves, for any snapping twigs or crunching leaves beyond the trees.

From Derek's farm to mine, it was faster to take the back roads, cutting straight across the top of the peninsula, instead of ducking down through town. But I had this pang that town might've felt safer. The quaint old brick buildings hugging either side of the road. The security of civilized silence. So different from these wide, wide woods. Those little sounds at the edges of my hearing—a flap of wings, the drone of insects, distant hoots. And that hissing, buzzing breath, like a cool slither darting around my brain.

But honestly, Main Street probably wouldn't have been any better. It was just a leftover pining from a time that had already passed—when Hollow's End was a real town, not a hollowed-out husk.

At least on the back roads, the emptiness didn't feel as *wrong*.

Black woods, black road, black sky.

Maybe that's why I didn't notice at first, when Claudette took a wrong turn.

But as the trees blurring past thinned slightly, broke ahead into emptier space—like we were approaching the top edge of Hollow's End, not driving through the thick of it—I realized: she'd veered left at that last fork. Left instead of right.

Dammit. Every second we wasted out here was another second the horde could find us.

"This is the wrong way," I said, as levelly as I could manage.

Claudette's breath paused against me for a fraction of a second. "No. It's the right way."

God, she was even more stubborn than Derek. The last thing we needed was a fight about directions. "Claudette, I know the way to my own farm. You have to turn back."

She didn't say a thing. Instead, she drove Buckwheat straight ahead.

Even kicked her a bit, to make her go faster.

"What are you doing?" My whole face flushed hot. "I told you—"

Ahead, gleams cut through the thinning forest, the opening night. Not the staring white eyes of the blighted. The hazard yellows of the barricading gates at the bridge, with all their stripes and reflectors.

And then it clicked. She wasn't taking me to Rainbow Fields.

She *was* going the right way—exactly the way she'd intended.

A steel structure, slung low and long, loomed near the

barricades. At first, it had been a big white tent. After the emergency responders had become a little more familiar with the blight, down went the tent. Up went steel.

The emergency triage clinic. Just a couple football fields ahead.

"C-Claudette, no." It choked from me, involuntarily.

"I'm sorry," she said. "Honestly, I am. And Derek's never gonna forgive me. But you have to understand, this is for his own good."

My heart seized in my chest. "Wait, please! I don't want to hurt Derek, either. That's the last thing I want." Maybe, if they kept me tied up at a safe distance, I could help them decipher Dad's journals—Derek had been so sure I'd have some insight, some key to the puzzle—but I knew the time for anything more than that had passed. "I won't come near any of you again!"

She shook her head, hard and stiff.

Buckwheat raced ever closer to the encampment at the bridge.

With every steely flash of the approaching clinic, all I could think of was those cold face shields. Those pointed questions. They didn't even consider helping those people in the forest. I'd take my chances in the Rainbow Fields shed, tied up like Benji Thomas, before I'd take my chances with them.

"No one who goes there ever comes back," I said, trembling. "You know that, right?"

"Well, anyone who goes to the forest *does* come back, like Amber did tonight," Claudette snapped at me over her shoulder. "Is that what you want?"

No. Of course not.

I'd tried so hard not to think about that—what I wanted. Because everything I actually wanted was dead and buried. But the blight was stripping my will away, and now, Claudette was crushing the dregs I had left. The ties on my wrists ached. My throat tightened; my eyes burned. "If my life really is over, I just want it to be on my own terms."

"I think it's a little late for that." She didn't say it mean. She said it sad.

That's how I knew we were done talking.

And, hell, maybe she was right. Even if the responders would only poke me and prod me and inject me and make me disappear, maybe that's all I was good for now, anyway.

"No." An answering whisper flickered through my mind. *"You will not go."*

I blinked, shaking off the voice. Had I even really heard that? The barest kiss of eerie light hazed down from the sky, pressed in around me, clouding my vision. That hungry pang that had started in Mrs. P's kitchen hit me again, stabbing my stomach, acidic and fierce.

My tongue went thick and syrupy. Warm saliva dripped down my teeth.

No matter how much I blinked, the fog wouldn't clear from my eyes—this misty veil between me and the world. It thickened. It ate in from all sides. My scalp squirmed, like worms were writhing underneath my skin, hooking in deeper and deeper.

The hunger sharpened.

Oh no.

I was stuck up here on Buckwheat, the clinic fast approaching, my hands tied and looped over Claudette. Her hair swung like an ash cloud in my face. Under that smoky mask, it smelled good. Like barley and the clinging aroma of coconut and pineapple. I leaned into it.

"Claudette—" My voice broke, heaviness squirming from my chest into my throat, my jaw, my lips.

She didn't answer. She didn't turn.

I was moving my mouth, but mold swallowed my words.

I needed to jump off Buckwheat now. *Now.*

I yanked and yanked, but the TV cord held my arms fast. Anchored to Claudette.

I was slipping. Drowning. I gasped for air.

"Wren!" Claudette yelled. "Jesus, don't make this harder than it has to—"

And then, she was gone.

The world was white. Soft white. My vision was caked over, like staring out through falling snow.

"Calm down, Wren. I'll take care of you," someone was saying.

The relief of it. The magic words I'd ached to hear since I first breathed in the blight, since my parents vanished.

"You can let go now," it said.

I could fall back into the pillows, where there was no pain. No problems.

I'd always loved watching the snow.

Something faint tugged at my ear. Something high-pitched and, honestly, really unpleasant. It was such a relief I didn't have to worry about that, whatever it was.

Distant motion pushed and pulled against me. Through

the muffled padding between me and the rest of the world, my left side reverberated with a hard clap.

Other vibrations rippled through me. My arms and legs were moving.

My mouth moved, too.

I tasted the sudden squirt of juice. It trickled down my throat, luscious and soothing.

At last, I was less hungry. I was finally eating.

I was eating.

What was I eating?

My eyes shot open, scattering back the fog.

My teeth were sunk down to the roots into Claudette's forearm.

Claudette's arm was up in the air like she'd been trying to shield herself.

The snarling beast reflected in her shock-wide blue eyes . . . that was me.

I reeled back in horror. My teeth, wedged deep, didn't come out easily. They tore her skin, spraying blood and leaving a blighted hole that steamed in the cold night.

We were both on the ground, lying alone together in the road. That impact I'd felt—we'd fallen off Buckwheat. I'd dragged Claudette down. Buckwheat stood several yards back. From her bug-eyed stare, her pawing at the road, I realized she was about three seconds from stranding us there.

Maybe that didn't matter anymore.

My brain was mincemeat.

Blood streamed down my peeling lips, and my gums throbbed. Claudette had taken my two bottom teeth with her. They were buried in the ruined flesh of her arm. She hauled herself up, one shaking leg at a time, until she stood over me. Her wounded arm hung tense, trembling. In her other hand she held her gun, the black hole of the barrel aimed at my head. Her every breath came in a jagged, laboring wheeze.

"You," she said, low in her throat. "*You.*"

She loomed over me, blotting out the moon, stars splattered across the sky behind her. "You've killed me. Too bad for you, I'm not dead yet."

The backpack, still looped around my shoulders, was anchoring me down. I lay belly-up, like a begging dog. I lifted my tied hands in open-palmed surrender, waiting for the click of her trigger. Or for that big boot of hers to stomp down on my unguarded stomach, to smash me like the vermin I was.

"Your eyes." She swallowed, but her voice still broke high. "They were white. Why aren't they still white?"

"I don't know," I said. I didn't know how this worked. "I'm still me, sometimes. You can shoot me anyway, but that's the truth."

With a storm of curses, Claudette stepped back.

But I didn't dare get all the way up. Slow as a slug, I raised myself to my elbows. My skin, damaged by the fall, stung against the asphalt. "Please," I said. "I think there might be a way to stall the worst symptoms. You have to get to my house. I can get you some bread—"

"Bread?" Claudette whipped around. She didn't point

the gun at me again, but it was still cocked to fire. "Is that your bright idea?"

"I know it sounds fake, but it's been working on me."

"Oh yeah?" she said, holding out her arm. "Seems like it's working."

She muttered curses as she flipped the safety on the rifle and set it down between her legs. Blood trickled from her wound and seeped into the woven bracelet on her wrist. The one made for her by Angie's little sister.

Who she'd never get to see again. Because of me.

"Shit." She traced the bracelet with a trembling finger. *"Shit."*

With a long, clumsy rip, she tore away the bottom couple inches of her tank top to wrap around her seeping forearm.

The sight of my teeth, still embedded in her flesh, stopped her cold.

She squeezed her eyes shut like she was going to be sick as she wriggled them free and flicked them to the road. Wiped the leaking tears from her cheeks with the back of her hand. And then she started wrapping.

In barely a whisper, I said, "I can help you with that."

She didn't even look at me. "You already helped plenty." She wrapped fast and hard, her fury showing in every harsh, tight circle of her makeshift bandage. Only once she was done did she march back to me. Her pale-blue eyes were cold and wild. Sweat and tears pinned stringy threads of hair to her forehead and cheeks. "Get up."

I didn't dare disobey.

The road lurched around me as I staggered to my feet. The ground felt unsteady, like pockets were sinking underneath me. "We should get you back to my house," I said, voice dribbling from my numbing lips. They felt thick and meaty, clumsy around the shapes of my words.

Something was wrong with me. Wronger than before. The blight was winning.

Claudette watched me through slitted eyes, coiling back on her heels like a rattlesnake. "If you think you're getting anywhere near my family, you are dead wrong. Emphasis on 'dead.'"

"I won't. I swear. But you still have a little time," I slurred. "Just for a little while, you could go back inside to see them—"

"No. I can't," Claudette said. "See, that right there is the difference between an ass like you and an ass like me." She grabbed my sleeve, yanking me toward her so hard I stumbled forward on the empty road. Toward the waiting clinic. "Guess we're doing this together."

Together?

My every breath ached in my chest. I wanted nothing more than to lie down in this road, let the asphalt swallow me up before I could hurt any more. Before I could hurt anyone else. But this—I had to fight for this.

"No!" I pulled away. "I'll go, okay? I'll go!" I forced my leaden tongue into the right shapes. "But not you. The answer could be inside this backpack. We have to give Derek, your family, at least a chance to figure this out—"

"A chance?" Claudette threw back her head with a bitter bark. Her eyes flashed with something like anguish, a twisted pain that strangled her voice. "Against the blight? You saw the size of the horde. Maybe the responders will only turn us into lab rats and no good will come of it, but they're the only 'chance' Hollow's End has. Face it—we lost, Wren. It's over."

It hit me like a punch to my heart. The same thing that doubtful whisper in my mind had been telling me all along: that we couldn't possibly make a difference.

But that's not what Derek believed.

And who knew what was inside the box. If we shrugged it off here in the road, the clinic could find it. Or the blight could.

I didn't know which was worse.

Claudette's fingers dug into my arm, tugging me forward. Toward the cold steel of the clinic. The arches of the iron-truss bridge blocked with flashing yellow lights.

I flung a frenzied glance at Buckwheat, abandoned in the road. She shuffled, tossed her head toward the forest behind us, her frightened ears flattening.

If only one of us was returning, even if just to deliver the backpack, it should be Claudette. But if that wasn't an option . . .

"Buckwheat!" I jerked away from Claudette. Hard.

So hard that Claudette tripped over her own feet, and I ripped my tied wrists out of her grip.

"Hey!" Claudette lunged after me, catching me by the shirt.

My flailing hands slapped, unintentionally, against her wet bandage.

She pulled back with a pained hiss, clutching at her wound. A fresh tide of blood seeping from her arm through her tied-off tank top.

"I'm sorry! I—" I turned just as her fist crashed into my cheekbone. Something cracked—her knuckles or my face. Pain radiated from my nose to my eye, and half the world went black.

I reeled with the blow, and my backpack dragged me down to my knees.

Buckwheat whinnied, her hooves clopping in a terrified shuffle. She still hadn't bolted, but I had no idea why.

"Don't think I won't knock you out!" Claudette grabbed a fistful of my shirt, at the hollow of my throat, and yanked me to my feet.

The world spun around me.

"Wait!" I threw my tied hands up, I shrank back—and then I saw them.

The eyes.

My voice died in my throat, but Claudette also stopped. Her own glare was widening into horror, locked on something over my shoulder.

Oh God, were there eyes behind me, too?

She dropped my shirt.

We spun around, back-to-back, facing the forest on either side. Trees lined the road like the bars of a cage, and from between their trunks came the leering glow of one set of white eyes after another. They'd snuck up while we were fighting. Distracted.

So that's why Buckwheat hadn't bolted. She couldn't.

And neither could Claudette or I.

The blighted had us surrounded.

*   *   *

At least twelve sets of eyes watched us. Behind them, more creatures slunk into position.

Buckwheat inched closer to us with a nervous whicker. She was the only one who wasn't blighted. A horse-shaped island of fresh meat. Still, I doubted they were here for her.

All those eyes were fixed on me and Claudette.

"It's time now." A rough chorus of whispers rose from the dark. *"To come home."*

The blighted spoke as one, from the trees, like they'd done at the Murphys' farm. The shivering scrape of one voice from too many mouths.

Claudette stepped back. "What the shit? They can talk?"

"My hands, Claudette," I whispered. "Please."

She shot me a wary glance, but what choice did she have? She dug a pocketknife out of her jeans and slit the cord.

It dropped, leaving behind numb white lines circling my wrists.

I inched toward Buckwheat, smoothing my hand up her side. Her skin flinched. If she ran, we were done for. I sank my fingers into the base of her stiff pale mane.

Claudette turned in a slow, controlled circle, aiming her rifle for the briefest of seconds on each pair of eyes, reminding them that she knew how to use it.

"Claudette. I've missed you." Only one voice had spoken, the closest one.

Claudette turned to face the sound. "I'll shoot."

"Even me?"

A figure stepped forward from the tree line. Moonlight skimmed the slope of its shoulders. The glow from its eyes cast a horrid sheen over its face.

It had been months, but even past its crumbling, moss-eaten state, I knew that broad cleft chin and those flat, wide cheeks. The dark, heavy brows. Just like Derek's. Claudette's barrel trembled.

"No," she said, but she didn't drop her gun. It seemed less an answer to his question than her answer to everything. To this final resolution of her dad's disappearance.

The blight had eaten deep into Mr. Flores's skin. Lumpy patches had slid from the muscles in his neck, revealing a dark red that squirmed with maggoty beads of silver. He took a few more steps forward, onto the edge of the road. Only fifteen feet away.

His mouth curved. It wasn't quite a smile—just teeth arranged in the rough shape of a grin.

Soon, this would be my parents. This would be me. Claudette, too.

"Dad?" Claudette spoke in the voice of some broken five-year-old. I never would've believed such a sound could come from her. From this heartless steel tank.

He nodded. Or, rather, he raised and lowered his head. As if he'd once observed the gesture and was now doing his best to imitate it. This thing wasn't Claudette's dad. Not anymore. The blight had his body to pilot, but it had swallowed Mr. Flores whole.

"*I can help you,*" the blight said through Mr. Flores. "*Come with me.*"

My eyes darted every which way, tracking the shapes slinking forward from the woods, hemming us in, in a tighter and tighter circle. Most on four legs, some on two.

How many creatures had Claudette taken down at her farm? How many bodies had she cost the blight? It knew exactly what she'd done.

"Claudette," I said, "get on the horse."

"*Wren.*" Mr. Flores turned to fix those ghastly eyes on me. There were no irises, no pupils, only that pale, haunting glow. Primordial as cave-deep fungus. "*You're right about them. The ones hiding behind their suits and masks and steel.*"

I froze cold. The responders? What did the blight know about the responders?

My eyes flicked down the long road to their clinic, sitting silent.

"*I see what they're doing in there.*" The blight squeezed Mr. Flores's voice, a voice that had once been so warm, into a rasping rattle. "*They collect my bodies. They try silly tricks to suck out my metal. To collect me. But metal is not all I am. They will not save you. All they want is to make more of me.*"

My gut clenched with fresh horror. Could that really be true? Our families had used the blight—argent vive, as they called it—but we'd only harnessed its powers from inside the stones.

To actively *create* more, like the blight claimed the responders wanted, why would anyone—?

Oh.

The money.

The ridiculous fucking money.

Of course. Mrs. P said it was only because of the argent

vive that our farms were able to produce miracle crops. If it could create one kind of moneymaking miracle, who's to say it couldn't manufacture others.

From behind me crept the stink of rattling, rotten breath. The staggering shadows pressed in past the trees, inching toward the road. Not as close as Mr. Flores. They hadn't quite touched asphalt. Stalking. But not pouncing. Not yet.

With a swallow, I turned back to what once was Mr. Flores—the blight's chosen mouthpiece. "Wh-why are you telling me this?"

Mr. Flores's fists clenched tight at his sides, the silver-thick veins of his forearms bulging past his torn sleeves, but the blight didn't speak. It was waiting.

Staring at me, like it wanted something.

And I had no clue what.

It almost reminded me of Dad: all his infuriating silent tests, how he would wait with his fingers steepled, pressed to his chin. To see if I'd say the right or wrong thing. So he could judge me accordingly.

"Isn't that what *you* want?" I asked it. "To make more of yourself?"

Mr. Flores's face sagged like he was disappointed in me. If this was a test, I had failed.

Every voice in the circle answered, in a raging whisper: *"This cycle will never repeat."*

Past Mr. Flores's crumbling teeth, the blight snarled, *"Even if that means I cannot stop here in Hollow's End. Even if I must then chase down every last person in that clinic. If I must continue over the bridge."*

The looming forest and the vaulting sky had never seemed bigger. I'd never felt smaller.

Claudette had fallen silent, freezing up, but even she took the tiniest step away from Mr. Flores. Closer to me.

The responders' barricades in front of the bridge, maybe it was just the distance, but they looked so thin now—like fragile toothpicks. The horde could surge over them in a heartbeat. I could see it: the blighted overrunning the bridge, splashing and thrashing across Harvest Moon Bay, skin and fur and hair swirling in their rancid wake. We'd tried to warn Meadowbrook the official stories were a lie—that this was more than a mercury spill—but no one believed us. The people there would have no idea what was coming for them.

I glanced from Mr. Flores to the circle closing around us, the moldy creatures creeping closer, slowly but surely.

Claudette and I didn't have time for this. Buckwheat was waffling under my grip. She seemed to be doing the survival math just like I was. Like a problem from my old algebra textbook: *Wren and Claudette are surrounded by a fifteen-foot circle of slavering monsters. If the monsters creep forward eight inches every three seconds, how long before they tear out Wren's and Claudette's throats?*

I pressed my hand harder onto Buckwheat's side, willing her to stay just a few seconds longer. "Claudette," I said, with all the force in me. "Now."

But she just stared at me, empty. She spun back to her dad, jaw slack.

It couldn't be in her brain already, right?

My arms shook as I grasped Buckwheat's shoulder and the firm hair at her withers. She snorted at the tug, but

I used that extra strength the blight itself had given me, summoning every last scrap of it, to haul myself up.

"Claudette." I held my hand down to her.

And then everything burst into a frenzied blur.

Mr. Flores lunged for her, closing the distance between them with the sudden surge of a striking snake. Claudette didn't shoot. She dropped her gun, and it fired against the pavement—a huge boom in my ears.

Buckwheat's, too.

The horse reared, slashing the air with her front hooves. She hit the earth and charged forward at a gallop that tossed me against her neck, bouncing my bones so hard the rest of my teeth threatened to clatter out of my head.

"Claudette!" I screamed over my shoulder.

I yanked at Buckwheat, trying to make her turn back. I kicked and pulled. But she plowed ahead with the force of a freight train.

The bridge, the barricades, the clinic, all melting into dark trees.

Claudette's rifle gleamed, useless, by the side of the road. The horde had converged into one seething, thrashing knot.

A chunk of blond hair flew from the center.

CHAPTER 12

It was a lonely, long ride back to my farm. Dismal and hopeless. The vast woods pressed in around me, smothering even the dim cries of night birds.

Claudette was gone.

They'd taken her like they'd taken my parents.

I wasn't far behind. Breath rattled in my moss-clogged throat. It made me think of the last time Dad snaked our shower drain, yanking up yards of snarled hair. It smelled like a sewer. If I coughed hard enough, the same thing might come out of me.

My vision was edged with a velvety glow. Like some dreamy Insta filter, everything taking on a ghostly sheen. It must've built gradually, so gradually I hadn't even noticed. And I knew it wasn't going away.

Buckwheat and I finally rode up in front of my farm. There was nowhere good to put her. I settled for making the supply shed as comfortable as possible, but her sides beat with a pulse that wouldn't stop thudding. She slurped from a bucket of water while I wiped down her lathering coat the best I could without a sweat scraper, or even a brush. Under my clumsy touch, she whickered and flinched, like she wasn't sure anymore if I was someone she could trust.

She visibly relaxed as I stumbled out and shut the door. It was the biggest favor I could do for her—walking away.

She wasn't the only one who needed me gone, but I couldn't leave quite yet.

Candles flickered through the living room window. They were here. Waiting. For me and Claudette.

I had to tell them.

I trudged past the driveway, past Derek's truck, metal shining through white paint where it'd smashed against his own house's siding. Past my truck, dented by Teddy.

"Wren?" From the porch ahead, someone whispered in the dark.

I lifted my head, heavier and heavier on my neck. "Derek?"

His silhouette waited on the porch steps. "I thought I heard someone ride up." He stepped toward me and exhaled in relief. "I'm so sorry. I'm so sorry we left you there. But you both made it."

He just assumed Claudette was here, too. Maybe off with Buckwheat. If only.

How could he still be standing here, waiting for me? Even after I opened that kitchen door and betrayed them all?

Then again, he'd realized a long time before I did—when you're lucky enough to have the love of your life born a few miles down the road, you didn't turn your back on that.

What I'd done to Claud, though . . . that was enough to destroy everything.

"Derek." My voice barely carried.

I wished so much I didn't have to tell him. I wished so much I could live in this one second a little longer, the last time Derek could imagine everything might still be okay. The last time he would wait for me with open arms.

"Claudette is . . ."

"What?" Derek froze, ten steps from me. "Claudette is what?"

"Sh-she's . . ."

The dreamy haze around the edges of the world brightened. Cobwebbed across my eyes. Static pierced like an ice pick into my brain. Instant, merciless, stabbing down my spine.

The blight seizing control.

"Derek, run!" I screamed.

Tried to scream. The electrical impulse died in my brain, never reaching my mouth. Something had cut the cable from my brain to my body. Hijacked the controls.

My lips turned up at the corners, mechanically engineered into a smile by invisible, internal hooks.

"Claudette's in the shed. With the horse." It came from my mouth, but it wasn't me.

"Oh, thank God. I thought you were gonna say . . ." Derek clutched at his chest, like he'd just about had a heart attack. "She better make it quick. Mom and Angie are freaking out, waiting."

No. *No.*

He had to realize this wasn't right. He knew I was losing to the blight. He had to run.

But Derek was always too good at seeing what he wanted to see. And the blight had handed him everything he'd been praying to hear. He wasn't running. He was just standing there with no weapon, no backup.

My body staggered toward him up the front path. Tiny steps, as small as possible, to hide the clumsiness of my stiffening legs.

"*Thank you,*" I heard myself say, "*for never giving up on me. For realizing before I did . . . when you're lucky enough to have the love of your life born a few miles down the road, you don't turn your back on that.*"

Oh my God.

Derek knew how unlike me it was to confess something that intimate. But no way he'd think I was under the blight's control now. How could he ever imagine it would be capable of saying something like that?

Because it wasn't. It stole that from me.

Something I couldn't have written in a locked diary without turning scarlet hot, from head to toe. And this is what the blight did with it?

Took something sweet and rotted it sour. Twisted it into the cruelest weapon.

The blight kept my head tilted down and my eyes peeking up to find Derek's face.

Past the snow in my eyes, I found the softness of his smile. The moonlight caught and glimmered on his dark, wet lashes, like he'd been waiting his whole life to hear those words. The exact kind of precious truth that would roll so effortlessly off his tongue but never seemed to make it past my own.

The heart in my chest was still mine, and the blood inside it curdled.

The blight made me take another step closer. Derek was already within arm's reach. It could grab him anytime.

It didn't need to do this. It was enjoying itself, toying with me. With him. The blight could dim the whole world for me, if it wanted. Put me back in that pillow suit—safe and cozy and warm. But it wanted me to watch this moment with Derek. To prove I was nothing more than its broken puppet.

Derek gazed at me with his melting brown eyes. "It wasn't your fault what happened, back at the house." His words came out choked. "You're just sick. But we'll find a way to fix this, okay?"

"I know we will. We can do it together."

This thing inside me was a monster. I could feel the happy glow of its vengeance, swelling by the second.

It held out my arms for a hug.

Surely, even for someone as kind as Derek, that was too big of an ask. No way he'd—

His arms were already wrapping around me.

His musky body spray filtered through, the warming squeeze of his arms. It was torture, how much I needed this—to collapse into him, to feel safe again for even a second. The blight was doing everything I longed for.

Stop, please. Leave Derek alone. I'll follow you into the forest. I'll do whatever you want, I begged.

Its thin laugh bounced back to me, echoing inside my

skull. This close, it rang hollow. Just as the blight had observed our human nods, our smiles, it had learned the shape of our laughs. But this sound had nothing to do with joy. It was pitiless.

It whispered back, *"I already tried being nice, Wren."*

It was angry at me, for opposing it again and again. For trying to stop it.

Now, it was going to crumble me to dust.

Derek, too.

The blight squeezed my fingers against Derek's back. My mouth was pressed against his chest, so close his heartbeat echoed in my ribs.

That same sharp hunger pooled in my gut again. My jaw started to open.

No! Not like Claudette. I'd sworn to myself I'd never hurt someone like that again.

I strained against my own jaw, but it only cranked wider. Deliberately. Spitefully.

A tiny groan inched up from my throat.

That one had come from me. Not the blight.

Derek's arms stiffened. ". . . Wren?" He pulled away, holding up the light of his phone to my face.

The glare of it stabbed into my eyes, penetrating past the fog to blind me.

The blight flinched me back from the bright beam, a slash of rage burning across my chest, crawling under my scalp.

"What happened to your cheek? Your mouth . . ." Derek's voice dropped to the barest whisper. "What's that on your mouth?"

Oh God, I hadn't gotten it all off.

My lips curled into a sneer, unsealing with a slow, sticky tear, wet and gluey at the corners. Gummed up with Claudette's blood. A low growl rumbled up from some deep, wolfish place in my chest I never knew existed.

Derek gasped. His boot crunched backward, as he stepped away from me.

My body charged.

The fog thickened, but I squinted through it, tore at it, trying to look out from my own eyes. Derek's dark outline scrambled for the porch, the safety of the house. He just had to make it to the door.

I had to slow my body down.

But my feet tore after him, driven by the insatiable hunger of the predator inside me.

I couldn't fight the blight. If it wanted my legs to move, they moved, no matter how hard I willed them to stop.

So I didn't fight. I helped. I threw all my momentum into my legs and drove it into the ground as hard as I could.

It worked. My body tipped, knees slamming into the hard-packed soil of our front path.

"Eat, Wren. You're hungry. Let us eat!"

My hands scrabbled under me, clutching for purchase. Something tore. My pinky. The bandage flapped; the nail twisted. I felt a distant pinch and wetness.

Derek took advantage of my stumble. His shoes clomped up the porch steps. He pounded on the door. "Mom, Angie! Open the door! Open—"

Fog thickened against my eyes, shoving me down. Drowning me in a cotton cloud.

The blight got my legs back under me. It lumbered me up the steps toward Derek's frantic knocking, his pleas to be let in.

My hand caught something. Something thrashing, desperate as a trapped hare.

My mouth opened wide to bite.

A hard, sudden jolt buckled my shoulder.

Derek was fighting back. The blight's cushioning muffled the shock. But I seized all the momentum I could from his shove.

My backpack clung like dead weight from my shoulders. If I could tip myself over, make myself heavy like an anchor . . .

Fall. Fall!

The world tilted, and through the swirling pale haze, the black sky winked at me as I tumbled off the steps.

I smashed down, hard.

No cushion to absorb the blow. The ground cracked against the back of my head, my ribs, the base of my spine. The blight had abandoned me just in time to leave me with the pain.

From the porch, Mrs. P and Angie were shouting for Derek and he was shouting back.

I wanted to tell them it was okay now, but I could barely draw a breath. My head rang. Cold air sliced against the open wound in my nail bed. I could already feel the bruise blooming on my back where it had hit the bottom stair.

Feet thudded on the porch, and the door slammed. A lock clicked. Then came the heavy, metallic slide of the door's chain.

I was alone.

Collapsed. Pain pounding in waves through my body. The frayed gasps from my lungs punctuated only by the lonely song of crickets.

I must've squeezed my eyes shut. When I finally dragged them open, all sound from inside the house had stopped. I was still lying in the dirt. I had no idea how long I'd been there. Minutes? Hours? The night towered around me. Clouds swallowed the moon into nothing but a ghostly whisper.

I was losing time.

I was losing my own body.

My head pounded against the back of my skull. My cheek ached from Claudette's punch. My injured hand was sticky with slowly drying blood, its little finger sore and raw. In the other hand, I clasped a swatch of flannel.

Derek's shirt.

I checked frantically around the edges but didn't find anything wet. No blood. I hadn't nicked him with my nails. He'd made a clean escape, thank God.

When I sat up, something heavy welled from my ear, trickling down the side of my neck. I touched it. Pure silver blight, a liquid galaxy, dribbled down my finger. It swirled with the stolen colors of Hollow's End. My field: violet, indigo, blue, and now green, too.

My vision blurred as I stared. My chest tightened with a sickening loathing too big to bear. For the blight. For myself—what it was making me become. Every part of me writhed with the desperate impulse to flee, even though it was too late. The second I yanked up that violet wheat, it was too late.

Like Dad's notes said, the blight was gnawing away at my insides.

Eating. Thriving. Burgeoning under my rotting skin.

Now there was so much in me that when I knocked my head, it sloshed out of me like an overfull cup.

My limbs felt heavy. I needed sleep. But if I let myself drift off, would I trance-walk my way into the heart of the forest?

The backpack dug against my aching shoulders as I swayed to my feet.

Dammit. I needed to get the bag to Derek, but there was no way they'd open the door for me now. Or ever again.

Maybe if I left it on the porch, he'd find it.

My feet dangled at the ends of my ankles. I tripped over them twice as I dragged myself around the side of the porch. I slumped down to lean against the outside of the kitchen wall, where Teddy so often begged.

I didn't expect the clean scent of bread that pierced through my clogging nose. A hunk was laid out beside me.

Derek had seen me feed Teddy from this window.

It had to be pity. It couldn't be forgiveness. Forgiveness was the last thing I deserved.

I poked my tongue at the front of my gums, the slippery holes where my teeth would be if I hadn't left them behind in Claudette. I scrubbed my sleeve over my mouth, flaking away the worst of the guilty evidence. I didn't want to wear it, and I definitely didn't want to accidentally swallow any more.

Keeping a wary watch on the forest, I reached for the bread.

Something scratched against the wood of the porch. Right beside me.

White eyes lit, popping the dark to life.

I jerked back against the wall. Tried to stand. My muscles resisted, exhausted legs shaking under me.

The eyes lumbered toward me, the creature's claws clacking closer. Maybe it was here to drag me off into the trees once and for all, like the blighted must've done to Claudette.

In a rancid wave, its breath rolled toward me. Its ashen tongue lolled in a pant.

As its red-brown snout came into sight, that familiar black button nose, I realized: "Teddy!"

In my drained state, Teddy wasn't necessarily better than an anonymous monster. She could hurt me just the same. Her jaw was strong enough to snap a rabbit's neck.

She sprang forward.

I cringed back, throwing my arms up to cover my face.

Her sticky tongue touched my forearm, the place where I'd bitten Claudette. She'd sink in her teeth, and then—

Half-warm wetness stroked the length of my arm.

Again.

Again and again and again.

"Teddy?" I croaked, dropping my arm.

That was a mistake. She dove straight in to run her putrid tongue along my cheek. Her tail beat in delight.

She wasn't attacking me.

When she'd lunged at my dad, when she'd charged at me and Derek . . .

Oh my God, she'd just wanted someone to pet her.

Tears spilled from my eyes. I reached out and ran my fingers over her forehead, behind her ear. I scratched, and her mouth opened into a big grin. She leaned her whole head into my touch, so hard she almost knocked me down.

"Good girl," I whispered.

That caused almost too much excitement. She pranced in a circle, and then shoved her head against my hand.

This time, she did knock me down. I slipped against the porch, and she threw herself after me, cuddling as close as she could get.

Strong as the blight was, it hadn't managed to take all of Teddy away.

There had to be hope for the rest of us, too.

Even me. I'd failed Claudette, but I hadn't bitten Derek. I'd done just enough to stop the blight—tripped myself, pitched my body backward.

Maybe that's why the blighted horde was so clumsy. Maybe they were resisting the blight in their own bodies. That could be why Teddy was always falling all over herself.

If my dog was still fighting, I sure as hell could, too.

I split the unicorn braid between us. I chewed around the gaps in my teeth as I pulled myself up. Shrugged my shoulders out of my backpack and unzipped it. If I couldn't get this stuff to Derek tonight, then all I could do was keep investigating myself.

By the light of my cracked phone, I found Dad's journal—the same one from before, thin and gray and anonymous on the outside. Inside, bursting with my dad's chicken scratch:

March 2

11 p.m. The argent vive has been on the Murphy farm for nearly 8 weeks now, and yesterday, Shauna Murphy called to say they'd found a hole in the yam field—their geode missing. The ground had been dug into with claws, by animals.

It can only mean that the argent vive is targeting the stones. But why? And how? The stones are designed to suck it in like a magnet and encase it inside. Obviously, there are limits. Here at Rainbow Fields, our quartz hit that limit long before anticipated. I don't understand how I could have miscalculated, but we clearly broke off too much, tasked the quartz at the center of the field with enhancing too much wheat. It's overflowing, a constant leak of argent vive into the earth.

Even so, I'm surprised the horde is capable of stealing an entire stone. Could it be that the stones are losing their power to trap it?

In Vial 37, I placed a cubic centimeter of rainbow quartz with 8 ounces of argent vive.

I'm happy to report the quartz immediately absorbed it.

So the Murphys' geode can't trap it anymore, but our quartz still can?

March 3

4:30 p.m. I still don't understand why the Murphys' geode no longer works, but I'm relieved the quartz remains so powerful, both at trapping and compressing the argent vive. If the argent vive keeps growing, we'll need a way to shrink it back down, or else—

He broke off midsentence. And then two lines later, he started back up:

Wren interrupted just now. She is beside herself that I won't let her help in our efforts against the blight, but she's far too involved as it is.

It seems she broke off an extra hunk of the quartz, back in December. This explains why the quartz started overflowing.

It's my fault, really. The more I sit with this, I know it never would've happened if I'd told her more about the quartz and argent vive from the start. How could she have known breaking the quartz would have such disastrous consequences? She's always been a little too smart for her own good. When I was her age, I never would have imagined that dividing and spreading the quartz could yield more wheat.

I wanted so much to leave her a legacy. Now, as the argent vive terrorizes our community, I'll be lucky if I can even keep her safe. She's furious at me, but I can't keep telling her half-truths. I've considered confessing the full story, but after all the damage the argent vive has unleashed on Hollow's End, how am I supposed to explain it to her?

She and her mother will both leave, I think.

It's a bitter pill to swallow—understanding more and more, with every passing day, how deeply I've failed her. Failed them both.

I knew Dad had been trying to protect me, but honestly, I'd thought he believed I wasn't capable of helping anyone. I'd assumed that was why he'd shut me out of the business of Rainbow Fields. Because he thought I would let the farm down again. Let him down.

It wasn't that at all.

All the time I'd stewed in guilt, he'd stewed in his own. We were more alike, really, than either of us realized.

Below, the entry continued:

At any rate, I can only conclude that the problem of the blight did indeed begin here at Rainbow Fields.

And yet, it manifested first at the Murphys'?

I wonder if it could be related to what just happened to the Murphys' geode. Could it be the difference between our stones? After all, the one who provided those four stones was Thomas Warren,

our own farm's founder, and it's no secret he kept
the best one for us. The rainbow quartz is by far
the most complex, and there are traces of it in our
wheat. It could be that the Murphys' geode is easier
for the argent vive to digest, and therefore, the
golden yams are, too.

Oh, I'm struck by a disastrous possibility.

As the argent vive ate through the Murphys'
golden yams, which contain traces of the geode, the
geode became less effective against it. Could the
argent vive be using the miracle crops to inoculate
itself against the stones?

If so, we should see the same effect with the
wheat and our quartz.

In Vial 40, I've crushed a stalk of violet wheat,
along with 8 ounces of argent vive. Once the blight
has digested it, I'll proceed.

March 8

11:30 p.m. It's taken five days for the argent vive in
Vial 40 to fully digest the violet wheat.

Today I added a cubic centimeter of rainbow
quartz. It still absorbed the argent vive, but more
slowly than before. A two-second delay.

My fears confirmed. The more wheat the argent
vive digests, the less effective the quartz is against
it. I don't dare continue in this vein of experiments.
What if I really am inoculating the blight? Building
its immune system.

What's worse, the purple flecks that appeared in Vial 40's argent vive as it dissolved the wheat seem to be redistributing. I found one in Vial 12, a batch that has never touched the violet wheat.

Could the argent vive possibly be one massive organism, somehow connected no matter its physical separation? If so, inoculating one batch of argent vive affects not only that batch, but all the argent vive in Hollow's End.

A devastating discovery.

We can't afford to let this get any more out of control.

I stared down at the journal in my bloody hand, blinking through blight-smoked eyes. He was right—we couldn't afford to let this get any more out of control. Unfortunately, it already had.

Even more than I'd realized.

Dad's notes confirmed what Mrs. P had told us, that the stones—the rainbow quartz, the Murphys' geode, the Pewter-Floreses' agate, the Harrises' cinnabar—trapped the blight, and somehow that blight inside gave them the ability to improve our crops.

But, as I'd also learned from Mrs. P, everyone across the four farms—including me—had broken our stones too many times, spread them too thin so we could increase our planting radius, and so the blight overflowed. Leaked free.

If Dad was right, as the blight came back to eat through our farms, it grew immune to the stones' trapping power. It ate the Murphys' yams until it could eat their geode.

It must've done the same to the Harrises' animals, and it had been gnawing on the Pewter-Floreses' ghost melons for months. If it hadn't already gotten their agate, it had to be close.

Our farm was the last hit. Maybe Dad's hypothesis was right—that because our rainbow quartz was the most complex artifact, the blight had saved it for last, first building up its strength as much as possible.

Now, the quartz could be the only thing left with any real power to trap the blight.

But the more the blight devoured our wheat, the less our quartz would work. Not just against the blight here in our fields, but on *all* the blight in Hollow's End. Dad had been coming to the same conclusion as me—it was one vast connected organism.

I glanced out to the dark fields. The whole farm smelled wrong. Already half-rotten, eaten up to green.

I needed to test if the quartz would still work against the blight. I could get a fresh hunk from the field, but maybe I didn't need to go that far. If Dad was doing tests with it, it's possible he was keeping some nearby.

A memory from my thirteenth birthday flashed into my head. My dad's weirdo gift.

"You're getting to be a proper adult," he'd said, "meaning you can start collecting your own proper secrets." Mom had pointed out that most parents wouldn't want to encourage that, but Dad had passed me his present anyway with a proud little smile—positive that, at least in that moment, he was getting to play the cool parent.

When I unwrapped it, I found a book, hollowed out with a secret compartment.

I didn't want to admit I actually loved it, not in front of Mom's disapproving frown. But I caught him in a hug after dinner, and I'm pretty sure he knew what I meant. It was only a couple nights after that when he first showed me the quartz.

I dug deeper into the backpack, lifting each book and giving it a small shake. As I picked up the dullest, plainest one, something thudded inside.

When I opened the cover, I had to smile. Just a little. A fist-sized hunk of rainbow quartz, saved for a rainy day.

I really did know Dad better than I'd thought.

I curled up on the porch, cuddling the quartz like it was a living creature.

Teddy stank like a swamp, but she was furry and her heart still beat. When she lay down between me and the forest, guarding me from the rest of the world, I threw one arm over her mangy shoulders. Her breath was even more labored than my own. Faint wisps curled from her mouth into the cool night air.

I was getting dizzier, drowsier, my mind fading, but I kept Dad's journal with us, and I read until the lines of his pen blurred to black.

I woke just before dawn with a ragged, hacking cough.

I spat over the side of the porch, as far away as I could get. I didn't want to see what came up. At least afterward my lungs didn't rattle quite so much. The mushroomy mold taste was fainter.

The sun peeked over the horizon, sending out feelers of orange and pink into the sky, as if to test if it was safe to come up.

And I could see it all clearly. The moonlike glow blurring the edges of my vision had faded.

Teddy let out a grumbling sigh. There was still a white film over her eyes, but underneath dwelled a touch of her old, friendly doe brown.

Maybe I just hadn't noticed the brown before. She only came out in the dead of night. Or maybe . . .

I held out my hands side by side. The hand I'd clutched against Teddy was still pale as death, the veins brackish and swollen. Like an overripe ghost melon. But on the other, the one that had cupped the rainbow quartz to my chest, a touch of color had returned to the skin. The veins looked more blue than silver. And my pinky . . . Crusted red flaked down the side, but the stinging ache was gone. Instead of an open angry gash, there sat a smooth, square fingernail. Milky pale and iridescent.

I pressed my tongue to my gums. The bloody holes at the front had smoothed over, two keen new edges just starting to poke through. New teeth? I was growing new teeth overnight?

I grabbed the quartz. Inside the glinting planes of white, past the arcing rainbows, something new and silver squirmed. It had sucked blight from my body, from Teddy, and trapped it inside.

It worked. It was healing us.

I wasn't cured, not by a long shot. Pinpricks of pain still dug into my brain, deep under my skull. But it was a start.

If only I'd realized the stone was in the backpack earlier.

Last night came back to me, one hammer-hard blow after another. The torn flannel of Derek's shirt in my hand. Claudette's blood in my mouth, her gun in my face. That trace of blond hair in the wind.

Above my head, the window creaked.

I pulled away from the wall. "Derek?"

Only his hand reached out, pushing another half loaf of unicorn braid to the porch boards. The window began to shut.

"Derek, wait!" I leapt up, just before the last centimeter sealed off.

He snatched his hand away and jerked back from the window like I'd bite off a finger.

Of course he did. God, that hurt.

I took two big steps backward, and instinctively held up my hands to show him they were empty. That I had nothing to hurt him with.

Then again, I'd already proven I didn't need a weapon to be dangerous.

Derek didn't dart forward to close the window and he didn't leave, either. He just stood, staring at me from the kitchen.

Maybe it was the gesture of surrender that had changed his mind. He'd clearly intended to have nothing to do with me.

"Where's Claud?" he asked.

But his eyes were lifeless, the color drained from his

cheeks. He'd seen the blood on my mouth last night. He already knew.

And I still had to say it. "She's with my parents now. With your—"

Derek didn't know that part. I caught myself before blurting it all the way out.

"Wren?" Derek tensed like someone was about to upper-cut him in the gut.

This was too cruel to say, especially now, with everything he'd lost. But what if the blight used his dad to draw Derek in, the way it had done with Claudette?

With every passing second, Derek's shoulders drew back another defensive degree. "If you've got something to say, you'd better just say it."

"It's what you were afraid of." I dropped my voice to a whisper, as if that would somehow cushion this blow. As if anything could. "We saw your dad last night."

All the fight Derek had braced for, it left him at once, in a slow, defeated crumple—chin slumping to his chest.

He breathed in desperate little gulps.

"She didn't shoot him?" He asked so quietly I had to lean in to make it out.

I couldn't believe he'd ask, honestly. I still remembered Claudette when she was twelve, leaning against her dad's truck with those long white ostrich legs, arms folded like she was just lounging around. But her eyes were fixed under the hood at every tiny movement Mr. Flores made. She sprang to his side when he said, "Wanna try your-self, mija?" He always called her that: my daughter. He always called Derek mijo, too, but the pet name seemed to mean more to Claudette. After all, her first dad didn't stick around for her. Whenever Mr. Flores called her his daughter, she gazed up at him like Teddy gazed at me.

"Of course she didn't shoot," I said.

Derek nodded, down at his own chest. "So they're both . . ."

"I'm so sorry."

He stood there, silent. For the first time, I couldn't read his face. It was just empty.

Finally, he spoke. "Me too."

The other night, in my kitchen, he'd looked like he was carrying the exhaustion of months. Now it looked like years. "You were right when you told me to let you go," he said. "I don't know why I thought that if you'd hurt anyone, it'd be me." He stared dully at me from the same window which I'd used to look out at Teddy. "I never thought it would be Claud."

"We can bring them back," I said. "Claudette and your dad."

"Bring them . . . ?" Derek glanced past the window and fields to the waiting woods. "For what? So they can turn on us, too? So I can lose Mom and Angie? Get bitten myself? I don't blame you for what you did last night, Wren, but this is what it's come to."

He shook his head. "I'm sorry. I'll keep bringing you bread."

He reached forward to close the final centimeter between us.

"Wait. Wait!" I cried. "It doesn't have to be like that. I think there's a way to heal them. To bring them *all* the way back."

Derek didn't say anything, but his hand paused at the window crank.

"The quartz." I reached down and picked it up.

At least this time he didn't flinch at my motion.

"It started reversing my symptoms," I said. "The bread, it has traces of the quartz, but they're just the tiniest of specks. Enough to slow the blight, but that's it. The quartz itself, though, it can suck out the blight and trap it."

Derek lifted his eyes to meet mine.

I saw his doubt. He couldn't afford to believe me anymore. Who knew if it was really me speaking from my own mouth.

"Look." I held up my hands so he could see the difference, twisted them this way and that. "Look at my nail."

"Your nail . . ." Slowly, he said, "You do look better today. More like yourself."

"And look at Teddy." I nudged her.

She yawned and stretched to her feet, shaking her moldy hide and licking her chops. Her tongue was just a little pinker, a little less sickly silver. There was a touch more auburn to her blight-mottled coat.

"She's been blighted for months. If the quartz worked on her, too, then all those people . . . Claudette, my parents . . ." I couldn't help taking one step closer, quartz clutched over my heart like a shield. "You weren't wrong about saving them. Or me. There *is* a way."

It was everything Derek wanted to believe. I knew it was.

Even still, he hesitated.

"Say that's true. Is the quartz really enough to help *all* of them? And even if we just started with our families, how are we supposed to get it to them?" he said. "They're gone now, into the woods."

Not to mention, I'd spent hours next to the quartz and it hadn't healed all of me or Teddy. It's possible it could cure someone with enough time. But the blighted weren't the type to sit calmly where you wanted them to. And if the blight was becoming more immune to the quartz with every devoured wheat stalk, time was the one thing we definitely didn't have.

Teddy tugged at my jeans, and I looked down at her.

"Teddy, what?"

She whined, and tugged again. She glanced over her shaggy shoulder to the rising sun. To the woods, lying like a shadow at the foot of the sky.

She always ran back to the forest before the sun came up. She'd never cut it this close before. Even these early rays had her squinting.

"She wants you to go with her," Derek said.

I was about to brush her off, but then I paused, looked back at Derek. "Maybe I should."

"Are you—? No!" Derek cried. "You can't follow her in there. You'll never come out."

"Well, how else are we supposed to figure out where they're going during the day?" I said. "We can't help anyone if we can't find them."

Derek shook his head. "That's way too dangerous."

"It's dangerous to stay here!" I pointed out. "The horde is only getting more aggressive. You think it's a coincidence they came to your house last night? If they attack us again . . ."

Teddy's whine grew sharper, more insistent. She nudged at me, leaned against my leg, but she was stronger than she thought.

I stumbled. "Ow, Teddy! Quit it." I pushed her off.

She looked at me, up at the sun, and back at the woods. Lowering her head, drooping her tail, she turned and started trotting off alone.

"No, wait! Sit!" I called after her. "Teddy, stay!"

Her ears flicked back, but she kept jogging forward. I wasn't her only master anymore.

Derek and I were out of time for debate.

"Look." I stuffed the quartz and Dad's journal into the backpack. I took off my ring, too, and zipped it into the front pocket. "Keep this with you, okay?" I passed it to him through the window. "Just in case."

"In case what?" Derek asked. "In case you don't come back?"

"I plan to. Just . . ." I shrugged, because there was nothing else to do. "Read the journal."

With that, I turned and took off after Teddy as Derek shouted my name out the window behind me.

CHAPTER 13

Teddy grinned at me when I caught up, her rotting tail smacking back and forth in a wag so joyful I worried that bits of her would fly off.

Under the sun's dim first rays, the wheat swished and rippled around us as we jogged down the path to the forest. It was still too dark to take in the full extent of the blight's decimation. A small mercy. Because it was sickening enough: the crumpling forms of the jagged, broken stalks, collapsing by grades into the earth below. The stench smacked me in the face—rancid like rotting blue cheese, like someone had taken one of Mom's worst casserole surprises and left it out for an entire summer.

I wondered if the blight had eaten all the way through green. If it had already made it to yellow.

"Wren, wait!" Derek's cry pierced the early-morning hum of insect wings.

I turned. "What are you doing?"

He closed the last steps between us, panting, clutching the rainbow quartz in his fist like a lifeline. "If you're going, I'm going."

I wished I had time to stand there a little longer, memorize a more accurate snapshot of him washed in that pale-dawn gold, the dark wheat shivering all around us.

I made myself turn away and follow in Teddy's moldy wake.

"No," I said over my shoulder. "You're not blighted. Let's keep it that way."

"We won't get close, right?" He strode after us. The trees loomed nearer. "If we're scouting, it's safer with two of us to keep an eye out. What if you go alone and they sneak up on you?"

"What if we go together and they sneak up on both of us?" I returned. "See how that's way worse?"

"Don't act like I'm no help at all." Derek got sharp. "This is as much my fight as it is yours. Claudette's in there now. My dad, too."

I see. In his mind, what happened to Claudette was as much his fault as it was mine.

I blew out a sigh.

A few steps ahead, Teddy paused to snap at a butterfly fluttering past her nose, bringing me to an unfortunately timed halt.

Derek stopped by my side. He reached out like he might touch my arm, but his hand hovered—stopping short of my blighted body. "Look, did you mean what you said last night?" He averted his eyes, suddenly shy. "You know, the few-miles-down-the-road thing?"

Wow. Even he couldn't bring himself to say it out loud. I figured that would've come easy to Derek, openhearted as he was.

Now the only one who'd actually spoken the words was the blight.

And that, I couldn't allow. This didn't belong to the blight.

I forced it past my tightening jaw. "When I called you the love of my life and said you don't turn your back on that?"

Derek rubbed his neck and nodded down at the dirt. "Uh, yeah. That."

He almost never got shy. I smiled involuntarily. "I did mean it."

Derek met my eyes. "Then you should get it. I won't give up on Dad and Claud. And I won't give up on the girl I've loved my entire life, either."

Heat bloomed under my cheeks, shooting down into my chest.

Just like that, I reverted to my ten-year-old self, wishing I had a sleeping bag to pull over my blushing head. How did he always do this?

The butterfly Teddy was hopping after flapped out of reach. She tossed a glance my way and resumed her trot.

"So . . . ?" Derek prompted.

Here I was, pretending this was my call. But, really, Derek was every bit as boneheaded as I was. I could tell him to come, or I could tell him to get lost. Either way, he'd follow. One way, he'd also be pissed.

"At the first sign of anyone blighted . . ." I paused. We hadn't even stepped into the forest and we'd already passed that point. "Anyone blighted who isn't me or my dog—if they see you, you run."

Derek nodded, biting his lip to stifle a laugh.

"What's so funny?"

He pointed back at the accusatory finger I'd locked on him. "You're doing your mom's 'I'm super serious' pointing thing again."

I wished I weren't blighted so I could swat at him. I folded my arms across my chest and marched after Teddy. "You left the backpack inside?" I asked.

He patted his empty pocket. "The Harrises' ring, too. Just in case."

In case he didn't come back.

God, I hated that he said that. To be fair, probably as much as he must've hated when I'd said it.

"Your mom is gonna freak out if she gets out of bed and you're not there."

"Don't worry," Derek muttered. "She hasn't moved since last night. Angie's with her." He grimaced. "Anyway, they'll forgive us for everything, you and me both, if we can get Claud back."

"We will," I said, stepping over the threshold from field to forest.

Almost immediately, it greeted me—a piping on the wind, like the very air was laughing at me.

I couldn't tell if it was a voice in the forest, a voice in my head, or just my own paranoia.

Derek's face didn't shift, but Teddy's ears pricked. Then again, she could've been listening to anything.

Twigs cracked under our feet. A few daring birds darted

from tree to tree, their song thinner than ever. Not many left unblighted here. Rot assaulted our mouths, our noses, our throats. Enough to gag on. It dripped from the branches like morning dew.

"*This way.*" The voice trickled into my ear. "*This way.*" Derek still didn't look up.

Teddy, however, lifted her head. With a wag, she veered off the path.

To the left. In the direction I found my own head tilting, like some invisible string was tugging gently at my ear. Not a command, exactly. A suggestion.

For once, I intended to listen.

Silver beads glimmered in the moss. They bubbled into the thinnest stream, weaving through the forest floor like a snake with no head. Under sticks and over logs, shimmering between lumpy mushrooms and the wet remains of leaves from last fall.

Maybe Derek couldn't hear the blight's voice. But this, he definitely saw. He tied my dad's old green bandana over his face, the first sensible thing he'd done all day.

Teddy took the lead. She nosed at the blight trail like she was greeting an old friend, snuffing up sickly splashes.

"Teddy, no," I said.

She looked up with a head tilt, blight dribbling down her mouth and chin.

"Never mind," I muttered. "Just . . . do your usual thing."

It had to be making her sicker, but at least we knew how to treat that now.

I followed behind her. I kept scanning the trees, but I didn't spot any lurking white eyes. Nothing coming at us from the front or sides. Nothing overhead.

Derek brought up the rear, keeping his arms in close, his steps tight—trying not to touch anything in this plague-ridden forest.

Whispers pulled at my ear, low enough that I couldn't make out words, only a hiss of breath. The wind propelled me forward, parting the hair at the base of my neck and chafing through to the skin.

"This way."

Every time that voice spoke in my ear, the muscles on either side of my spine clenched so hard my back ached.

We walked a long time. It should've gotten lighter. Day should've been breaking. But the deeper we drew into the forest, the more the canopy scratched its talons over the sky.

Teddy's ruff stood taller. Her steps fell more carefully.

Derek's shoulders hunched.

The glimmering trickle beckoned to a circular clearing ahead.

The blight trail began to fatten. Fumes of withering mold and musty dander clung to my face like a mask. The stream swelled from the width of my pinky to the width of two fingers. Then three. Four.

It got thick as my forearm, my leg, my torso.

It spread, and spread and spread and spread, until it fed into a puddle.

A pool. A swamp.

A lake that ate up the entire circumference of the clearing. Thirty feet across, glistening with eerie stillness.

We stopped at its edge, paralyzed at the vastness. Our missing summer was in this lake—the warmth of it, simmering like a hot spring. A balmy sheen reaching out to glaze over my exposed face and hands.

Our stream wasn't the only one feeding into it. Blight seeped in from every side, snaking through the trees from uncertain destinations.

"Holy shit," Derek whispered.

My heart spiked, and I elbowed him in the rib. The horde had to be close. Where else would they be? This was more blight than I'd ever seen. More than I'd even known existed.

How much had there been to begin with? Just enough to fill four large stones? And now . . .

How much of Hollow's End had it devoured, to grow this massive?

The blight puddled, languid and viscous. The colors of my own wheat glittered up at me, diamond-bright against that deep silver: violet, indigo, blue, green, yellow . . .

My farm—all I had left of my family—was slipping out from under me, like everything else.

The whispering in my head surged louder, and feverishly fast. I couldn't make out words past all the different voices: high, low, soft, rasping. There were other sounds, too: animal grunts and groans, rustling like the flutter of bird wings.

I clutched my skull, brain lighting with a thousand wiggling pinpricks, like my scalp was falling asleep, but deeper. Inside my head.

"Welcome home."

The one voice I'd come to know so well spoke loudest of all. Louder than ever before, like it was on top of me, all around me.

Something lukewarm slipped from my eye, and I hoped to God it was a tear.

Doubled over, I reached for anything to hold on to, and found the solidness of Derek's arm. "Do you hear it?"

"Hear what?" he asked. "Wren, are you okay?"

I shook my head, forcing myself up to meet his widening stare. "They're here."

"Where?"

"I don't know." The horizon was nothing but trees. The branches above our heads had too few leaves to hide the blighted among their gnarled knots. "Maybe there's a cave nearby. Some secret entrance."

Teddy barked, tired of waiting. She looked over her shoulder at me, slapped her paws against the ground like she wanted me to play, and ran straight for the puddle.

Nosing around in blight trickles was one thing. Splashing into a puddle that big? An extremely bad idea.

"No! Teddy!" I charged after her, diving to grab her around the middle.

She barked again, wagged her tail, and darted away. In her world, we were playing chase.

"Dammit, Teddy!" I lunged after her again.

I missed.

She ran headlong into the blight. I threw a hand over my face to block the inevitable splash.

But it didn't come. Teddy charged out onto its surface,

the liquid heavy underneath her. Her paws sank just an inch. She turned back, grinning, to see if we were still playing, her upside-down reflection in the quicksilver wagging along.

Then, with a thick slurp, Teddy's feet sank into the puddle. It slipped over her legs and tail.

Oh my God, I'd thought it was an inch deep. Maybe two.

The ripples swam over her back, her neck.

"Teddy!" I took two weak steps toward the edge, as if I could possibly reach her.

It closed over her head and sucked her all the way down.

This was no puddle at all. Just like in my dream, it was deep as the tar pits that had swallowed the dinosaurs.

And now it had swallowed my dog.

The lake's surface already lay perfectly placid, like Teddy wasn't drowning underneath. Its smooth luster revealed nothing but a reflection of the clouds overhead, and the scraggly branches that scored across them.

A thick sucking noise caught my ear—a small pop like some seal was breaking.

"Wren!" Derek cried in warning.

Something sticky touched my ankle.

Groping fingers. A hand, dripping with blight. It stretched up from under the lake and clutched me like a coiling viper.

I couldn't stop the scream that burst out of me as I leapt back.

Or tried to leap back.

My foot was trapped. And the creature's head and neck and shoulders broke the surface. All drenched in blight, dribbling from its scalp and sliding down its face—streaming and streaming.

It caught the shore with its free hand, clawing against the earth.

I tugged at my caught leg and kicked at the creature's head with my free foot. My ankle ached under its strangling grasp.

Derek ran to me, knotting strong arms across my chest to pull me back.

The shine of white blurred my vision. The whispers got louder. The blight was trying to seize my body.

I gritted my aching teeth and blinked back the snow, my mind more resistant than it was last night, thanks to the quartz.

But the creature's slippery fingers slid up my calf. They dug in behind my kneecap. So hard I yelped.

Across the lake, ripples stirred, circling out everywhere. More and more disturbances underneath.

"Derek, go!" I shouted. The second those beasts rose to the top, it would be too late for both of us.

He did let go, with one hand—or maybe the thing pulled so hard that he lost his grip.

My leg gave out, and I crashed to the shore on my knees. This close to the reeking pit, my eyes burned. It was like drowning in roadkill, and I wasn't even inside yet.

This gaping maw of a pit . . . it was like the vial from Dad's journal. The mouse floating, suspended, encased tooth-to-nail in silver—while the blight ate it alive. Dad was right, wasn't he? The blight digested its horde from the inside by night. But by day . . . this is where they all went. So it could digest them from the outside. This lake might as well have been the blight's stomach.

Every person, every animal we'd lost was down there now. Blight seeping into their every inch.

Gnawing away.

Melting them into more of itself.

If I went in, no way would it be me that crawled back out.

I'd been so naive to come here. To think I could survive any of this.

The figure was at my eye height now, half in, half out, its scrabbling fingers clutching at my shirt. Its eyes shot open to meet mine—luminous white orbs blinking around melting silver. It lifted the trickling lines of its lips into a smile.

The toe of my shoe dipped under the lake.

And then something smashed against the creature's head, wiping the smile from its face.

The fist-sized chunk of crystal quartz Derek had carried with us. He'd wielded it like a weapon, cracked the creature over the head with it.

He bought me the second I needed to scramble free, backward, onto the safety of the bank. Molten silver coated my shoe. My legs stuck to the dirt, blight clinging like tar, but I hauled myself up to stand.

"*You should be careful.*" The blight spoke from its wounded mouthpiece. A dirty trickle of blood-red seeped from its forehead. "*Careful who you hurt.*"

My body begged me to run.

But Derek stopped only a few feet from the quicksilver lake. He stared as the blighted creature slithered onto the ledge and pushed itself up.

I took a second look myself.

At the bony face, masked with silver. The slick hair that clung to its skinny shoulders. The long arms with hard-carved biceps. And on its left forearm—a bite-shaped dip under the gilded skin.

"Claud?" Derek whispered.

"Little brother, I could show you so much."

Her body wore that dripping silver like a liquid suit. Or maybe, it was the other way around.

Every square inch of me, living and breathing, filled with horror.

Derek froze, like Claudette had when she saw their dad.

I grabbed his wrist and yanked hard. "We have to go. It's not her anymore."

Claudette's luminous eyes stayed locked on his. *"Did Wren tell you what she did to me on that lonely road? You wouldn't leave me for dead the way she did. Not when I'm still alive."*

The blight rippled down the long line of her nose and split back, like someone peeling away a mask from both sides. Underneath, her eyes held their old stony blue. The red skin of her cheeks flaked in strips from the bone. She gasped for breath, lips stained purple.

"Fuck, it hurts!" Claudette's voice, hoarser than ever, rasped from her throat. She scrunched her sliced forehead, where blood ran down from the sharp edge of the quartz. "Everything hurts."

Her gaze found our faces as if seeing us for the first time. "What are you jackasses doing here?" she said. "Run, *now*! *Ru—*"

Silver slimed into her mouth, over her face, smothering her scream.

We'd frozen, numbed in horror, exactly where the blight wanted us. The edge of the lake rippled closer, this seeping puddle coming to swallow us whole. More heads broke its surface.

And Claudette . . . She was back in her silver mask, eyes shining white, teeth grinning yellow.

She lunged for Derek.

We scrambled away, toward the labyrinth of trees between us and safety.

Claudette lurched after us. She staggered wetly over leaves, crashing down again and again.

So she was fighting for us, even now, tripping the blight to slow it down—but it couldn't be easy, not with it suffocating her, controlling her limbs like a puppet.

Every time she fell, it picked her up.

And Derek kept turning back to look, slowing us by milliseconds we didn't have.

I gulped down breath after wheezing breath, grasping his wrist with an iron grip. "Stop looking! Come on!"

I wanted to tell him we'd come back for her, that we weren't going to leave her here forever, but I had no more air to waste on words.

Up ahead, a creek burbled through the trees. If we could just make it that far, if we could cross, maybe that would slow down the blight. Maybe it would wash from Claudette's skin.

I dragged Derek around tangling roots and moss-slick rocks. Around the creeping puddles of quicksilver streaming into our path, trickling out from the lake to chase us.

We were so close to the creek, only a dash away—

When Derek tripped, on a slippery patch of blight. His hand was yanked from mine. Biting droplets sprayed against the back of my calf as he collapsed to the ground.

His stumble pitched me forward.

I splashed into the shallow creek, my knee plowing hard into silt, cloudy water surging into my face. I thrashed free and blinked against the sandy water streaming from my eyelashes, spitting out the taste of fish scales.

"Derek!" I coughed.

He was on the ground, reaching for me, as the thing puppeteering Claudette caught the leg of his jeans. Blight seeped instantly into the fabric, running down in streams.

Behind them came the animals—the barking dogs and crying foxes. More and more charging toward us.

Derek hacked at Claudette's arms with the quartz, trying to loosen her grip.

The blight wearing her body let out an unearthly shriek. Blood trickled through before silver closed back over it.

But now the charging dogs were within reach.

With a snarl, one of the biggest, a mold-chewed Harris dog—Teddy's brother—latched on to Derek's other leg.

My whole world narrowed to slow motion, to micro-moments: Derek's gasp. The pained crumple of his fore-head.

The creek's whispering wash, now roaring in my ears, drowning out all real sound.

The dog biting down, through the denim of Derek's jeans, burying its teeth up to its gums.

An instant gush of crimson—redder than sun-soaked rose wheat.

Stained wet fur around the dog's lips as it thrashed its teeth even deeper.

My own blood evaporated into raging steam heat. I charged forward.

"Wren!" Derek's strangled voice pierced through to me. *"No."*

I lurched to a stop. I could throw my body into the fray, let those dogs tear me to pieces, but then there really would be no hope for him. For anyone.

Just like when he'd had to leave me and Claudette behind at his overrun house—another unforgivable, but inescapable, calculation.

My mouth opened to argue, to plead, to scream at our current reality.

The approaching pack of Harris dogs, running to join their ringleader, snapped their slavering attention from Derek—to me.

Derek flung me a desperate glance. "Go!" He hurled the quartz.

It splashed into the stream just past me. If he'd had any

chance, he'd literally thrown it away. To make me turn back.

I snatched it from the water.

All I could say was, "I'll come back for you."

"*No need,*" Claudette said, hands digging into Derek's shoulders, holding him down while the dogs grabbed his legs. "*We'll come to you.*"

As she smiled, new orange glimmers danced to life across her silver-coated forehead, sparkling in among the other stolen colors.

All but our red.

"*The other stones are gone,*" she said. "*Once the quartz is, too, we'll be ready to cross the bridge. All of us— together.*"

Derek strained against Claudette and the dogs, pushing up from the ground even as they tore him back down. Blight dripped from Claudette's chin onto his neck, splattered in beads across his face.

"*Wren!*" he screamed.

I'd been so focused on him I hadn't seen the approaching shadows falling over me.

Mom. The blight from the lake coated her, clung and oozed in an iridescent shimmer that slimed over her face, her skin, her red plaid shirt. Her eyes were empty lanterns as she splashed into the water after me, stumbling with arms outstretched.

From my other side: another splash.

Dad. The silver film dripped from his face, revealing his cracked freckled skin. In places, it was stripped back so far it found the parts of him where there were no freckles left.

Like a sunburn scorching deeper than skin. His nose was red raw, a bloody line gashing down his face.

He reached, too.

They blocked me from Derek, even as the thing that wasn't Claudette began to drag him away. As he scratched his own ten-fingered tracks deep into the dirt.

I couldn't help him.

Mom's nail-less fingers grabbed the collar of my shirt.

I shoved her back. As she crashed into the creek, I scrambled from the sloshing dirty water.

I ducked Dad.

I ran from the monsters my parents had become. I ran, even from Derek, because that was all there was left to do.

CHAPTER 14

I ran in breakneck panic, staggering through the toxic forest. At first, I didn't look back. I couldn't.

The blood pounding in my head muffled the growls behind me—the clumsy trips and staggers of the horde, snagging in branches and slipping on leaves and stream banks.

They weren't getting louder. They weren't keeping up.

I was jackrabbit-fast. But every step I put between me and them—Derek, Claudette, my parents, everyone—ached. Stab after stab to my throbbing heart. Like I was running on spikes that gouged all the way through, driving a wedge up into my rib cage. I was cracking myself in half.

Why did I let him come? I should never have involved him in the first place.

I'd been right to break it off with Derek after what happened with Teddy. If you really loved someone, you left them behind. Before you dragged them down with you.

I'd just wanted his help moving the fence. Saving the

wheat. I was scared, and lonely, and so wildly selfish to call him that afternoon. Now I'd drowned both him and Claudette in that festering blight pit. I'd as good as done it with my own two hands.

I stumbled on a root, only just managing to catch my palm against the trunk of a tree.

My lungs were a gasp away from bursting, and I still hadn't made it out of the forest.

I darted a look behind me.

The trees stood still. Silent. As far as I could tell.

I knew what I was running from. But where was I even going?

Rainbow Fields. On autopilot. Like some scared little kid. Like it was my blankie and would make it all better. But it couldn't, could it? It was the root of the blight in the first place.

From overhead, there came a juddering whir.

I smudged the sweat away from my eyes. High above the trees, piercing the faint blue sky, a helicopter churned.

The emergency responders, out for their rounds.

The thought of those squeaky white suits, the cold masks hiding their faces, made me grind my aching teeth. All I could hear was the echo of the blight's slithery voice, when it told me the responders were only here to make more of it.

But there was plenty of reason for it to lie.

I didn't really know the responders' intentions. As for the blight, I knew *exactly* what it meant to do—to digest Hollow's End to juice in that stinking lake. To cross the bridge into Meadowbrook and do the same to the people there. And why would it stop? It would just keep growing. Growing and devouring.

Let's face it, I was helpless.

Claudette had been right: We needed someone to save us. Someone who wasn't me.

This was our last chance. *All* our last chances.

I threw up my hands, waving wildly. When they found out I was blighted, who knew if I'd survive them. It was like flagging down a wolf—hoping to God it could save you from a bear.

The chopping blades hovered in the air directly above me, whipping my hair around my face. The leaves underfoot.

They saw me.

My knees slackened with dizzy lightness. Help was coming. Someone was going to take this off my hands, and then I could collapse.

I'd found a treatment, what they claimed they were looking for. I had to believe that if someone handed them a real answer, something that could help people, they'd put it to good use.

Except then the wind lessened. The mechanical roar began to fade.

The helicopter started to lift back up.

Leaving me here. On the ground.

I blinked. No. They couldn't.

"Wait!" I leapt up and down, waving so hard my shoulder twinged. "Wait, please! We can treat the blight—I can show you, I swear!" I yelled.

The helicopter rose into the sky, higher and higher.

"You can't just leave us here! We're going to die!" I strained onto my tiptoes, the wild force of my scream grating against my throat. "Would you just be fucking human beings? I'm right here! *I'm here!*"

Even as the helicopter got smaller and smaller, I couldn't stop. I kept flailing, a muscle in my back snagging into a tearing burn. A raging tremble shot through me, from the soles of my feet, through my sweat-soaked shirt, my furious hot face, my pounding scalp. It ripped the scream right out of me—a spewing cloud of all my aching loss and fear and fury. Something thick and sludgy tore free in my throat, choking me into a painful cough. Hot tears and snot streamed down my face.

High above my head, the helicopter veered off. Away from the woods. From me.

After all, the responders never went into the forest.

Apparently, not even when a girl was stranded right under them, and they were safe above in hazmat suits.

The blight really was telling the truth, wasn't it?

They weren't here for us. They were here for *it*—to harness the blight and use it to manufacture their own money-making miracles. To turn our silver blight into caged gold.

As for the actual people of this town, they'd always intended to leave us here to fend for ourselves. Or, more accurately, to die.

No one was coming. No one was ever coming to help us.

It was like someone had cut all my strings. I collapsed against a tree, my back scraping bark all the way down.

Blight seeped from it like sap, trickling into my hair, oozing through my shirt.

As broken as Hollow's End turned out to be, it made up my bones. Maybe it would be fitting if I just lay here until the blight stripped my flesh into fertilizer.

My eyes leaked, a whisper of salty water eaten up by the soil below.

All I could see was Derek.

His gasp and his scream. The dog ripping into his leg. Claudette dragging him away while he clawed at the dirt. And reached back—for me.

The blight had everything now.

Even the other stones. It would come for the quartz next, our only remaining hope. And how was I supposed to stop it?

That lake might as well have been infinite. A black hole in the earth's crust, stretching to the planet's very core, funneling us all the way down.

Behind me, a stick snapped. Leaves crackled.

Something was coming.

Of course. They'd heard me scream.

I couldn't run anymore. I couldn't even get up. It was all I could do to raise my eyes, to at least witness whatever was here to drag the last of me into that quicksilver lake.

The shape shuffled, slow and steady, out from the trees.

Stiff-spined, it shuddered toward me, wearing the sweater I'd helped Mom knit last fall.

In spite of everything, I almost smiled.

At least I got to see him again, while my mind was still mine. "I'm glad it's you, Dad."

There was a chance he could still hear me through the fissures of whatever prison the blight had locked him in. However far it had buried him beneath the surface. He hadn't been blighted long. He'd eaten that unicorn braid his whole life. Maybe it had given him the tiniest bit of immunity.

Although, obviously, not enough.

By now, he'd mostly shed the blight from the lake, but it still clung to him in places, dripping down the calves of his jeans, past his ankles—leaving gleaming toxic puddles with his every step.

His jaw sagged like he might say something, if only he could remember how to talk. His head tilted, rolling on his neck like it was too heavy.

Mine felt that way, too.

In an awful way, it was just so right he was here. He was always the one who found me when I'd done something wrong. Appearing in my bedroom doorway with that dour grimace, a disappointed sigh: I didn't get every last particle off the pots I'd washed; I put away my gloves and shovel in the shed too sloppily; I got a B on a math test; he'd seen that quick glance under the table at my phone during dinner.

Back when those tiny mistakes were the worst damage I'd done.

Dad kept staggering toward me, stumbling over the ragged forest floor. His mouth opened and closed. Like Amber Murphy's had. Teeth testing the empty air.

God, I couldn't look at him like this.

I squeezed my eyes shut.

If I didn't have to see this lumbering creature that he'd become, maybe I could pretend that things were how they used to be: The wood of the blighted tree behind me was only my desk chair. My dad come to visit me in my room.

I still remembered how he'd found me that night not long after my thirteenth birthday, surprising me with a knock at my door.

"Wren?" He'd stood in the doorway, squinting like my decor hurt his eyes.

It probably did. While the rest of the house interior was dull, I hoarded color in my room: My Great Grandma's old quilt, embroidered with square after square of our rainbow wheat. A sapphire-rich blanket underneath that. Lilac paint on the walls. A round daffodil-yellow area rug, fuzzy under my feet.

I wondered what I'd done wrong this time. My stomach had squeezed tight, crumpling like a ball of paper.

He looked toward the window over my bed, to the quiet waves of rolling wheat, dyed ocean-dark by night.

"You like it here, don't you?" he asked.

I could barely comprehend it. He might as well have been asking if I liked breathing or eating or sleeping. Rainbow Fields was life, survival. A fact, not a question.

He chuckled a little, at the face I made. Whatever he saw, it must've been what he'd hoped for. "Have you thought about your future? If this . . . the farm . . . is something you'd want for yourself?"

It was all I'd ever pictured. Me and Derek, and Rainbow Fields. We were supposed to have kids named Luis and Delilah. I'd show them myself, like Dad had shown me, how to pour their love into the soil, how to care for something as precious as our living rainbows.

I could see that version of my life so easily.

I didn't *not* want it.

Of course, I was a little curious what it might be like to be anywhere but here. To live any life but the one I'd always taken for granted. But I knew better than to admit that to Dad.

I picked at a stubborn speck of dirt under my nail and tried not to swivel in my chair. "Well, you're gonna need someone, right? To take it over someday? You can't run it forever."

"Right." The smallest of sighs lifted and dropped his chest. "But if it's not what you wanted . . ."

It was so obvious. How much he needed it to be something I wanted. It was too painful to watch him drag the words out, stiffening with each syllable.

"I can do it, Dad," I said. "Derek said he'd help."

That crumpling point between Dad's eyes smoothed back out. A hint of a smile flitted at the corner of his mouth. "Hollow's End is lucky," he said, "to have a generation like yours. Very dedicated. Hardworking."

Dad didn't say a lot of stuff like that, but if he paid a compliment, it was never empty. Twin suns of pride burned in my cheeks.

What a fucking waste.

As I lay there against the tree, the blight bit through my shirt—cold, metallic.

I opened my eyes.

The torn knees of Dad's jeans were level with my face. He loomed over me, exhaling heavy mold-clogged breaths.

"I'm sorry," I told him. "For what it's worth, I really did try, Dad. I found your journals." It felt so far away now. I shook my head. "I tried to protect the farm while you were gone. I figured out what you were on to. About the quartz."

I held the chunk up for him, like it was one of my softball trophies.

I had to be kidding myself, hoping he could be proud of me anymore. But maybe the sight of our quartz would be soothing to him on some level, even if only a subconscious one.

He locked on to it with his softly glowing eyes. They looked slightly grayer, closer to his natural color, than white. Maybe a trick of the light.

"But I didn't figure it out soon enough. And now I just don't know how . . ." My voice cracked. "Even if there was a way to save the farm, you've been powering it on blight all this time? Dad, I don't even know anymore, if that's worth saving."

His head lolled up. And then down.

A nod? He *agreed* it wasn't worth saving?

Right. My laugh came out in a bitter bark. The blight was the one pulling Dad's strings. That's who I was talking to now. It was just using Dad to toy with me, the same way it'd used me against Derek.

I was too deadened to even be angry. To feel anything

at all. "So, you really are gone then. You're not my dad. Fine, just get it over with and take the quartz."

He bent down to me.

I braced for his trembling fingers to latch on to the fabric of my shirt. To seize the stone and snatch it away.

But he only laid his hand on it. Just like I had, when he first showed it to me.

Gently.

Like he was touching a newborn's head.

The humanness of the gesture, stilted as it was, shocked me. I sat up, careful not to jostle his hand. "Dad, can you hear me? Are you actually . . . ?"

He just stood there, wheezing rattles sucking in and sucking out.

I stayed there with him, staring up at his peeling face.

If anything, I should hate him, after all the secrets he kept. The mistakes he made. It was so nonsensical, but here I was, just desperately afraid I'd disappointed him worse than ever.

"Do you hate me?" My voice barely scraped past my lips. "I let us all down. The last six generations of our family. I lost Rainbow Fields. I lost everything."

He reached his other hand to my face and touched my cheek with quivering fingers. He hung his head.

His eyes closed.

Slowly, trembling the entire way, he drew his hand back and dug into his pocket.

He pulled a closed fist out and unwrapped each finger like the air itself weighed a thousand pounds. Like it was pushing against him.

From his hand, a glimmer of something dropped, vanishing under the patchwork blanket of scratchy dead leaves.

That was all.

He released the quartz and nearly fell over, tripping on one shoeless foot. He started off again, through the trees, back the way he'd come.

"Hey, wait!" I reached down to the leaves to rescue what he'd dropped.

My fingertips found it—the cool band of silver.

The final ring: the upside-down triangle, a line intersecting the bottom. Earth.

The Murphys' ring.

How could he possibly . . . ?

"Dad!" I hauled myself up by the rough bark of the blighted tree. He was already gone, melted into the forest.

Had he been one of the faceless shadows in the tree line, back on the Murphys' farm? The one I saw break away from the rest to pursue the lost silver glimmer? Like Teddy, there'd been a little of him left, after all.

I squeezed my eyes shut, clutching the clammy ring in my palm.

I couldn't save Hollow's End alone. But Dad had just proven, I wasn't. Maybe the farm was doomed, but he wasn't gone yet. Neither were Mom, Mr. Flores, Claudette, or Derek. Not unless I abandoned them.

I blew out a slow, shaky breath. And I forced my feet forward. With every shaking step, my legs unfroze a little more. Rediscovered their footing.

I jammed the ring onto my finger.

Okay, Dad.

This wasn't over. Not yet.

When I found my way out of the forest, the blight was waiting for me.

It crept up the stalks of the glistening orange wheat, bending them to the earth. It had torn its way through the rows, from the violet at the back, beelining all the way toward the red at the front. Racing to taste at least some wheat of each and every color. Maybe that's what it needed to be able to eat the quartz.

At the edges of the field, some wheat in each opalescent shade still swayed. Except for the violet. All of those stalks lay scattered, rotting, reaching out across the earth as if groping for kinder soil.

It'd taken the blight months to achieve this kind of devastation on the Murphys' crops. But things were changing. The horde was larger. The blight was stronger.

It ate faster.

The only thing totally untouched was that circle in the very center of our wheat field. The tall, luscious patch that glittered deeper emerald than the stalks around it. My parents always worried someone might notice, but, of course, no one even knew what they were looking for. No one except the blight.

I pumped my legs, pushing up the path from the forest to my house.

The Murphys' ring sat heavy on my thumb. I clutched the quartz so hard it chafed, rubbing my palm raw.

Behind my every blink, Derek's lost, frightened eyes flashed at me. The tortured strangle of his scream.

I had to find some way to fix this. To stop the blight. Dad seemed to think it might be possible—why else would he have bothered to get me the Murphys' ring? And why would the blight have tried to make me throw it away in the first place? Inside that silver box, there had to be an answer.

And if there was, I needed to know before nightfall, when the horde would freely wander out from the forest. When the blight would come back for me and for the quartz.

Judging by the high sun, it was early afternoon, so that only gave me a matter of hours.

First things first. I needed to get back into my house. I needed to find the backpack I'd given Derek. I needed to—

An awful weight slammed into the back of my skull.

I staggered on the path, a weak hand reaching toward the pulsing pain, another dropping to soften my fall.

I couldn't see. This time, it wasn't the white gauze of fog and snow. The whole world faded—to a spiraling, lightless pit.

CHAPTER 15

I beat the emptiness back from my eyes one blink at a time. And I was almost sorry I had. Something pressed into my throat, ice-cold prongs of metal, and with my every move, they tightened, pricked my skin.

There was only one thing that could be. From Teddy's early training days: a prong collar.

I was leashed to a workbench, sitting among sawdust and dead grass from the mower. The shed.

Next to me, Buckwheat whisked her tail and slurped from the bucket I'd left for her.

"Hi, Wren." The voice was so dead, so flat, I almost took it for Claudette.

Of course, it couldn't be.

Angie sat propped against the shelf opposite me, arms crossed hard.

Dull light filtered through the dust-caked windows behind her—haloing the cloud of her hair, armoring her shoulders in a pale glow. The light glinted against a polished rock resting beside her, one taken from our private garden. It was dotted with a drying splotch of blood.

I blinked from the rock back to Angie.

"You hit me . . . ?" I didn't mean for it to come out like that, so dazed and lost.

Angie was out of patience, her glare deep and shadowed. "Where the fuck is Derek?"

Submerged in that simmering quicksilver lake—the blight gnawing and gnawing at him. I winced.

"Wren!" In a rattling crash, Angie kicked over a bucket with her electric-pink sneaker. Her voice was quivering, her chest heaving with shallow breaths. "I *saw* you! From the window, I saw you go into the forest together. Where is he? What have you done?"

I wanted to hold up my hands in surrender, but she'd knotted them with a stretch cord. A much messier knot than Claudette's. Angie wasn't someone meant to be hunting and hurting and trussing. All those cat and cupcake headbands, her candy-scented ChapStick and sunshiny smiles. And this was what Hollow's End had driven her to.

It was the blight's specialty, after all—taking something sweet and twisting it sour.

Now, here she was: leashing me in a barn like Benji Thomas's parents had done to him. Because all the good options were gone.

At least she hadn't shot me in the face like Claudette had considered doing.

Like Claudette probably would have done, had she seen what Angie saw.

Angie's eyes were puffy. Bleary. Her glimmering eye

shadow from yesterday was smeared down her cheek. I wondered if she'd even slept. If she'd been up all night, hoping there could be some mistake. That Claudette might still come back.

I opened my mouth to try to give her an answer, but all I could see was Claudette trembling as she'd touched that bracelet Angie's little sister had given her, the one stained by her own blighted blood.

How she'd had to watch her future with Angie trickle away.

Angie sighed at my silence, shaking her head. "Derek is missing. Mrs. P is practically comatose. I can't get her to eat or get up or do *anything*. Claud would want me to look after her family. That's what she'd do, if she . . ." Angie's rock-hard resolve wavered. A sudden shine glossed her eyes. She pressed her hands to her temples, digging her nails into her forehead like she was fighting the worst headache of all time. But when she looked up at me again, her jaw was set. "You're going to tell me where Derek is. And then I'm going to call the clinic to come pick you up, before you can hurt anyone else."

"Angie, I'm not what you think I am," I said softly. "There's more of me here than there was last night. There's a way to treat the blight. We can help them."

"*Them?*" Angie demanded.

My exhausted neck dipped, and the pain of the prongs forced my head back up, to look her in the eye. "Claudette. And, yes, Derek. We went into the forest to find her. It . . . didn't work out as planned."

Angie stilled. For a long time.

"How many of us are you going to kill?" she asked, her face slack. "Did you come back for me and Mrs. P, too? Did you think we'd be delusional enough to trust you?"

"Claudette and Derek aren't dead," I said.

"If they're not dead yet, they will be."

"No." The heat of my raw frustration surged from my veins, exploded into my heart. "They don't have to be. That's what I'm trying to tell you! But they *will* be, just like my parents, and me, and everyone else in Hollow's End, unless we do something about it today. If I'm right, the blight is coming here tonight. So you can lock me out of my own house forever, you can leave me leashed like a dog, you can even call the clinic on me—but first, I *need* you to get me my backpack! Please. Just bring me my backpack."

Angie leaned back harder against the shelf behind her, letting the heat of my words fall flat in the empty air. Her brown eyes flickered as she gave me a once-over, chewing her bottom lip.

"Why," she asked, low and grim, "would I bring you your backpack? So you can tear up everything inside?"

"So I can open the box. Because I finally, *finally,* have the Murphys' missing ring!" I held up my hand, as best I could, to show her. "Or you can open it. Or Mrs. P, for all I care—we need *her* ring, too. But if there's any chance that box could help us, we need to know. Now."

Angie sat there, her back in light, front in shadow. She looked down at the floor.

"Wren." Her voice was worn ragged around the edges. "Do you have any idea how long I waited to find someone like Claud? She was it for me. Do you have any idea what you've taken from me?"

Actually, yes. Derek was gone now, too.

I squeezed my eyes shut against the ache, searching for calm.

"Angie, you only came to Hollow's End in the first place because you would do anything for Claudette. Isn't that still true?" I asked. "I don't know what'll happen if we keep trying, but I know exactly what'll happen if we don't."

Angie didn't speak.

She looked over her shoulder, back out to the light of day. The few hours we had left.

With the smallest, tightest nod, she left—slamming the shed door behind her.

Angie was gone a long time. Rain started plinking onto the corrugated iron roof above my head. Trickling down that corner near the shed door that Dad had said a million times he was going to reinforce. Buckwheat heaved with a sigh, lulled by the patter into a standing doze.

For me, every drop was a needle at the back of my neck. Another second wasted.

At last, Angie inched her way back into the shed, clutching the backpack's dripping straps on her shoulders. Behind her came Mrs. P. The silver ring gleamed on her finger.

Rain matted her corn-silk hair to the top of her skull. It clung wetly to her cheeks, down the back of her slumped neck. Her eyes were red-rimmed and raw. She wasn't blighted, but she walked like someone else was piloting her body.

A living ghost.

She crumpled to the floor across from me, legs tossed to the side like a rag doll's.

Her whole family was gone. And I was the one who'd taken them.

Angie tugged the door until the cranky wood squeaked tight against the floor. She kneeled beside Mrs. P and touched a soft hand to her shoulder. "Mrs. P wanted to join us. Because you said there's a way to get Claud and Derek back."

"I hope so," I said. "We won't know for sure unless we open the box. Are you going to let us do that, Mrs. P?"

She stared down at the water-flecked ring on her finger, like she hadn't even heard me.

"Mrs. P?"

Finally, a craggy voice croaked from her throat. "Your parents ever tell you, Wren, about the Hollow's End initiation rites we used to do?"

I shared a questioning glance with Angie.

Above us, the rain pelted down, counting out our dwindling time. But this could be important. The key to what we needed.

"No . . . ," I admitted.

Mrs. P was sitting there, just a few feet back, but she might as well have been miles away. "Once the kids in a founding family were at least thirteen, we'd all get together in the Murphys' barn," she said. "Did you know I had two sisters? When they saw what was in that box, they swore to leave Hollow's End, as soon as they were old enough. My farm shouldn't belong to me. Each family is supposed to pass theirs down to the oldest child, but I was the only one willing to stay."

There was a lot of water on Mrs. P's pale cheeks, and I couldn't tell anymore what was from the rain.

"I try not to be superstitious, but once the blight came, it was hard not to think we were . . . haunted. Or maybe cursed," she said. "I'd never told Derek's dad our deepest family secrets, and when I finally did, in January . . ."

Under Angie's hand, Mrs. P's shoulder shook harder. So that was it. Why she and Mr. Flores had fought. Why he'd left to clear his head with a walk in the forest, one from which he never came back.

"He wanted to tell Derek and Claud the whole truth, too," she said. "I couldn't let him. What if they decided to leave? That's why the Murphys buried their ring, you know, because a couple of their boys moved away last generation after opening the box. And the other three families agreed to discontinue the rites—to stop sharing our history. So your grandpa sealed that box away. Really, I thought it was for the best. You don't need to know the story of our miracle crops, not in order to farm them. Bringing old secrets to the surface only makes kids ashamed of their legacy. Hate their own home."

"But my dad gave me this ring," I said. "He must believe I have a right to know what's inside the box—"

"I know." Mrs. P wouldn't look at me. And that icy edge to her voice—the one I'd heard for the first time when we brought the box into her kitchen—it was back. "But even still. Don't you hear what I'm saying? Opening it will ruin everything we have left: our legacy, the farm—"

"The farm?" Angie pointed through the shed window to the rotting melons. "*That* farm?" she asked, incredulous. "Look, my family owns our brewery. We take pride in our business, and it's hard when it suffers. And honestly, I love your farm, too! God help me, but those creepy melons are downright magic at night. I thought maybe Claud and I would . . ." Her voice faltered, but she swallowed and pushed on. "I saw a life here."

Like Derek and me. Our farm, our wheat.

Angie swiped at her brightening eyes. "But that's not going to happen now."

Mrs. P froze, watching her. The steel in her eyes melting into something softer.

"Your farm . . . your farm is dying, Mrs. P," Angie choked out. "It's dying like Wren is. Like your family is. But Wren just said maybe we can get them back, that maybe there's still a chance. So I don't know what it is you're clinging to, but you need to stop. You need to wake up."

Mrs. P squeezed her eyes shut. She clutched her ring.

"What good is a legacy if it's always been a lie?" Angie implored her. "Mrs. P, there's nothing here to protect."

At last, Mrs. P nodded.

She twisted the ring from her finger, wincing as she tugged it past her knuckle, like it hadn't come off in an awfully long time.

She deposited it in Angie's palm with a grimace.

Angie pressed her fingers closed around it with a slow

nod. Like she understood the trust Mrs. P was putting in her.

I held my hand out with the Murphys' ring, for Angie to take.

That one, she snatched lightning-fast. Like a brush with my skin might blight her. She scrubbed the ring clean with a cloth from the floor of our shed.

"Where are the rest?" she asked.

"Backpack," I said. "Front pocket."

Angie slid the other two rings out and deposited them on the floor with a chorus of little clinks.

All four triangles, upside down and right side up, studded along the bands carved with crescent moons.

She lifted out the box, gasping at its heaviness, and set it down, too. Smooth and plain except for its strange "silver and gold" saying, and the lock, with its four round symbols, waiting for their keys.

She lifted each ring, one at a time, and slotted it into place.

Air. *Click*.

Fire. *Click*.

Earth. *Click*.

Water. *Click*.

And then Angie flipped back the lid.

"Oh," she said, with a tilt of her head, a scrunch of her mouth.

I craned to see past the raised rectangle of the lid. "What? What is it?"

"It's . . ." Angie reached in with two fingers and lifted out a single piece of paper. Ink-smudged, yellowed, age-eaten at the corners, it looked like it might crumble to join the sawdust on the floor. "Um. I think it's a recipe?"

Mrs. P buried her face in her hands. Like she couldn't bear to look.

"A recipe for *what*?" I demanded.

"For . . ." Angie's eyes widened. "Oh my God."

Her fingers flinched like the paper was suddenly living vermin. She touched the edges as lightly as possible, holding it up for me to read.

Scrawled in uneven ink—thick in some places, watery in others—with large looping letters:

The Preparation of Philosophic Mercury; or A Study in Argent Vive

Adapted by Thomas G. Warren in 1874, from Eirenaeus Philalethes's circa 1678 "Praeparatio mercurii ad lapidem per regulam et lunam"

The philosophical manipulation of mercury must be accomplished by two processes: by removing what is superfluous, and by introducing what is wanting. The resulting argent vive serves as an unrivaled agent of purification, uplifting any property to its highest nature. Now is the hour of silver and gold.

Marry sulfur with three parts mercury to one part silver. So are combined one offspring whose father is gold and two offspring of silver, the mother.

Heat to release vapors. Stir thrice.

The breath of life requires the acquaintance of both flora and fauna. Flora is introduced with a block of coal, to provide vegetation, for therein is peat. Fauna, of utmost import, provides the necessary salt. Be it the bitter salt of lifeblood itself, a full body's worth.

Place the concoction, along with coal, atop the tongue and stitch sealed the mouth.

May each hand and foot of the vessel be inscribed with a rune, one for each element. May left hand be air, left foot be earth, right hand be fire, and right foot be water. And may suitable stones be chosen to correspond with each element: air embodied by rainbow quartz, earth by geode, fire by cinnabar, and water by enhydro agate. By designating these runes and stones, so shall each stone direct the manner in which the argent vive will enact upon the outside world.

Ensure the body is freshly warm, for this is the precise temperature required. Remove from all light.

As argent vive ingests, it shall melt through the body, and draw and quarter itself into each stone atop hand and foot.

Thus from death shall spring life, and so shall it be. Our black earth is a fertile earth.

So, our families hadn't *found* the blight at all.

We'd created it.

When I could finally force out words, all I could manage was, "Mrs. P? You knew about this?"

She didn't uncover her face as she spoke. "Thomas

Warren called it alchemy. Something his father taught him, and maybe his father before him. He had those stones, the tools to mix it, the books . . ."

I shook my head. "What does it mean, about the blood? Whose body? The hands and feet? Th-the mouth they stitched shut . . . Was it . . . an animal?" God, I really wanted it to be an animal.

Mrs. P, at last, dropped her hands.

"No," she said. "It wasn't an animal."

And she told us. All the founding farmers, husbands and wives, drew coins from a hat. One was colored red. They'd agreed: they could all starve, or one of them could make a sacrifice to save the rest. Agnes Murphy drew the red coin. But her husband, Cormac Murphy, couldn't live with the rules they'd set down. He fought back.

Mrs. P didn't know who landed the blow that killed Cormac: one secret the founders resolved to keep buried.

In the end, Agnes took the geode intended for her farm. Obstinacy wouldn't bring her husband back from the dead. And Cormac would've wanted, she said, for his sacrifice to mean something.

So it was murder.

Silver, mercury, sulfur, coal, and blood.

The argent vive . . . the blight. That's how all of this started. With the murder of one of our own.

Whatever Mrs. P saw on my face, it pulled a miserable little moan from her. "Oh, honey . . ." She pushed her shoulders back, the same way Derek did when he tried to collect himself. "When my daddy showed me and my sisters that box, you know what he said? 'Just you ask yourself—*really* ask yourself—what you would've done if you'd been in their position. If doing nothing meant your kids were going to starve.' I think my sisters left because they weren't even willing to ask."

I didn't want to ask, either.

"Couldn't they have left Hollow's End?" I asked instead. "Started over somewhere with better soil, or moved to a city and found some crappy job?"

Mrs. P smiled thinly, in a watery, hesitant way, like she was about to break it to me that there was no tooth fairy. "Those things cost money. If you don't have any to begin with . . ." She spread her hands with an obnoxiously helpless sigh. "Well. What's done is done. For a hundred and fifty years, the argent vive has served our farms, absorbing our crops' impurities to make them into miracles."

The paper fluttered from Angie's hand.

All of us stared down at the one-page recipe on the shed floor—the murder pact that had destroyed Hollow's End.

Now is the hour of silver and gold.

Jesus.

It seemed to be one of the core tenets of alchemy, this idea that everything has a higher nature. But maybe the mistake of alchemy was assuming that higher nature always had to be silver or gold.

It was the sickest kind of irony, that in theory, the argent vive had been created to make the world a better place.

Underneath the smell of the wet wood of the shed, the mineral-rich soil that clung to the tines and trowels of the tools surrounding us, that oversweet stench of lurking rot was thickening in my throat. On the new pinky nail the quartz had helped me grow overnight, creeping up from the cuticle, there it was again: mold.

Just the sight of it nearly crumpled me with exhaustion.

But I swallowed against the cold prongs of the collar. And I held myself up. We needed to figure this out, before I ran out of time. Before we all did.

"If the argent vive was supposed to be so good at making other things better"—I gestured to Buckwheat with my tied shaking hands—"then what went wrong?"

"Well." Angie rubbed her chin. "Maybe it wasn't meant to handle four farms' and a hundred and fifty years' worth of 'better.' If it's cleansing other things by taking those impurities into itself . . ."

Right. If all the crop's impurities kept getting sucked in by the stones and absorbed by the argent vive . . .

"You're saying, for a hundred and fifty years, the argent vive made other things better," I said, "but in the process, it made itself worse."

"Much, much worse," Angie said.

From living silver to toxic waste.

"It's just a theory," Angie added.

Mrs. P nodded. "I'm afraid you may be right. But it still doesn't explain . . . I could understand if it stopped working, but for it to do what it's doing now? It's almost like . . ."

"Revenge?" Angie suggested, crossing her arms in front of her chest. "If the blight really is alive, then it suffered on your farms for an awfully long time—and it doesn't sound to me like anyone gave it a choice about that."

"No. That's not . . ." Mrs. P stiffened, glancing to me and the silver stains on my clothes. " 'Living silver' is only an expression."

But her downcast eyes darted away—just like Derek's had time and time again as he'd refused to admit I was blighted.

She knew it was alive. She was just very practiced at rewriting truths into something more comfortable: Your parents will turn up tomorrow. The horde will pass, as long as we stay quiet.

It was never only us she'd been lying to.

But even now, the blight squirmed under my skin. "Mrs. P, I promise you, it is very much alive."

"Well." Mrs. P swallowed. "If that's true, I don't think the founders knew that."

Angie shrugged. "I'm not sure it matters what they knew. It matters what they did."

We sat with that, silent. The roof rattled over our heads.

Strangely, I almost felt sorry for the blight. Could it be true, Angie's theory about revenge?

Beneath my throbbing scalp, my brain pounded.

It made a certain type of raw sense. The people who'd created the argent vive only to imprison it were long dead, but their descendants profited at its expense. So did the town. Even the folks who flocked in from Meadowbrook every Sunday to buy our miracle crops, and the others who came from all over for the festivals. Those people had no idea what the story really was. But like Angie said, maybe the blight didn't care what they knew.

It cared what people did. The ripples they created.

But was revenge *all* this was?

My eyes landed on the discarded recipe before me. The body. The blood . . .

I didn't think it was literally Cormac Murphy's spirit that lived on—more like a Frankenstein's monster of our ancestors' creation. A new consciousness, born only to live caged.

Yet, no matter how much grime and debris the blight had accumulated along the way, it had been some tiny part human, all this time.

I thought back to the way it had looked at me through Mr. Flores's body down the road from the clinic. How it'd almost reminded me of Dad, the way it watched me, waiting for something I couldn't guess the right answer to. How disappointed it had been when I'd assumed it wanted to make more of itself.

It hadn't made sense to me. If it genuinely didn't want more of itself in this world, then why did it keep growing and devouring? The blight was coming out earlier in the daylight. The horde it commanded grew larger and larger. It spread itself farther and farther.

But then I remembered, in a new light, what it had said: *This cycle will never repeat.*

How, through Mr. Flores's cracked lips, it had added, *Even if that means I cannot stop here in Hollow's End. Even if I must then chase down every last person in that clinic. If I must continue over the bridge.*

Was that actually what it wanted, to keep going?

Or was it just that desperate?

"Wren?" Angie waved a hand between me and my distant stare. "Why are you crying?"

I reached up with my tied hands to brush my fingertips against my cheek, catching a strangely cool drop from my eye.

A smudgy gray tear.

I wasn't actually sure anymore if it had come from me.

I reached out for the recipe, to read it one more time.

"What's that?" Angie asked. "On the back?"

The ink stain?

I flipped it over.

There, at the bottom, was a line so faint, the ink so smeared and watery, I'd overlooked it before:

What is done may be undone. Yet, be it so, from life shall spring death. And the earth shall be fertile no more.

"Angie, Mrs. P . . . ," I said slowly, "we have to fix this before the horde comes back at nightfall. And I might actually know how."

All it would take was magic and a miracle.

All it would cost was my entire past. Maybe my entire future.

CHAPTER 16

B y the time Angie, Mrs. P, and I finished what we'd set out
to do—a grinding, exhausting process that had taken
nearly every hour we'd had—we emerged from the shed to
find the afternoon rain clouds had long since parted. And
the first stalks of red wheat had buckled and fallen. Blight
was already bubbling up from the soil at their roots.

It had tasted the whole farm now, inoculated itself
against each color at a time. Even still, we hoped the blight
wasn't *entirely* immune to the rainbow quartz yet. We
were banking pretty hard on that.

Eventually, Angie and Mrs. P went inside to rest and
prepare, but I stood on my porch and stared out at my
farm one last time as the sun sank behind the looming forest. The backyard still looked okay. Our personal fruits
and vegetables a little smaller, more tentative than they'd
usually be in June, confused by the weather. But they still
stood. Our shed looked the same as always. It served as a
makeshift stable now, but maybe not for much longer. I

was taking Buckwheat out tonight for what I desperately hoped wouldn't be her final ride.

If I squinted at the first rows of the field—the remaining pearl-bright stalks, twisting crimson in the wind—I could almost trick myself into seeing what I always used to see. The magic of our farm. Our miracle.

Everything beyond that, though, was limp, slimed with silver. The sour-sweet stench of rotting wheat hung in the air. Such a sad, far cry from the enchanted oasis it had been. A place that had felt safe. A place that had taught me, since before I took my first steps, that magic was alive.

A place we'd all hoped was invincible.

A place that had proven just how wrong we'd been.

Deep down, the fertile soil had always been stained. Poisoned. By us. It was just that our sins were only now oozing to the surface.

I hadn't planned, at sixteen, to say so many goodbyes.

I guess that's one thing I was learning: you were lucky if you got to plan them at all.

At least, finally, my breath was flowing freely. I used to take that for granted—the basic ability to pull air in and out. From the fields, the blight wafted its foul scent up to greet me. But for the first time in days, the air inside my own body tasted sweet and pure.

My legs stood strong. My eyes saw clearly. More than clearly. They caught every shining, iridescent particle in the misty air. Ones I'd never noticed before.

The farm, dying as it was, glittered before me.

Through the sun's quieting rays, the faint arc of a rainbow slanted through the sky.

It'd always been my favorite sight as a kid—the handful of times we'd had one grace our fields. Our farm's namesake stopping by to give its blessing. I loved them so much Mom would always run to get me if she spotted one. Even Dad. If we were out in the fields, he'd tap my shoulder, a small but unmistakable smile creasing the corner of his mouth as he pointed overhead.

This one was faint. A wispy seven-hued trail stretching from behind our house, over our fields, out to the horizon behind the trees.

I stood until the shadowy woods bled up to stain out its light. Until the whole sky washed purple as violet wheat.

Until it was time to bring out Buckwheat.

They started appearing in the tree line—pair after pair of those glowing firefly eyes winking in the dark.

Angie and Mrs. P were in their positions. I was in mine.

The hardest part now was waiting. Waiting and hiding behind the silo, my breath and Buckwheat's both shallow. Funnily enough, we stood over the churned-up ground where I'd once planted that extra hunk of quartz, where I'd grown my own new rainbow wheat. Dad had dug up that piece back in March and returned it to the center of the field. As I'd discovered this afternoon, he'd dug up *all* the little pieces he and Mom and the rest of our family had cracked off over the years and piled them down there, too—I think in hopes of slowing the quartz's leaking. From back here, I could see he'd also uprooted my test wheat. But, even if this patch behind the silo now looked like nothing, it was because of this, my secret little experiment here, that the blight had broken out when it did.

It was only fitting that I had to wait in the muddy spot I'd created.

I clenched my fingers in Buckwheat's mane, the fresh wounds Angie had helped me carve into my palms stinging. Inside my boots, my socks dried sticky to the bleeding soles of my feet.

Had the blight noticed it couldn't find me anymore, that it couldn't see inside my mind or spy on my thoughts? It had to be searching for me.

Owls circled over the field, molting torn feathers with every flap, combing over my house. Searching, searching.

I wasn't far from the forest. Maybe only a hundred feet.

Close enough to smell them as the blighted tore out from the trees. Like always, the animals led the way—deer and moose and dogs and foxes. Tonight there were more than ever: horses, raccoons, crows, and songbirds. All eyes casting that phosphorescent glow.

They plunged into the wheat, ripping the last of my family's farm to shreds.

With each crush of fangs against wheat, I felt their teeth sinking into my own flesh. As they tore stalks from the earth, they plucked out my fingers. The stalks snapped, and my bones ached with each crack.

It was wrong to be up here on Buckwheat's back, so far from the fields as they bled. I wanted to sink sobbing into the earth, pull the soil over my head until the cool dark swallowed me whole and cradled me at its core.

Finally, the last of the blighted, the humans, arrived to join the horde.

I sucked in a breath and held it as the first of them stepped out from the tree line. Blight from what must've been the lake clung to his ankles and feet.

The light was dim, the sun's last rays, but I'd never mistake his gait, the proud lift of his shoulders and chest.

Why did it have to be Derek?

Because he was the freshest, the smoothest working body? Because the blight wanted to hurt *me*?

Claudette wasn't far behind. Her jaw hung slack, like the blight had melted away her mind, and her spirit along with it. Now that she was free of all the lake's silver, the missing hunk of her hair was clearly visible. The raw open skin of her scalp. The wound the horde had ripped into her while Buckwheat had carried me away.

Among the silhouettes that staggered free of the forest, I knew many others, too. The Murphys. The Harrises. I'd wondered how long it would take—to spot Mom and Dad.

There.

They lumbered up to the wheat, stomping on it as if it wasn't everything they'd built and worked for. Their livelihood, their home. As bitter as Mom could sometimes be, the wheat had still been sacred to her. Whatever ounce of rebellion Dad had spent on giving me that ring, it must've been his last. If there was even the tiniest speck of control left in either of them, they never would've trampled the crops. I knew now without a doubt, I couldn't count on them.

Not them, not Derek, not Claudette.

The desperate loneliness almost crushed me. But something held me up now, shielded my bones like a second glimmering skeleton. Armor from the inside out. A coolness soothing as a breeze, strong as a gale, that said: *No, you're not alone.*

I waited—muscles clenched, barely breathing—while the blighted tromped toward the heart of my farm.

The center of the field.

The thing that wasn't Derek led the way, thrashing the wilting emerald wheat out of his way. The other humans followed.

They stopped at the tallest patch, and searched the ground, ready to dig. Ready to haul up our rainbow quartz and—do what with it? Drag it back to that toxic lake to digest it? That had to be what it had done to the others.

Derek's body stopped at exactly the right place. He looked down, then leaned closer to confirm what I knew he'd find.

An empty hole.

He reeled back with outrage. His moon-white eyes looked up, cast over the farm, and found—

Angie. In the bed of Derek's pickup truck, holding a large burlap bag.

"Looking for this?" she called, with a big sunny wave, head to toe in her customary bubble-gum pink.

Bless her. She had to be shivering to her very core as every blighted creature on my farm, the ones roving and ravaging the wheat—stopped and turned. Pair after pair of eyes, all aimed at her.

Mrs. P blasted the truck's high beams.

The creatures that could threw arms over their faces. They stumbled. Many fell.

But they still scrambled over each other in a mad rush, charging for the truck.

We knew the light wouldn't stop them. All we wanted was to slow them down.

Mrs. P roared the engine to life. Angie barely had time to drop and brace herself before the truck took off down the driveway.

She lowered the bag and hoisted her gun.

Shots pierced the air. Most went wild, striking grass or gravel. In spite of Claudette's efforts, Angie wasn't a great shot. Not when she was stationary, and especially not when sliding around the bed of a racing pickup.

They headed for the open road as all the beasts chased after them.

The deer and black bears and dogs were gaining fast.

Moose kicked their long legs, bounding through the wheat. All the Harrises' animals appeared now—the pigs and sheep and goats and horses—outpacing the Harrises themselves. The Murphys. My parents.

Angie, Mrs. P, and I had expected all this.

But the hawks. They swooped down at Angie, wings billowing like capes against the fading sky.

Mrs. P swerved the truck, spinning its wheels to throw off the birds' aim, but these hawks were used to snagging running prey.

The truck's wild swaying only slammed Angie back and forth, and slowed the truck down enough that the deer began pelting its sides. The blight didn't usually dispose of its creatures recklessly, but now it threw those deer away as they dashed against the metal of the bed, the doors, the tires, with sickening slams and mangling crunches.

Angie shrieked, no longer even shooting, just clutching her gun and flailing for purchase.

"Remember," I'd told her, "if it looks bad, throw the bag."

It had gotten bad way faster than we'd anticipated, but it was time.

Throw the bag, Angie, I willed.

The bears were catching up.

Three of them. The one without its jaw, and two others in better shape. Bigger, faster. With hard loping strides, open mouths and blight-dripping teeth.

More deer darted out, to cut off the driveway from the road.

Finally, Angie picked up the bag. She hurled it from the truck bed in a high vaulting arc, to land in our front yard.

The bears, the creatures hemming in the truck, pulled back, veering around to converge on the bag. But the first to reach it was Mom.

She grabbed it up in a stilted jerk, untied it, and tipped it open.

Out poured a pile of dirt.

A decoy.

The bears roared.

I should run, I knew. The horde was as far away as they were going to get. This was all the lead Mrs. P and Angie could buy me.

But I couldn't leave them like this. Not without letting the blighted glimpse me, lock onto some new target.

I charged Buckwheat out from behind the silo to stand before the tree line. I was about to yell, to attract their attention, but then I looked over my shoulder.

All those white eyes were already staring back.

Their haunting gaze dried up my mouth, shivered into the aching arches of my feet clenched in their boots.

The blight saw the backpack on my shoulders.

I jammed my heels against Buckwheat's barrel of a body and drove her straight into the forest.

This time, I had to find my destination without the blight leading the way. It was too busy chasing after me. God, I hoped Angie and Mrs. P were safe.

A sharp branch whizzed dangerously close to my cheek, and I ducked against Buckwheat's neck, gripping her bare back and slick sides with everything I was worth. "You got this, girl," I whispered.

If she didn't—if she slipped on a patch of blight, caught her hoof on a root, was run down by that pack of Teddy's blighted kin . . .

She was the last of the healthy Harris horses. If any creature was capable of outrunning that horde, it had to be her.

I urged her on. She flicked her ears at the sounds of crunching leaves, cracking sticks, and angry growls, all closer and closer by the second.

Branches swiped at my head and whipped my arms with the force of Buckwheat's speed.

Behind us, too close, dogs howled, eerie echoes bouncing off the trees.

A red shape flashed behind the trunks to our right. Another to our left.

Harris dogs: hunting us down like wolves.

Buckwheat snorted, eyes wide and rolling. Foam flung from her mouth; steam billowed from her nostrils. She was already going as fast as she could.

The big dog to our left swung in, diving for her ankle.

Buckwheat screamed a terrified whinny. I shouted at the dogs, hoping it might scare them back.

But the big dog was undeterred, snapping at her back leg. It caught the air the first time, then recalibrated and charged for another strike.

The dog to our right swung in, too. With a fierce growl, it grabbed the first by the scruff. Yanked it back with strong, steady jaws, clearing Buckwheat's path.

I allowed myself one glance back at the red-brown dog schooling her big brother, shaking him by the scruff, and I couldn't help my grin.

"Good girl, Teddy!" I called.

She wagged her tail before trees ate her up from my view.

We were getting close. The stench rolled out to meet us as the trees thinned ahead. The clearing loomed on the horizon.

"Just a little farther." I stroked Buckwheat's neck. "I promise."

Fifty feet from the lip of the quicksilver lake, she skidded to a halt. She threw her head back and screeched out a shrill bray.

She'd carried me as far as she could.

Before she broke free of my control entirely, I dropped to the ground and took off, racing for the lake ahead.

Buckwheat ran for quieter trees.

The blighted horde let her go. It was me and my backpack they were after.

Ahead, the toxic lake shone under the night sky.

Molten moonlight covered the forest floor. Rippling pestilence.

Last time I was here, when Claudette had nearly dragged me under, nothing had frightened me more than the idea of drowning in that rotting tar pit, blight seeping in through my nostrils, my mouth, my ears, filling me to the brim with poison.

I was still terrified, honestly.

But I hadn't come this far to chicken out now.

Backpack and all, I charged into the lake. I braced for the slickness against my calves, for it to crawl all the way up my legs, torso, neck, mouth, brain. The way it had slurped up Teddy earlier.

Instead, my legs met empty air.

The thick silver parted before me, around me. Even as the lake got deeper, as the ground beneath me sloped and revealed the crater the blight had carved out of the earth to create an oasis for itself, the quicksilver divided. Walls of it climbed around me, only a tunnel above my head clear, spotlighting me under the moon.

It was afraid to touch me.

Was it afraid of the quartz it knew I was carrying? Afraid of whatever plan it suspected I had?

I clutched at the straps of my backpack, scared something might burst through the strangely placid silver surrounding me and snatch it away at any second.

I pressed ahead, walking to the deepest part of the lake, where the stinking mercury walls around me were at their tallest.

I looked up at the branches and the night sky above like it was the last sip of water I'd ever take. Even if this plan went right, the awful truth was, I didn't know what would happen to me.

"*Wren.*" That whispering voice spoke next to my ear.

I wheeled around to face it.

Through the wall walked the blight's favorite new host. Freshly coated, head to toe, in silver. Shedding those mercury beads onto the dirt beneath us.

I could just make out the rough shape of Derek's face under that molten mask. The sharp line of his forehead, the broad curve of his cheekbones.

The blight's glowing eyes leered. "*You mean to kill me with a rock?*"

In a vicious flash, it seized the backpack from my shoulders, tearing it away.

The blight unzipped the bag and tipped it upside down, just like at the farm—but nothing came out.

When the blight looked up at me, it snarled with Derek's teeth bared.

"*Where is it?*" it demanded. "*What have you done?*"

My own reflection stared back at me, distorted and strange, rippled by the planes of Derek's face. I looked so small. So pale. So terrified.

I forced myself to stand tall. Derek already loomed over me at his six-foot height, as it was. I didn't need to feel any smaller right now.

I looked straight into his silver-slicked face. "I destroyed it."

The blight hurled my backpack to the dirt. *"I know it's here."* It stepped toward me. *"And you really think, because you've loosened my grip, I can't get you again?"*

I pushed my hands into my pockets to hide their trembling. And the symbols carved into my palms.

"A child's mistake." Droplets spat from Derek's lips like living spite, sizzling against the freckles of my cheeks. *"If you won't give me an answer, then I'll take one."*

It reached for me, hands dripping down my sleeves as it clawed at my shoulders.

Thin tendrils—snaking and solid—climbed out of Derek's mouth.

My brain blared a red-hot warning, every primal instinct screaming it was my last chance to run.

But I grounded myself like an ancient tree, massive roots coiling deep into the earth.

As the blight leaned into me, I reached up and set my hands on Derek's shoulders. Like we were dancing. Like we'd danced at the New Year's party.

Derek's lips pulled into a sneer. Silver ooze bubbled through my fingers, searing against the open cuts on my hands.

We were only a couple inches apart now.

I watched as the blight realized my eyes had changed. They weren't the white of the blighted anymore. Not even my original color. After what we'd done this afternoon, Angie had looked into my new eyes and gasped. She'd held up a compact to show me.

My irises were fractured rainbows. Smashed iridescent shards kaleidoscoped against the background of my natural gray.

"No." The blight tried to pull back.

It realized exactly what I'd done to that rainbow quartz. I hadn't lied. I had destroyed it.

This monster couldn't have known how much it had cost me. That hunk of quartz was the key to everything I loved most in the world. My farm. My home. My family's magic. With every chink of my chisel, every rasp of the grinder against the stone, I pulverized my own heart to powder. Any hope for the future we'd planned.

I wanted so much to leave some small piece intact. Some tiny hope we could cling to.

But the original recipe had called for the entire stone. I couldn't take any chances. I chipped away until there was nothing left, like I was grinding away my own skeleton, bone by bone.

All for this moment.

The blight wasn't going to escape me. My grip was iron.

My left palm was carved with the symbol for air. For my family, the Warrens. My right palm: fire, for the Harrises. I stepped my left foot on top of Derek's, the sole carved with earth, for the Murphys. And, at last, I stepped with my right foot. Water. For Derek's family, the Pewter-Floreses.

I gathered all the fight left in my belly, for everyone I

loved, for Hollow's End, and I drove myself forward to plant my lips on Derek's.

The blight tried to suck those twining, grasping tendrils back into its host and hide.

But I'd already latched on, drawing on the magic inside me. The rainbow quartz—the final stone—ground to dust, that I'd poured into water and then poured down my throat. Let it become part of me so that it could fight.

So that it could trap.

The blight had already told me it had broken down and devoured the other stones. Everything else in its original recipe was already still inside it.

As for the fresh blood, the warm body, I could provide that.

That would be it: all the original ingredients reunited. Even if the blight was almost wholly inoculated against the quartz, the recipe said: *What is done may be undone.*

So the ritual itself must have some power over the blight.

I just hoped to God I was interpreting it right.

The blight from Derek's face ran down my own, streamed through my eyelashes, spilled into my mouth with its moldy embrace. The quartz in me searched out the heart of that squirming, miserable mass and sucked it in.

I gagged as the blight lashed against my lips, the inside of my cheeks. It was thrashing away, trying to flee.

No way in hell. I bit down, and a hot surge of putrid liquid spurted over my back teeth. I chomped harder, gnashing into it until those trickling toxic beads lost their hold on each other—and began to fall backward down my throat.

Writhing tentacles scratched and scrabbled at the soft lining of my esophagus, gouging. It pushed and stretched against the thin skin of my throat, like it would burst through me with a wild spray of blood and sludge.

I didn't want to die like this, split through at the throat, esophagus exploded and dangling in open air.

I choked, eyes flying open in panic.

Derek stared back, only an inch away—his eyes dark brown and frightened and utterly his own. The silver had peeled away from his shocked face.

His hands found mine and pulled, trying to break free. Even now, trying to save me. Trying to stop me from saving him.

Not this time, Derek.

All the way back in my kitchen, before we went to look for my parents, I'd told him not to come with me. He'd said that it was his decision. That he should get to choose which risks were worth it to him.

Now, I curled my fingers through his—squeezed—like he'd done for me on the drive to the Harrises', when he told me I was family.

I tried to tell him without words: He was worth it to me. And I wasn't leaving him behind.

His face crumpled; his lips softened against mine. He squeezed back.

As Derek held me, fog took my eyes, cobwebbed over my vision as thick as cream soup.

I was doing what the quartz was meant to do: sucking in the blight, condensing it, and containing it. I'd become the vessel, a fragile container, for this force so much bigger than myself. I fell into the prison of my own body as the blight railed against my very blood, my bones.

It thundered through my wincing brain. *"Stop this now!"*

But I didn't have to obey, and I wasn't going to.

I turned my skin to armor, imagined the rainbow quartz—and whatever remaining power it had, whatever extra power this ritual could give it—blocking the blight's escape from my every single pore.

Not one bit was getting free.

Outside the walls of my body, the blighted lake crashed in around my head. Derek's, too, our fingers still entwined, my mouth still pressed on his, drinking out the blight like venom. My feet left the earth. My body floated, suspended in a sea of silver.

I didn't gasp for breath. I didn't need to breathe. Was I already dead?

I'd made sure to do this at the lake because I'd seen how every time I splashed into the blight, it behaved like mercury. It beaded out, and then the smaller beads linked up with the bigger beads until it reformed as one. Now I knew it didn't just behave like mercury. In large part, it *was* mercury. If I could drink in the lake, the biggest part of itself, maybe the rest would have to follow.

With the recipe's reassembled ingredients flowing inside me, I called all the blight here, to me. To my body.

Every speck of blight from Derek, from this lake, from Hollow's End. My parents and Claudette and the other decaying people and creatures at its shore. The trees and their corrupted roots. The soil of our farms.

Each particle was grabbed by a mote of rainbow quartz inside me, compressed and smashed smaller and smaller under my skin. Like Angie and I had ground down the quartz, now the quartz was grinding down the blight. Making it less and less. I'd wondered if the quartz would be enough to protect me from sucking in that much toxic quicksilver, but it must've been—because I didn't keel over dead on the spot.

White fog hugged my body from all sides. The cushion of my skin had never felt so thick, so bloated. And I lost hold of Derek. I was flat on my back now, at the deepest hollow, the center where the lake had lain only moments before. I must've drunk the whole lake.

I reached out and dug my hands into the soil, to grab on to something on the outside.

Inside, I held the blight down, the same way it'd held me down while it bit into Claudette. Made me betray my loved ones. Turned our town, one by one, into its own frothing army.

That shivering voice rang out through my mind: "*You think you can hurt me? You're nothing. Animated stardust gasping for a heartbeat. You'll fall to bits in under a century. Organic matter recycled before, waiting to be recycled again.*"

It still thought I was trying to hurt it.

Like it had wounded us. Like we'd wounded it.

Now I knew what it felt like to be crushed inside a rock, drinking in every impure scrap of Hollow's End. My blood boiled like acid. My veins scraped under my skin like they were churning with gravel.

At least in my case, I'd made the choice to do it to myself.

The argent vive didn't get to make that choice.

Our founding families gave it blood. They saw it squirm. They knew it was alive.

They'd set out to make living silver, and that's what they'd done. They knew the cost, and they were fine—just fine—letting someone else pay for it. First, Cormac Murphy, and then the argent vive itself.

We'd made it a monster, when it was never meant to be one.

I didn't think it actually wanted to have to destroy us, all the people who so deeply misused it. It just wanted us to *stop*. And if it had to chew us all up to make that happen, so be it.

That's what I'd failed to understand on that bleak road when the horde had hemmed me and Claudette in, when I'd incorrectly guessed that the blight wanted people to make more of it.

But that was the last thing it wanted. For more argent vive to be created, for more people to exploit and torture it.

From me, the blight had only wanted to see if I understood.

I hadn't then.

But I did now.

My eyes dripped with tears. Mine, or the blight's, or maybe both.

Nothing could ever make up for what our families had done, but I could try, like Mom had told me, to be better. Do better.

Calm down. I spoke to the blight in my own mind, like it so often had to me. *I'll take care of you.* I used its own words, remembering the blissful relief of them. How much I'd longed to fall back against pillows, where there'd be no more pain.

Let's put it back, I said. *All the way back, to how it was before they did this to you. How it was supposed to be.*

Wary, the blight watched and waited—burning with more than a lifetime of fury.

On my fingers, I wore all four rings, reunited for the first time in God knows how long. The silver dollars we'd obtained off the back of the blight's misery.

I'd once been so sure our farms were ours—our crops were ours, our money was ours—because we'd *earned* them. We'd worked so hard.

We did work hard. But we still hadn't earned any of this.

We'd stolen it.

To the blight, I said, *These four rings, I think, belong to you.*

"Yes," it said.

I stripped the rings from my fingers and crammed them into my mouth. I couldn't sew it shut like they'd done to poor Cormac Murphy, but I pressed my hands over it to trap them inside me.

The blight dissolved them—melting them from solid metal to liquid silver on my tongue. Squirming them down into my throat, my very tissue.

With every pulse, the silver of our farms beat out through my blood.

And with every pulse, I felt the blight's grip inside me

311

loosening. All that burning rage and clenched fury releasing, just ever so slightly. Its first tiny taste of relief—and the last step taken on Cormac's body in the ritual.

I'd already recombined the ingredients. The blight was here, clutched up tight inside me. Technically, according to the recipe, I think this was all that was needed to unmake it.

Maybe, if I just willed it to happen now, it would?

But that's not how I wanted to do this, not if I could help it. The blight had never gotten to control what happened to it. I intended to at least give it control over this.

You can let go now, I said, like it had said to me. *Will you?*

Again, it said, *"Yes."*

On my back at the bottom of the empty lake, I squeezed my hands into the soil.

Everything the blight had swallowed while we kept it trapped under our farms, every coarse and ordinary scrap it'd sucked from Hollow's End, leaving the extraordinary to glow and shine elsewhere while it made itself muddy and sour and ruined . . . we switched it all back.

We gathered the silver from Derek's farm, the gold from the Murphys', the rainbows from mine, the fiery sparks from the Harrises'.

We replaced them with drab and dull. Normal.

Last of all, the blight swallowed the rainbows inside me.

It ate everything back up until there was no more magic that belonged to Hollow's End. After all, there never really had been.

The skin between me and the rest of the world wore thinner and thinner. The fog retreated.

The argent vive sighed through me, an almost endless exhale.

A final death rattle as the living silver unstitched itself into nothing but regular, raw ingredients.

And then it was just me, back pressed against earth, hair tangled with soil. The full moon looking down.

I gasped for breath.

Something stabbed against my throat, hard and sharp and unforgiving. The recipe's ingredients were still inside my body. Now that the argent vive had gone, taking its magic with it, they had turned from liquid back to solid.

I clutched my throat, the blockage in my windpipe poking against my skin.

My chest heaved for air that couldn't come.

The recipe had, after all, warned me what would happen if reversed: *from life shall spring death.* I just hadn't realized this was how it would happen. I'd thought if I survived sucking in all the blight that maybe I would be okay.

But no.

Hollow's End was free, but I wouldn't get to see it. I was going to choke to death on enduring sins. At the bottom of an empty pit. Alone.

"Wren!"

No. Not alone.

Derek lifted me by my shoulders, his skin rubbed raw and bloody, his lips peeling.

His hands were still trembling. But he wrapped them

around my stomach and pulsed them against my diaphragm, hard.

Cutting edges twisted in my throat.

Derek shoved again under my ribs, and I heaved.

With a nasty ripping drag of metal and burning matches and dead ash and copper, I retched everything out onto the earth.

A silver dollar, a lump of coal, a hunk of sulfur, a swallow of mercury.

And blood. Blood that kept coming and coming. It wasn't my own. Clotted and rotting, ropey and thick. This blood had been dead a long time.

The last of the argent vive, magic and all, unmade.

Thanks to Derek, I was still here to see it.

When I looked up from the bottom of our crater, the entire forest stared back at us.

Mom and Dad and Claudette and Mr. Flores and Amber and all the rest. Amber sank to her knees, clutching herself. Dad looked almost as hypnotically dazed as before, except now his eyes were clear and frightened and round. All of them were returning to themselves after days or weeks or even months.

My gaze snagged on the damage that had been done. Gaps where teeth should be, torn nails, shredded skin sloughing from muscle.

The trauma of horrors planted deep.

And no idea how to move forward from here.

CHAPTER 17

We stumbled our way out of the forest, one step at a time.

Then, one day at a time.

We returned to rotting farms, the final decay of the cash crops we could never grow again. Rotting bodies, which would heal the way my purple-scarred thumb did—worse than they were before. The blight, far more powerful than any bacteria, had kept open wounds uninfected. But now, the infections would come.

Some of the animals—the injured ones, like the bear Derek had shot in the jaw—had staggered down dead within minutes.

At least all the humans came home. Even some we didn't expect—from the emergency triage clinic. Once the blight was gone, the blockade vanished, too. Overnight.

Of the dozen people who'd turned themselves in to the clinic, three came back. Mrs. Thomas, Benji's mom, was one of them. She confirmed what the blight had reported:

Containment cells. People in faceless white hazard suits attempting to suck out the metal from under their skin.

She was never able to identify who they really were, what agency they were with.

At least they didn't get ahold of our stones. Or the recipe. Dad and I burned that ourselves, with grim satisfaction.

But we still worried about how much they knew. Just how much research they'd managed to accomplish. I'd heard them myself, back on the Harris farm, referring to some mysterious recipe from the 1600s. At minimum, they suspected what the blight really was.

I hoped to God they never figured it all the way out.

Mr. Flores walked with a cane, at least for now. Maybe forever. Jagged scars carved down his neck where the skin had rotted away. Derek had one by his ankle, where Teddy's brother had torn into him. Claudette's arm sported a craggy dent, thanks to my teeth.

And when she made it out of the forest with the rest of us, Angie had hugged her so hard, they both dropped to their knees, heads on each other's shoulders, sobbing.

My family came away with wounds of their own. Mom's strong hands were plagued by persistent tremors. Dad's memory was fuzzier. I routinely had to run after him with his keys.

For me, faint triangles haunted my palms and the soles of my feet. Silver and sulfur and coal had scraped my throat into a new shape. My voice had changed from birdsong to something wilder. With deeper hollows, raspy outskirts.

In a way, I preferred it. I could've done without the

coughs that shook me awake, though, and the ache that came with them.

Most especially, I could've done without the silence of our farm. How when I woke in the night, and everything around me lay dim and deep and vast, I couldn't stop myself from listening out the window—searching for the rustling lullaby that wouldn't come.

Rainbow Fields was just a name now.

Our wheat was gone. We'd dragged ourselves home and found the last surviving dregs sapped of their color, drained down into the dirt.

I knew it would hurt to see it like that. I didn't realize it was going to be like losing an actual piece of my soul.

And, just as I'd feared, it cost me my family. At least, my family as I'd known them.

Saving Hollow's End hadn't saved my parents' marriage. Mom could barely even look at Dad anymore. She'd rented a place in town for a while, promising she'd stay nearby at least until college so I could switch back and forth every Sunday. After that, we'd just have to see.

She still helped on the farm for now. She took maybe a little too much satisfaction in razing that field to the ground.

Dad said we'd start over once we'd tilled and renewed the soil, which was suddenly so pale and lifeless. We'd replant ordinary wheat, and other new things, too. Lavender, basil. Soybeans. The Harrises were kind enough to give us some of their corn. The Pewter-Floreses gave us pumpkins to plant for the fall.

We didn't really have it all figured out. It wouldn't be easy to turn a profit without our rainbow wheat. It might be completely impossible. Dad said we just had to try.

So that's what we did.

One day at a time became one week at a time.

At last, our unseasonable chill loosened its icy grip on Hollow's End. Trees sprouted their overdue leaves, and the summer air rolled in, hot and sticky—buzzing with the lazy pulse of cicadas, warming the soil and the pavement of our driveways, melting ice cream from cones. Promising us with its sun-kissed glow that the world was softening back into its intended shape.

It was still hard to look at Teddy, especially by daylight. To see all the damage the blight had done to her. But one day, before I could habitually wince away from the sight of her tail—it caught my eye. At the tip, where that gleaming chunk of bone had glared, there was . . . skin. The baby fuzz of pretty chestnut-brown—not red—fur slowly and steadily growing back over the wound.

I'd spent so long not looking at her, I hadn't even noticed she was healing.

Soon, Teddy darted through the open fields again, chasing birds and rabbits and driving Dad nuts.

Weeks became months. Summer became fall.

Trying became easier.

On a golden-leafed October Saturday, I creaked past my screen door to sit with Derek on the porch swing. Teddy surged by my legs, teetering the precious plate I'd laid across our mugs. I steadied it and rolled my eyes while she dropped an oblivious, adoring chin on Derek's lap.

He slid his phone back into his pocket and scrunched his hands into her scruff.

Once sated, she ran out to dart around the fields.

Derek smiled at me, especially when he saw I'd brought his favorite striped mug. I always did, and he always smiled.

I snuggled in beside him, passing him the mug of Dad's red-hot mulled cider.

"Claudette?" I asked, nodding to his phone.

"Yeah. Dad's birthday is in a couple weeks." He paused, cider almost to his lips. "I remembered to tell you, right? Hope so, because I definitely told Mom to make the reservation for all of us."

"You did *not* remember to tell me." Before he kicked himself too hard, I added, "But I already had it in my calendar from last year. Tino's, right?"

"If I didn't tell you, how did you know it was Tino's?"

"Because your mom takes us to Tino's for literally every special occasion."

"Come on, that's . . ." He stopped and considered. "Well, true, actually. But, yeah, Claud wants to bring Dad a case of beer from Angie's family when they drive back for the weekend. Personally, I'm not sure how he'd feel about his underage kids chipping in for beer. Also, he doesn't really drink much anymore."

"She gonna do it anyway?"

"Of course." Derek sighed. "Anyway." He looked at the plate cradled in my lap. "Is that it?"

I nodded down at it solemnly.

The very last slice of unicorn braid. Despite our scrimping and saving and diligent freezing, it'd had to end sometime. Mom and Dad had agreed on one thing—they set the last slice aside for me. It wasn't a heel, either. They'd left me a luscious middle piece.

In the kitchen, I'd cleaved the soft braid clean down the center.

"Did you want butter?" I asked. "We have some good honey butter from the Harrises. I just figured I'd have it plain. Really taste it, one last time."

"I think that's right," Derek said. "Let's have it the way it is."

I passed him his slice, and I picked up my own.

"Ready?" he asked.

"Almost."

I just needed to sit there for a minute, that last half piece in my hands, and press it with my fingertips. I needed to remember this sensation, to prove to myself later that this had been real. That rainbows had once been mine.

"Okay," I said to Derek.

We touched our last bites of bread together like we were clinking glasses and popped them into our mouths.

My teeth sank into that silky vibrance. It tasted like it always had, like peppery red, malty-rye orange, grapefruit yellow, celery-seed green, salty blue, eely indigo—and, at the end, my longtime favorite, blackberry-sweet violet.

The unicorn braid slid down my damaged throat.

And then it was gone: the final remaining vestige of our miracle.

Gone were the days of our Hollow's End harvest festivals.

Carnivals and cakewalks. Glow-in-the-dark melonade and sliding into Derek on the Tilt-a-Whirl. Twisting wheat into shining wreaths. Hot apple rainbow fritters.

All our farms had lost so much.

The Murphys didn't even try to salvage their land. They packed up and left town before any of us could speak with them.

But slowly, our soil was coming back to life. With our hard work, it grew darker and richer. We had quite a few more tricks at our disposal than they'd had in the 1800s. Our family's second chance to till the untenable soil. To do less harm this time.

Derek's farm still had its pumpkins. They weren't magic, but they were fat and plump, and they sure did sell out every Halloween.

The Harris animals had lost some speed, and their brilliant-red coats were muddied and faded. And yet, they were still plenty perfect to me—especially Buckwheat. I stopped by a couple times a week so that she could crunch green apples from my hand. We rode together in a ring, safe and slow, with all the time in the world. No more breakneck chases deep into the woods.

Even here at home . . .

True, we didn't have rainbow wheat anymore. But I looked out into the fields, where Dad was working. Mom was here, too, today. I'd helped her finish hanging the last of the art in her townhome last weekend—lots of bright, cheery colors. She'd sighed with something like relief, to see all the pieces she'd kept in our attic now back up on her walls.

Teddy was out there, too, ducking and diving around them with her goofy lolling tongue. The farm looked empty, barren. Under the soil, though, I knew that wasn't true at all. I'd scattered many of the new seeds myself. Regular old winter wheat. In the spring, it'd rise fresh and pale green, then boring beige. The first thing we'd actually planted on our own. Without the living silver, pulsing, writhing, suffering, under our feet.

To be honest, I kind of looked forward to seeing it.

"So that's it," Derek said, nodding to our empty plate. He wasn't grinning anymore. A slight quiver tugged at his mouth. "The last of the magic in Hollow's End."

"Are you sad that it can't be what we pictured anymore?" I asked. "We can't have Rainbow Fields together. Or at least, it won't be easy. Dad's not sure whether the farm will even make it, without the wheat."

Derek nodded. "A little, but . . ." He shrugged. "We still have everything we need. Whatever happens."

I looked down at his hand in mine. How tight he held me. How careful he always was not to brush against that old burst vein in my thumb, because he knew how much it hurt.

I couldn't help kissing him, melting my mouth against the softness of his. His arm tightened around my waist, and mine tightened around his shoulders. And it was the most miraculous thing, how the unicorn braid lingered on his lips.

I wondered then, if I would taste it every time I kissed him.

Actually, I knew I would.

ACKNOWLEDGMENTS

Growing up, I was that kid with her face crammed in R. L. Stein books, bookshelves stuffed with ghost stories. Reading scary stories made me feel brave, sometimes even powerful. Especially when the characters were my age, and when they overcame the monsters in the end. So maybe it makes sense that *What We Harvest* is what I wrote when I stopped planning what to write—when I put away the outlines and stared down the blank page.

After decades of working toward being an author, this has been my miracle book, the one that finally brought my dream to life. And while I planted the seed for this story—an image of the prettiest wheat and the hungriest blight and the girl who would fight against impossible odds—it has taken the care, creative energy, and expertise of an entire community to nurture it into the book it is now.

First, I want to sky-write an enormous thank-you to the shining team at Delacorte Press. Krista Marino, my ingenious editor, your passion, insight, and thematic vision made this book sharper and realer with every revision. Thank you for poking all the holes so we could fill them, and, of course, for the glorious horror movie recs, too. From every conversation with you and the fabulous Lydia Gregovic, I leave twenty times more inspired—and I don't know what more an author could ask for. Another huge thank-you to Barbara Marcus, Beverly Horowitz, and Judith Haut for believing in *What We Harvest* and giving it such a wonderful home. I'm so grateful to Elizabeth Johnson and Colleen Fellingham for the careful attention and clarity your copyediting has given this book, and to Renee Harleston, my fantastic sensitivity reader, for your astute and generous feedback. I'd also like to thank Marcela Bolivar for bringing the magic of Hollow's End so gorgeously to life in her jacket art, Ken Crossland for the interior design, and Kelly McGauley, Elizabeth Ward, Jenn Inzetta, and Tamar Schwartz. Every one of you helped to make this dream real for me, and your work means so much to me.

Christa Heschke, my brilliant agent, I want to scream to the world about your rock-star representation. Kind, attentive, always on point. Thank you so much for your advice on everything from shaping this story to the nitty-gritty, business-of-being-an-author questions, and for celebrating with me and cheering me on. I'm constantly grateful to have you and the fantastic team at McIntosh & Otis, including the ever-thoughtful, ever-lovely Daniele Hunter, and K Dishmon, who was the first to fall in love with this story after Pitch Wars.

And, speaking of Pitch Wars, I owe so much to Brenda Drake, Kellye Garrett, and the whole team who donate their time and energy to help querying authors find their footing. Most of all, I need to thank my mentors. In Pitch Wars 2018, Laura Lashley and Ian Barnes, you were the first to pull me out of a slush pile, to believe in me and my work. Your pro tips and ridiculous gifs helped me grow so much as a writer. I couldn't have written this book without your mentorship. Once I did, in 2019, Kylie Schachte and Aty S. Behsam, you gave me a second opportunity as a Pitch Wars mentee, and your work on *What We Harvest* brought its beating heart onto the page. Kylie, your love for this book made me fall deeper in love with it, too, and your support at every step in this process has meant the world to me. Also, you've read it a billion times. The least I could do was dedicate Teddy to you.

Thank you, too, to the larger writing community and all the inspiring people I've met in places like Pitch Wars, #22debuts, and the Write Team Mentorship Program. I want to give an especial shout-out to two critique partners, Ashley Winstead and Amanda Quain. Ashley, your uplifting emails came at times I really needed them. Thank you for believing in my work, for your thoughtful critiques, and for sharing your own writing, which ranges from spectacularly funny and sexy to gut-smashingly twisty. And, Amanda, your perceptive notes and positivity are always so energizing, and your own writing is such a sugar-and-spice-laced delight. I'm thrilled we're debuting in the same season and get to yell about our books together. I'd also like to thank William Loizeaux, trusty family friend and veteran author, who has been a longtime source of inspiration and has shared key wisdom such as: make sure to maintain a life outside of writing (thanks, Bill—good call).

To my dear friends and early readers, gigantic hugs. Maia McWilliams, my fellow novelist-in-crime going on . . . oh God, twenty years? You are mind-blowingly talented, and I need to thank you for the writing sprints that keep us both on track, the superb eye, the no-nonsense edits—and for the extreme nonsense elsewhere. Emily Friend, my partner in many a walk around a lake and many a late-night chat. Thank you for advising on visuals (the glowing ghost melons send their fond regards), for always having my back, for insisting my weird writing choices aren't *too* weird, and for your beautiful art. Katie Zelonka, you wonderful human, you never fail to inspire with your big mind and big heart, and with all the magic you find and create. Also, thanks for running that super-cool dog-walking business with me (hey, couldn't have written Teddy without it). And, Sara Wilf, I cherish your deep and wonderful curiosity, and our long and looping conversations that never want to end. Thank you for staying in touch no matter where we each go.

Finally, one hell of a toast to the family members who are my anchors.

To Mom. For sharing your own love of writing. For your infinite support, especially on all those nights you listened to my young self babble about my books while you were cooking and I paced the kitchen floor. For the extensive edits and notes and smiley faces. For reading about that jawless bear in chapter 3 not once, but *several* times—because if that isn't love, I don't know what is.

To Dad and Pam. Dad, for teaching me to pursue passions and love words. For being the very first reader of my very first book, and for giving me the courage to keep writing ever since. And Pam, for all your deep care, and for one of the all-time best gifts I've ever received. When I was fifteen, you had a copy of my first book bound, allowing me to keep a piece of my dream on my bookcase, until I could finally put my published book on the shelf beside it.

To Shawn. For being not only the best big brother in existence but also the other half of my brain. For the epic brainstorming and editing and inspiration. For instilling my love of monsters and magic in the first place. And, you know, for writing all those plays with me, too.

To Ollie and Sophie, my furry writing companions, for the unconditional (okay, slightly conditional) affection.

And, of course, to Grant. For your endless love and rock-solid support. For your deep thoughts and feedback, and for those mini-Bundt cakes you kept bringing me during Pitch Wars, back before we realized I'm gluten intolerant. I am so grateful for you every day. Life partner is the best way to describe it—nothing I do is possible without you.

ABOUT THE AUTHOR

Ann Fraistat is an author, playwright, and narrative designer. Her coauthor credits include plays such as *Romeo & Juliet: Choose Your Own Ending* and alternate-reality games sponsored by the National Science Foundation. Born and raised in Maryland, Ann lives with her husband and ever-adorable cats, Ollie and Sophie. *What We Harvest* is her debut novel.

annfraistat.com
@annfrai